A Crime in 5C

A Murder at the Morrisey Mystery

Book Four

Eryn Scott

KRISTOPHERSON
PRESS
Publishing

A Crime in 5C

Meg Dawson's world is turned upside down when her Aunt Penny makes a surprise appearance at the Seattle apartment building she once called home. But hidden within the true reason behind Penny's visit is a mystery that could rock the very foundations of the Morrisey community.

During her visit, Penny breathes new life into the beloved Morrisey Masterpiece Classic, an annual building scavenger hunt. Tensions soar and rivalries ignite among the residents, including between Meg and Laurie. But what starts as a friendly competition soon takes a dark turn when apartment 5C is broken into and a body is discovered.

Suddenly, the scavenger hunt transforms into a deadly game, with Meg and her neighbors unwittingly caught in the crosshairs. As the stakes rise and suspicions mount, Meg must figure out who killed the woman, and why, before it's too late.

**A Google map with the actual scavenger hunt
locations is linked on my website. If you'd like
to see the locations first, or check them while
reading, head to erynscott.com and hover
over the Books tab at the top menu. Click on
Bonus Material, and that's where you'll find
a link to the map.*

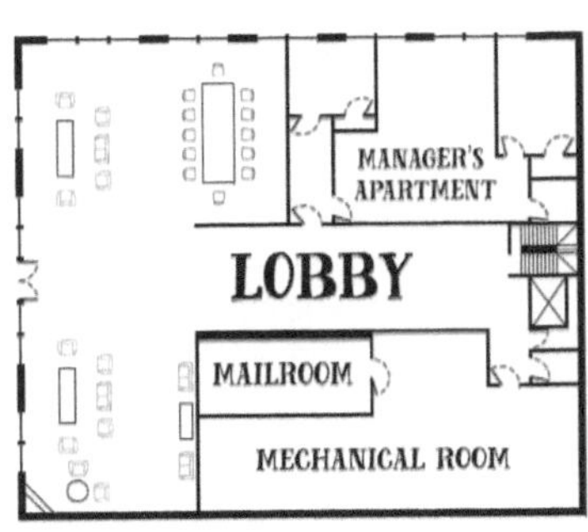
MANAGER'S APARTMENT
LOBBY
MAILROOM
MECHANICAL ROOM

THE
MORRISEY

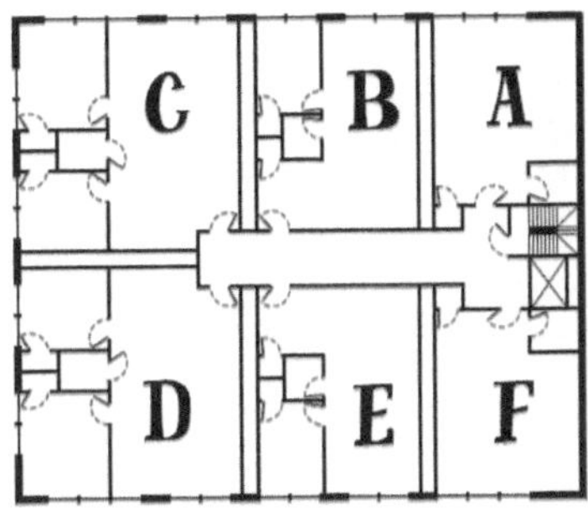
C
B
A
D
E
F

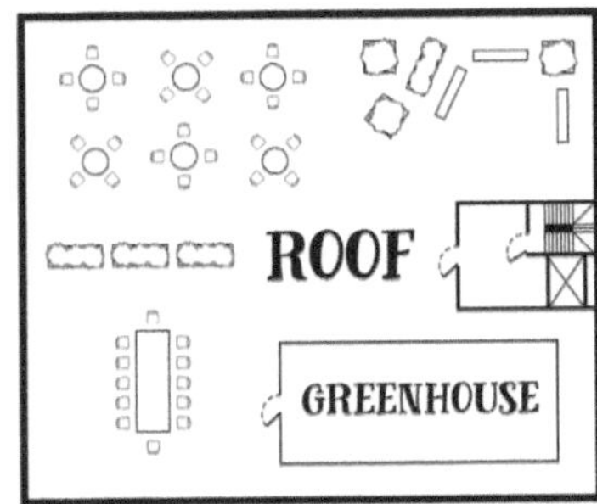
ROOF
GREENHOUSE

LIST OF APARTMENTS AND RESIDENTS

ROOF

5C - ALYSSA VERLICE	5F - BAILEY LUNA
5B - IRIS FINLEY	5E - ZOE DAVIS
5A - MEG DAWSON	5D - EDNA AND TAYLOR FELDNER

4C - W. UNDERWOOD	4F - PAUL KELLY
4B - LAURENCE TURNER	4E - WINNIE WISTERIA
4A - RONNY ARBURY	4D - GREG, OLLIE, LEIA PORTER

3C - KATE, OWEN, FINN, BRYCE O'BRIEN	3F - FATIMA AND URBANE JUNT
	3E - ANDREW SASIN
3B - OPAL HALIFAX	3D - SHIRLEY AND BETHANY ROSENBLOOM
3A - JULIAN CREED	

2C - DANICA AND DUSTIN MCNAIRY	2F- HAYDEN AND TEAL NUTTERS
	2E - ARTURO CORTEZ
2B - DARIUS ROWLAND	2D - VALARIE, VICTORIA, NOEL, MIA YOUNG
2A - CASCADE GRYFFON	

LOBBY

BUILDING MANAGER - NANCY LEWANDOWSKI

ONE

The comfortable background noise of the city streamed in through Laurie's open apartment windows, bringing with it a cool breeze that warned of fall. I was mid-sentence when a weight landed on my chest, making it impossible to breathe, let alone speak.

"Leo, buddy, you've gotta move off my ribs," I wheezed, wriggling under the mass of dog.

He licked my face instead. I used the last of my air to grunt out a laugh at the small land-hippo panting down at me from where he was perched, using my crushed bones as his new bed.

"You gonna finish that sentence?" Laurie's voice traveled over to me from the kitchen. I could picture him craning his neck to see what could've caused my sudden silence.

"Help," I croaked, waving a hand in the air.

Footsteps approached. A low chuckle rumbled out of Laurie's throat. "Leo, off."

The pit bull leapt off me, but not before elbowing me in the spleen, stepping on my stomach, and accidentally clawing my thigh.

Closing my eyes for a moment, I said, "I've never been so happy to be bruised." I followed up the statement with a groan as I sat up.

Laurie's hand closed around mine, pulling me to my feet. "He's not a puppy anymore. He shouldn't jump on you like that," Laurie said, sounding like he was addressing me, but from the way his words sharpened and his eyes slanted toward his dog, I knew the admonishment was more for Leo's benefit.

"It's my fault for not being around as much," I said in the dog's defense. "Which brings me back to what I was saying before he sat on me. I sold my last painting at the Hastings Gallery today. My exhibit is officially over." Beaming, I looked up into Laurie's brown eyes, studying the exact moment my news hit him.

His pupils widened. His eyebrows rose. His mouth spread into a wide smile. I drank it all in, memorizing each subtle sign of his delight.

"That's amazing!" He wrapped his arms around me, picking me up and squeezing me to him.

"Oof."

Laurie set me down. "Sorry. Looks like I'm as bad with your personal space as Leo is." He ran a hand over the back of his neck and sent a sheepish grin toward his dog. "I'm just happy. You worked so hard on those paintings. I'm glad you can relax now that it's over."

"Me too." I puffed out my cheeks and plopped back on Laurie's couch.

It had been a long summer, and while the majority of my hard work had been front-loaded toward the beginning of the season while I created the pieces for the gallery exhibit, I'd gone back weekly to check on my paintings.

Leo jumped on the couch again but curled up next to me instead of on top of me this time.

"What was *your* win from today?" I asked, patting the seat on the other side of me until Laurie settled.

Eyes lighting at the reminder that we'd both had good news to share about our days, he said, "Oh, I helped Mom and Dad settle on a tile they both liked." He crossed his fingers, hoping the decision stuck.

Laurie's parents were redoing their kitchen, and the choice of tile had been a contentious topic, one that had pushed back the install date three times already.

"Now that I've heard your news, though, I feel like mine isn't that exciting," Laurie admitted. "Maybe I should've gone first."

Head falling back in a chuckle, my outburst earned me another lick on the cheek from Leo. I swiped at the dog spit and squinted happily at Laurie. "Well, I suppose not every day can come with a promotion."

He'd started the week with a job offer for a higher-paying position, one where he wouldn't have to travel anymore. I was selfishly ecstatic. I leaned into him but jerked away as I remembered another win I'd had today.

"Actually, I have one more." Patting him on the leg to emphasize each word, I said, "Guess who got a compliment from Taylor this morning?"

Laurie's body shifted so that he was facing me. "No way."

I lifted my chin. "She said she liked my shirt."

Taylor Feldner, the nineteen-year-old great-granddaughter of Edna Feldner, had moved in with her great-grandmother on the fifth floor a year earlier, and yet I could count on one hand —okay, two fingers—the number of times she'd even talked to me on purpose.

Laurie's eyes dipped to the shirt in question.

My cheeks heated. "I mean, it *is* Alyssa's shirt, so technically she complimented Alyssa, but she was really excited when I told her about Alyssa's fashion philanthropy program."

That was what my neighbor, a buyer for Nordstroms and a person whose loungewear was nicer than my best outfit, called it when she let us borrow clothes from her extensive closet. When she'd first moved in, it had started out as her donating her unused clothes to the other women on our floor instead of taking them to the local thrift shops. But ever since Zoe moved in, officially turning the fifth floor into a *girls only* zone, Alyssa had taken to leaving a key in the light fixture next to 5C and letting us go in and borrow clothes whenever we needed to.

"She sounded excited about the clothes. I think it earned me some major cool points." I smiled proudly.

Taylor was only about five years younger than me, but she felt decades cooler with her blasé attitude, constant use of large pink headphones, and a boyfriend who looked like he might be a DJ.

Coughing out a laugh, Laurie said, "Aaand, just like that, you lost them by calling them *major cool points*."

Moving to slap him on the shoulder, a knock on Laurie's

apartment door interrupted me. We both jumped as Leo let out his usual three warning barks.

"Leo, crate." Laurie pointed the dog toward his standard spot whenever he was about to open the door.

The well-trained dog trotted over to his open crate and flopped onto the cozy collection of pillows and blankets inside. He huffed out any disappointment as his eyes followed Laurie toward the door. I stayed put, but peered over as Laurie swung the door open.

"Whoa." He lurched back, causing me to jump to my knees on the couch so I could see better.

Standing at the threshold was Laurie's fourth-floor neighbor, Wendell Underwood, holding a snake as thick as his arm. I couldn't quite see how long the reptile was, but it was one of those scenarios where I figured not knowing was the better option.

"Oh, hey, Wendell." Laurie scratched at his cheek, probably not proud of being so startled.

"Sorry to surprise you, Laurence, but I wanted to let you" —he peered around Laurie to see me on the couch—"and Meg know that Nancy just called an emergency building meeting." He lifted the snake a few inches, causing Laurie to lean back in response. "I'm just putting Monty away, and then I'll see you two down there."

Laurie pushed the door shut as Wendell wandered back toward apartment 4C. The planes of Laurie's face were taut with worry. "What do you think the meeting's about?" he asked as he strode over to where Leo was still sitting in his crate so he could shut him inside. "Good boy, we'll be right back."

But I couldn't answer his question for more than one

reason. First, I had no idea. Second, I couldn't get out a full sentence because I was giggling too much. "Monty," I said with a heaving laugh as I climbed off the couch. "Monty Python!"

Worry cracking into a smile, Laurie shook his head. "I'd like Monty a whole lot better if I wasn't face-to-face with him." He slid an arm around my shoulder, pointing us toward the door. "Or, better yet, if I never knew he existed. I have to share a wall with that guy." He shot a glower toward Wendell's apartment as we entered the hallway.

"Not technically," I said, holding up a finger as Laurie held open the stairwell door for me. "This is one situation in which the passages are less creepy and more of a snake buffer."

We'd boarded up the small passageways in between each of our apartments after someone had used them to sneak inside and kill another resident.

Laurie shuddered and followed me down the stairs. "Yeah, but Wendell is one of the people who *liked* them. He thought they were cool," Laurie whispered, glancing over his shoulder to make sure our reptile-loving neighbor wasn't behind us.

"True, but yours is blocked off. You're fine."

He eyed me as if he didn't believe for one second that I'd be this cool and collected if it were me who lived next to a giant snake, but we made our way into the building lobby, and the cacophony of noise stole our attention.

Nancy Lewandowski stood behind her building-manager podium. Her short reddish hair seemed even more spiky than it usually did. Was she trying out a new gel, or had she been tugging at it as she often did when she was stressed?

"Don't worry about chairs, everyone," Nancy called out. "This is just going to be a quick, stand-up meeting." Her voice wavered, and she plucked the small reading glasses from her nose and set them on the podium next to her.

"No agenda? No list? She's just winging it?" I whispered, basically just listing observations, but Laurie tensed next to me, knowing how bizarre this was for the always overprepared Nance.

Before he and I could make any conjectures about the cause of this change in behavior, Nancy's eyes flicked over to the stairwell where Wendell walked out—snake-free now—and gave her two thumbs-up. The front doors to the lobby opened and Alyssa jogged inside, obviously having come straight from work. She cringed in apology to Nancy for making her wait and stood near the back of the room.

"Okay, that's everyone." Nancy scanned the crowd as they quieted. "I'm sorry to bother you all on a Thursday evening, but I wanted to impart some news to you. Now, I don't want pandemonium when I tell you this." She stabbed a look of warning at a few points in the crowd. "At this point, we're not sure what it means."

Pandemonium? I swallowed down the worries rising in my throat, glancing up at Laurie, who shared my discomfited expression.

"Casey Kincaid has passed away." Nancy placed her hands on either side of her podium, like she was bracing for something big.

Whispers peppered throughout the crowd of residents. The name sparked something in my memory, but I couldn't place where I'd heard it before.

"Was he the guy that played Batman in the newest movie?" Art called out from the front of the group.

Nancy scoffed, taken aback. "No, Art. He owned this building."

Sounds of recognition flowed through the lobby.

"What happened to him?" Darius asked. "Was it gout? My old buddy, Tom, just got that, and he swears it's going to be the death of him."

Bristling, Nance tightened her grip on the podium. "It wasn't gout. He had a boating accident."

We all winced in unison.

"So, you brought us here to tell us we're getting kicked out?" Winnie Wisteria's loud voice cracked through the gathering, causing everyone to wince a second time.

"Wait. We're getting kicked out?"

"We're going to be homeless?"

"This is awful!"

Shouts of disbelief buzzed in my ears as the din reached a crescendo. Their concerns were valid. While we each owned our respective units, either outright or in escrow, Kincaid owned the building itself. Depending on who it went to, they might decide to buy us out of our homes—a clause we'd all had to agree to when we'd purchased our apartments—and then either renovate or demolish the building.

But the Morrisey was more than a building. It was our home. And the panic surging through the residents spoke to the level of attachment we felt for the place. Winnie let out a wail fit for a horror movie.

"I said no pandemonium!" Nancy slapped her hands on the podium, cutting a glare in Winnie's direction. She waited until the group settled to continue. "At this moment, we don't know what it means. I just didn't want you to hear it from another source and feel like I'd kept you out of the loop. Okay? I'm sure there will be a long process of going through his will and figuring out what his wishes were, but rest assured that we will advocate for our building."

That settled the crowd as much as anything could. Realizing that this might be her best opportunity for a clean break, Nancy clapped her hands together and dismissed us.

"What's going on?" My best friend appeared next to me, her eyes widening as she took in the lobby. "Aw, man. Did I miss a building meeting again?"

"Barely," I muttered under my breath. "It was just a stand-up meeting."

"Ripley here?" Laurie asked, leaning in close as he followed my line of sight.

I nodded in confirmation because the weird truth about my best friend was that she was a ghost, and only I could see or talk to her. Laurie, however, had earned his Best Boyfriend Ever badge a million times over when he'd found out about my little secret and hadn't run straight for the hills. In fact, he'd adjusted to my ability to communicate with ghosts better than I had, which was a little annoying, and not at all surprising. Laurie was good at everything.

Before I could explain the reason for the meeting to Ripley, Iris Finley walked over to us.

"What do you make of that?" Iris shoved her hands into the pockets of her skirt—because, of course, the garment had pockets. She was such a stereotypical librarian with her pearl-buttoned cardigan, glasses, and ballet flats that I sometimes wondered if she dressed that way on purpose to mess with people.

Laurie answered for us. "It's a little worrisome, but it doesn't make sense to freak out until we know if there's something *to* freak out about." At that, his eyes shifted over to where Winnie Wisteria and the Rosenbloom sisters were, for lack of a better phrase, freaking out.

The middle-aged sisters wafted their hands toward their eyes, as if that might do anything to quell the tears streaming down their cheeks. Winnie had somehow gotten her hands on a paper bag and was hyperventilating into it, hunched over like she'd just been socked in the stomach.

Iris exhaled through her nose, rolling her eyes at their antics. "How was your day, Meg?" The question was stiffer than her starch-pressed skirt.

"Ugh. I was hoping she wouldn't still be awkward," Ripley complained.

I hid my flinch, but felt the same disappointment as my ghostly companion. Her stilted small talk wasn't a huge surprise. I knew the risks behind going to Iris to ask for any tidbits of information about my father. But after months upon months of getting nowhere by ourselves, Ripley and I had become desperate. My father was the only mystery surrounding why Ripley's spirit still hadn't moved on, we were sure learning about who he was would hold the key to whatever unfinished business was keeping her here.

Iris was my aunt's best friend. And seeing as Aunt Penny was the only one who knew anything about my dad's identity, Iris was the less-scary option. Aunt Penny might've refused to tell me anything about him over the course of my life, but that didn't mean she hadn't let anything slip around Iris over the years.

Our plan had—obviously and spectacularly—backfired. Now I still didn't have any information about my father, and my neighbor was treating me a lot like Laurie had treated Wendell when he'd been holding Monty the Python, like I might strike at any moment.

"She sold the last of her paintings at the Hastings Gallery." Laurie wrapped his arm around my shoulder, coming to my rescue and answering Iris's earlier question about my day.

Iris's blue eyes softened, and she shifted from a poorly passing robot into the woman who'd been like a second mother to me. "Oh, hon, that's wonderful. I'm so proud of you. I know Pen is too." She reached forward and squeezed my hand. "Which one was the final painting? Want to tell me about it as we walk up?" She swung her gaze toward the stairwell.

Swallowing, I was about to tell her I wasn't going up to the fifth floor, that I'd been hanging with Laurie, when he interrupted my confession.

"You go ahead." He squeezed me to him in a side hug before letting me go. "I've gotta do a little research into Monty. You know, figure out where his cage is situated in Wendell's apartment. Make sure he *has* a cage with a secure lock on it." He winked at me as he stepped toward where his next-door neighbor stood talking to a group of second-floor residents. "I'll bring Leo up to your place in a few."

I bobbed my head in some sort of trancelike acknowledgment, following the perfect man with my eyes for longer than was probably comfortable for those around me.

"Earth to Meg." Ripley snapped her ghost fingers in front of my face. "You're ogling again."

"Right." I scrunched my eyes shut. When I opened them

again, I focused on Iris, who grinned at me in a way that made me feel like maybe—just maybe—she'd forgiven me for prying. "The painting," I said, getting myself back on topic as we walked toward the stairs. "Uh, the one that was last to sell had the Space Needle upside down, acting as a record needle, playing the tricolored Alice In Chains vinyl."

My exhibit had been a mixed-media mash-up of iconic Seattle spaces and grunge music. I'd collaged local landmarks with pieces of musical importance to the Seattle grunge scene, like the Fremont troll holding a cassette tape of my favorite Pearl Jam album, *Ten*, instead of the Volkswagen Beetle it actually has clutched in its stony fingers.

"Oh, I loved that one!" Iris held the door open for me as we entered the stairwell. "I can't believe it took so long to sell."

Shrugging, I said, "Yeah, I'm still surprised the Nirvana baby flying in place of the Pike Place fish was the first to go."

As we climbed and chatted about my art, Bailey Luna and Alyssa Verlice slowed so they could walk with us up to our floor. Ripley stayed close but floated above us since it was so crowded. She hated when living people walked through her spirit.

The other residents fell away as they peeled off onto their respective floors, and then it was just the fifth-floor women as we scaled the last flight. Everyone was there except Zoe, who worked nights, and Edna Feldner, who rarely came to these meetings anymore, now that she had her great-granddaughter Taylor to fill her in on the information. Taylor, however, seemed to be elsewhere because she wasn't with us as we stopped in front of the fifth-floor door.

"Do you have any other gallery exhibits coming up?" Bailey asked, holding it open for us.

"Not as of right now. I need a little time to recover. It was a lot of work." I shot a knowing look at Ripley, who'd been by my side for all my late nights and artistic meltdowns.

But Ripley wasn't paying attention. Her concentration was locked on the end of the hallway, on apartment 5C. Alyssa let out a strangled cry as she noticed, just after Ripley had, that her door was wide open.

Two

The women of the fifth floor stood there, frozen for a few seconds. Alyssa reached out for my hand, squeezing it tight with shaking fingers. On instinct, I reached out and took Iris's on my other side.

"Is it Brad?" I whispered, keeping my voice as steady as possible.

Alyssa's head whipped back and forth. "He's working tonight," she squeaked.

"That dude has a *job*?" Ripley scoffed, giving voice to my exact thoughts.

If Iris was going out of her way to emulate every librarian stereotype, Alyssa's boyfriend, Brad, was doing the same thing with the list of deadbeat-boyfriend qualities. He was always holding a bag of some kind of crunchy snack—chips, Cheetos, pretzels; you name it. His scruffy beard was in a constant state of chaos, and the man almost exclusively wore sweatpants.

Now, I'm not one to throw stones in this area, being someone who spent the majority of my day in paint-spattered leggings. It was just an odd choice of partner for Alyssa, someone who cared so much about fashion and ... well, looks.

"Should we call someone?" Bailey asked in a voice so timid I had to glance over just to be sure she wasn't backing into the stairwell where it was safe. She wasn't leaving, but her fingers were tugging on her long braids, giving away her trepidation.

"I'll check." Ripley rushed forward, disappearing into the apartment. She'd followed me in there many times to look for outfits, so she had ghostly access to the place.

I was about to let the others know Ripley had it covered when I remembered they couldn't see her. Instead, I pressed my lips together and waited for my ghostly friend to return.

Letting go of my hand, Iris stepped forward. She tugged on her cardigan. "I'll go in." Bravery emanated from her, and I found myself walking back my earlier judgments about her typical librarian ways. Well, I wasn't sure librarians *weren't* brave per se. It just wasn't part of the stereotypes surrounding them.

Fingers clenching together in the absence of Iris's hand, I released a pent-up breath as Ripley emerged.

"No one inside," Ripley reported, giving me peace of mind as Iris entered Alyssa's apartment.

Bailey walked over, surprising me even more. But instead of following Iris, she stopped at 5D and pressed Edna Feldner's buzzer. "I'm going to see if Edna or Taylor heard anything."

One would think that the sheer number of times Bailey had to ring the woman's buzzer would've prepared us for Edna to open the door instead of her great-granddaughter, but we'd all experienced Taylor taking just as long to hear the door over the music pumping through her headphones as her hard-of-hearing great-grandma.

"Edna. Hi." Bailey gestured over to Alyssa's open door. "Did you hear anything next door in the last thirty minutes?"

It was an objectively silly question, made even more ridiculous when Edna crinkled up her face, tilted her ear toward Bailey, and said, "What?"

Iris stepped out into the hall at that moment, shaking her head. "There's no one inside."

Alyssa emptied her lungs in relief. "When we came back from a building meeting, my door was wide open."

Our elderly neighbor frowned as the women of our floor filled her in. The deepening crevice in the middle of the woman's forehead could've just as easily been from concern as it could've been that she couldn't hear a word they were saying. But she finally tottered out into the hallway and peered into Alyssa's apartment.

"Oh my!" she gasped, a frail hand flying to cover her mouth. "Darling, you've been robbed!"

Alyssa darted inside, the rest of us on her heels.

"What? Where? How do you know that?" Alyssa spun around in a circle, frantically searching her apartment for clues.

Edna, who wore thick glasses, gaped at Alyssa in a way that made it ironically clear that *she* was questioning Alyssa's ability to see well. She wafted a shaky hand at the two-bedroom apartment, a mirror of her own in every way but one.

"They trashed the place!" Edna cried out, motioning to the clothes lying on almost every surface.

The open doors to Alyssa's bedroom and spare room, which she used as a walk-in closet, displayed the same level of scattered clothing, shoes, handbags, and accessories.

Bailey coughed in discomfort as Iris and I exchanged an

uneasy glance. Edna had obviously never taken Alyssa up on her fashion philanthropy program. If she had, she would've known that this was how things always were.

Alyssa appeared put together on the outside with her sleek dark hair and perfect outfits, but she was a bit of a slob behind closed doors. Actually, maybe her boyfriend choice *did* make sense, now that I thought about it.

We all tensed, ready for an awkward encounter as Alyssa digested the offending statement, but our neighbor just chuckled. "Edna, you're so funny," she said, brushing off her comment as she began searching through the place to ensure everything was still there.

As the fears slowly leaked from my brain, they created room for more rational thoughts. Given space, my earlier conversation about borrowing clothes clicked into place. "Wait. Is the key still in the light fixture?" I asked, rushing back to the hallway to check Alyssa's hiding place. Laughing triumphantly when my search came up empty, I rejoined the fifth-floor residents. "I told Taylor about the key today."

Bailey, Iris, and Edna turned toward me. From the confused way they stared at me, they weren't following.

"This morning, I passed Taylor in the hallway and she complimented my shirt." I plucked at the fabric as if they might not know what a shirt was. "I told her it wasn't mine, and explained how Alyssa lets us borrow her clothes. I showed her where the key was hidden."

Understanding dawned across Iris's and Bailey's faces. Alyssa poked her head out of the bedroom to listen.

"I bet she's the one who left the door open, and she must've forgotten to put the key back." I grinned, relieved that such a potentially scary situation could be explained away in such an innocent way.

Alyssa leaned her weight into her doorframe. "Omigosh, that makes me feel so much better. Phew."

A high-pitched tone cut through our celebrations. Edna had her finger in her ear, and the more she fiddled, the weirder the pitch became. Finally, she pulled her finger away and loudly said, "Sorry, my hearing aid was on the fritz for a second. What are you all so excited about?"

"It was Taylor," Iris said, stepping forward and gesturing Edna back toward the hall. "Meg told her about the key and how Alyssa lets us borrow clothes. She must've taken the key and left the door open."

But Edna dug in her heels, refusing to follow Iris. "There's no way Taylor did this."

Of course, Edna *would* think the best of her family member. Clearing her throat, Bailey stepped forward. The three of us softened our expressions, tilting our heads ever so slightly as we decided how to tell this woman that Taylor was most definitely the kind of person who might leave a person's apartment wide open. She was dismissive at the best of times.

Before we could choose a representative to break the news, Edna cut the air with a gnarled hand. "She left for Iowa this morning to visit her parents for a few weeks. She's not here."

Mouth dropping open, I pointed to the hallway. "But she was coming home when I was leaving this morning," I repeated, wondering if Edna hadn't heard that part. "She could've gone over to borrow something before she left for the airport."

Edna shook her head with so much vehemence I worried she might fall over. I wasn't alone in my concern. Iris splayed her hands out in the air around the older woman, ready to catch her.

"Taylor went to grab coffee with a friend, but only because she was packed and ready to go. The moment she returned—which I'm guessing was right after she saw you—she grabbed her suitcase and headed back down to the lobby where that boyfriend of hers picked her up to take her to SeaTac," Edna explained.

From the doorway, Alyssa began murmuring worried phrases.

"She's right. The door wasn't open when I left for the stand-up meeting." Bailey's eyes locked with Alyssa's. "Whoever broke in here did it while we were downstairs."

With that, Alyssa flipped back into panic mode, searching the space more frantically than she had before. She darted into her second room, having finished her search of her bedroom. My lips parted, and I was about to offer a few suggestions about who else might've done this, when a screech of agony came from the walk-in closet.

We raced forward to find Alyssa pointing a trembling finger at an open space in the rows of hanging clothes.

"No! No, no, no, no." She was pacing, fingers grabbing at her shiny hair.

"Is something missing?" Iris asked in a voice that felt mockingly calm compared to Alyssa's distress.

As if she felt it, too, Alyssa's eyes snapped up to meet Iris's. Anger burned behind her gaze. "The dress. The thief took *the* dress."

Despite Alyssa's very clear emphasis on the word, Bailey replaced it as she repeated the statement. "They took *one* dress?"

There was a dismissive air lacing her question, and I was surprised she didn't finish it with a snort.

The rest of us in the room grimaced, including Ripley.

Alyssa went preternaturally still. "Yes, *one* dress," she spat out the words. "It was a sample I was supposed to bring to my bosses to convince them to sign a local designer. Despite the fact that it was worth hundreds of dollars on its own, it represented a contract that could potentially be worth hundreds of thousands of dollars."

Cowed, Bailey looked down at her sneakers.

"The designer is going to kill me," Alyssa said, picking up her pacing again. "He's going to wring my neck. He's going to lose it, and then he's going to strangle me." Her voice had reached a pitch so high it might have been a match for the sounds emitted by Edna's hearing aid.

I stepped forward, placing a supportive hand on Alyssa's arm. "What can we do to help? Do you want us to call the cops? You could report the theft and—"

"No," Alyssa interrupted me, her eyes going dark. "No. I don't want this to get out until I have a plan." Her attention drifted away, and she stared into the middle distance for a moment before looking back in my direction. "I'll figure something out. You should all get back to your evenings." Holding her hands out like little shovels, she urged us forward, practically pushing us out the door.

Iris looked over her shoulder, worry coating her words as she asked, "Are you sure?"

"Super sure," Alyssa answered with a manic smile. "Thanks for your help, ladies."

And with that, she slammed the door shut in our faces.

The four of us stood in the hallway for a stunned moment, but Edna quickly peeled off to her apartment and Bailey waved goodnight as she did the same. That left just Iris and me. Suddenly, all of our earlier ease dissipated, and we were back to awkwardness.

"This is dismal," Ripley said, speaking up now that there were fewer people around.

I couldn't help but agree.

"Look, Meg." Iris sucked in a breath, as if steeling herself for what she was about to say. "About what you asked the other day, about your dad..." she added.

Like I could forget. I gulped, wondering if she was about to spill something, but trying not to get my hopes up. Ripley floated closer in anticipation.

"...I really think you need to let it go." A line formed in between her eyebrows. It was the same expression she wore when researching a tricky subject or searching for a book at the library that wasn't where it was supposed to be.

It was a dead end.

Still, I didn't know what to say. Luckily, Laurie chose that moment to come walking into the hallway from the stairwell. Leo panted happily as he saw me, and he flipped his ears back into greeting mode and wiggled his whole body like a happy little seal. I knelt to meet him as Laurie let the leash go slack.

"Well, I'll let you two get on with your night." Iris tugged at her cardigan again. "It sounds like Alyssa will figure out what to do about her stolen dress."

I'd only barely glanced up at her before she was stepping toward her apartment door and disappearing inside. Ripley let out a low whistle. Laurie arched an eyebrow in question.

I inclined my head toward my door. "I'll explain everything inside."

"Everything?" Laurie asked.

"You have no idea, man," Ripley muttered as I let us into my apartment.

THREE

By noon the next day, I'd told the story about the break-in at apartment 5C twice.

Laurie had been concerned about everyone's safety, but his worry ebbed once I mentioned how the burglar had used the key Alyssa left in the light fixture to get inside.

"At least it's not like they picked the lock or anything," he'd said, breath rushing out of him in his relief.

Zoe, the second person I told, was also troubled by the news, but for a very different reason than Laurie had been last night. "Dude, I usually don't mind working nights, but lately, it seems like I'm missing out on all the good stuff." She signed the receipt for her lunch and glanced at me to see if I was ready to go.

Standing, I let her lead the way out of the restaurant where we'd gone to eat.

"And this was after Nancy called a meeting to tell everyone that the owner of the Morrisey died?" Zoe held her hand up to shield her eyes from the September sun. Her long, dark hair swung behind her as she turned to face me, cocking an equally dark eyebrow.

"It was a big night." I chuckled.

Zoe snorted. "So, what? Was the guy who owned the building super old or something?"

"Middle aged. Boating accident." I let my expression go slack. "He actually dated my aunt Penny for a while when I was little."

I mentioned that as if it were a fact I'd forgotten, and not something I'd been too young to remember, as was actually the case. Ripley had been the one to remember that tidbit last night when she, Laurie, and I were hanging out.

"Wild." Zoe checked right, then left, before jogging across the street toward the small city park that took up the triangular piece of concrete outside our building.

We passed by a walking tour that had stopped in front of the totem pole in the middle of the park.

"—it was stolen from the Alaskan Tlingit tribe by businessmen who were up north on an expedition. They 'gifted' it to the city—" The tour guide used air quotes around the word before continuing on in his speech.

"People giving things away that they didn't own in the first place? Checks out," Zoe deadpanned as we wove our way through the gathered crowd.

"Yeah, and that's not even the genuine totem pole, either. The first one was set on fire by an arsonist. They recreated it in the forties. This one's a replica."

Shooting me an impressed look over her shoulder, Zoe said, "I can see someone's taken that tour before."

"I haven't, actually."

"You just know that much about local history?"

"Maybe I do." I lifted my chin in defiance as we approached the Morrisey.

"She learned about it because of the Morrisey Masterpiece Classic, actually," Ronnie Arbury, who I hadn't even realized was right behind us, said as he grabbed the door from Zoe. He squinted one eye. "That had to be the 2011 MMC, I think. *This local artifact was destroyed by arson and replaced in 1940,*" he repeated the clue that had led us to the totem pole.

Zoe stopped in the entryway of the lobby, hand on her hip. She spoke slowly as she repeated. "Morrisey Master—"

"—piece Classic." Ronnie bobbed his head as he finished the name for her. His attention drifted to me. "It's an annual scavenger hunt we used to do as a building. Meg's aunt organized it, so we haven't had one since she moved to Scotland." Sadness surrounded his statement.

Zoe pursed her lips suspiciously, like she thought Ronnie was pulling her leg. She turned toward me.

"It's all true." I held up my hands in a defensive posture. "There were three rounds of scavenger hunts. The first took place here at the Morrisey. If your team advanced through that round, the clues broadened to Pioneer Square, and finally to all of downtown for the third round." Fondness tugged my lips up into a grin. "I forgot how much fun those used to be." I turned to Ronnie, hoping to reminisce some more, but found his focus had strayed past me.

He was squinting toward the mailboxes. When I turned, I saw what had caught his interest. A group of residents were crowded around the mailboxes. Well, crowded was the wrong word. They stood in a line, each pressing an ear up to the wall of mailboxes. Ronnie moved toward them, as if pulled by a tractor beam of nosiness. I guess I was one to talk, though, because I followed right behind him, Zoe on my heels.

For once, Ronnie Arbury—grocery deli manager, wannabe thespian, champion of awkward improv acting, and person who'd stuck his foot in his mouth more times than I could count—read the room correctly and stayed silent. He simply pressed his ear to the wall alongside Darius, Opal, Art, and Nancy.

The most humorous part of the whole thing was that their super-obvious eavesdropping positions were unnecessary. I could hear the conversation happening in the mailroom just as well from where I was.

"—father is a problem. I thought the father was bad, but I'm really worried about the kids," the person inside said, forgetting that the mailroom was not soundproof.

"Penny?" I blurted before I could stop myself. My hand came up to slap over my mouth, but the damage was done.

My fellow Morrisey residents scowled at me from their places on the wall. Even Ronnie studied me with frustration, which stung most of all. I officially had less sense than Ronnie Arbury when it came to keeping my mouth shut. They scrambled away from the mailboxes, getting as far from the scene of their eavesdropping as possible before the mechanical room door opened and my aunt stepped out, followed by Iris.

"Meggie!" Penny opened her arms as she strode toward me, only sparing a quick glance to the side as she noticed Nancy and Opal studying a potted plant near Nancy's apartment door, and Art and Darius who'd just decided to face the opposite wall like she was some sort of predator that wouldn't see them if they couldn't see her.

Pushing past my questions and reservations, I closed the distance between us, slipping my arms through hers as she wrapped me in a hug.

"Hey, kid." She squeezed me tight. "Surprise."

I *felt* like a kid again. There was something about Penny's familiar scent—black licorice from her favorite writing snack, black jellybeans—and how she lifted me a little as she hugged me tighter, that stripped away any sense of adulthood I'd created over the past six years since I'd moved out.

"Surprise?" I repeated, dumbfounded.

Penny's eyes shifted over to Iris, where the woman had stopped next to her. Iris's cheeks were blotchy with red spots and her fingers worried at the hem of her blouse.

"Yeah," Penny finally said. "I came to visit you, of course." She huffed as if it was obvious.

My eyes narrowed. "Why didn't you call? And why were you holed up in the mailroom whispering with Iris?"

Penny coughed. Her throat moved through a hard swallow. "I, well, there's—"

A crisply indrawn breath rang out from behind me. I turned to find Ronnie Arbury doing some middle-aged-man version of jazz hands. Zoe looked at him sidelong before taking a small step away.

"You're here to do a Morrisey Masterpiece Classic, aren't you?" Ronnie's question was less of a query and more of an order.

It wasn't the worst guess Ronnie had ever yelled out loud.

The annual scavenger hunt *had* always taken place in September, a ritual to close out the summer.

So, I suppose it shouldn't have been a big surprise when Penny said, "You caught me." A grin spread over her face, and she pointed affectionately at Ronnie. "I thought I'd surprise the building!"

At this news, the other residents who'd been pretending not to be involved in the conversation rushed over, chattering with excitement about the competition. A hand closed around my arm, and I jumped to find Zoe standing by my side.

"Oh! Sorry, I forgot to introduce you." I pulled her over to the group. "Penny, this is Zoe. She lives in 5E."

Penny peeled her concentration from the other Morrisey residents to look at the surly young woman next to me. "The bartender! Right!" She held out her hand. "It's so great to meet you, Zoe."

Zoe smiled politely, a customer service mask I'd seen her wear during her shifts at the speakeasy around the block. My friend obviously wasn't as excited to see my aunt as our neighbors were, and she obviously wasn't feeling inclined to hang around. "I've got to get ready for work. Walk up with me?" She hooked her arm with mine, pulling me toward the stairwell.

"I'll come by to see you in a bit," Penny called after me.

The whirlwind of feelings solidified into actual dizziness as Zoe hauled me into the stairwell and spun toward me.

"Whoooa," I said, the word coming out in a fragmented way that made me sound like a cowboy attempting to slow a wild horse. "What gives?" I said, starting up the stairs so I might put some distance between myself and my aunt.

Zoe followed, fixing me with an anxious look. "This isn't good. Is it?"

Nostrils flaring, I said, "Well…"

"Meg." Zoe's tone was sharp. "I heard what she and Iris were talking about: a father and kids. She's here because you've been asking about your dad. Iris tattled, and now Penny's here to shut you down."

Wincing, I nodded. "I'm pretty sure that's what's happening."

Zoe patted me on the back as we climbed the stairs. "Sorry."

My friend understood the harsh realities of researching the identity of a long-lost father better than most people. She'd moved to Seattle to find her father after losing her mother, only to find that her dad had passed away back before she could walk. She'd never even gotten the chance to know him.

"Thanks." I reached up and patted her hand, letting her know I was okay.

She broke the contact, letting her hand fall away as we continued to climb the flights up to the fifth floor. "And is she staying with you? How's that supposed to work?"

I shrugged. "I'm sure we'll figure something out. I can always stay with Laurie if she wants the bed."

It never bothered me when people didn't understand my relationship with my aunt. She and I were close—the only family we each had—while simultaneously being two very independent people. Well, Penny was independent. I only *seemed* that way because I'd always had Ripley by my side, no matter what. But it was like waving a red flag whenever I told people my aunt, the woman who'd raised me, had moved over four thousand miles away, and I didn't know when I was going to see her next.

Zoe expecting me to find Penny's lack of communication and gatekeeping surrounding my dad's identity as frustrating as she did also wasn't a surprise. Penny wasn't a selfish person, but she definitely made choices I didn't always understand. Ripley had talked me through a few big blowups when I was a teenager, and we'd come to the conclusion that "Penny was gonna Penny." I could either accept my aunt for who she was, or risk being frustrated and offended about things outside of my control.

As much as Penny joked about the characters she wrote in her Scottish romance novels having minds of their own, the woman was used to being the boss in all ways that counted. She was not only her own boss, but the creator of her characters, settings, and plots. She pulled all the strings, and sometimes that expectation transferred to her interactions with real people.

"Have a good shift," I told Zoe as we reached our floor, and we broke off to our respective sides of the hallway.

"Thanks. Come by tonight if you need a break. I'll fit you in."

The Cooler speakeasy, where Zoe worked, was so exclusive that it was accessible by reservation only, and those spots filled up quickly. But every once in a while, Zoe texted saying she had a last-minute cancelation, or that it was slow enough that I could sit at the bar and chat with her.

"Thanks. I'll let you know."

Unlocking my door, I pushed it open to find my black cat, Anise, waiting for me.

"Well, hello, my beautiful girl," I cooed, kneeling to scoop her up into my arms.

"Aww. Hi. You're not so bad yourself," Ripley answered from the other side of the room.

I wanted to laugh at her joke, but I had information to impart, and I wasn't sure how long Nancy and the Conversationalists would be able to delay Penny downstairs. "Penny's here."

Ripley's attention snapped over to me. "What?"

Inhaling through my nose, I tried to stay as calm as I'd pretended to be around Zoe. "She just showed up. Did an awful job of covering up her true intentions downstairs, and Ronnie took advantage of her stumble by suggesting she's here to run the Morrisey Masterpiece Classic. Now she's stuck planning that." I giggled despite the concern furrowing my best friend's features.

"True intentions? Like, stopping you from researching your dad?" Ripley crossed the room.

"I don't see what else it could be. I overheard her talking to Iris about fathers and kids, so..." I lifted my shoulders, then let them drop.

Puffing out her cheeks, Ripley let the situation settle over her. "Okay. All right. No, we can work with this. Actually, it might be good."

"Good?" I scoffed. "How? We're going to have to pause our research for however long she's here. I'm guessing her plan is to follow me like a hawk to make sure I don't find anything."

Ripley lifted her hands, palms up. "There's nothing to stop. We aren't getting anywhere, anyway." There was a level of defeat in her tone that made my stomach drop, but then she added,

"Penny might be the only person alive who knows the identity of your father, so this is probably for the best."

Setting down Anise, I tried to comprehend what Ripley was saying. "You want to ask Penny directly? Again? And what makes you think we'll get a different answer from the other times I've asked?"

"Psh. No." Ripley studied me like I might be crazy. "I know she'll say no if we ask her outright. *I'm saying* that we should trick her into spilling her secret while she's here."

I chuckled. "Ah, so you're even more delusional than I thought."

But determination shone in Ripley's eyes. "You said yourself that she's off her game."

"When did I say that?"

"She just got duped into running an intricate multiday scavenger hunt by a man who frequently wears his shirts inside out." Ripley glanced at me through dark lashes. "Penny's already destabilized. We just have to push her in the right direction, and I think she'll lead us right to your dear ol' dad." Ripley flicked her index finger to signify the amount of pressure she anticipated having to use to sway her.

I hoped she was right, but something told me it wouldn't be that easy.

FOUR

I had to give it to Penny. Ronnie Arbury may have tricked her into running a Morrisey Masterpiece Classic, but she was sticking with the lie.

The next day was a Saturday, and the building was summoned for a non-urgent meeting around lunchtime.

Nancy couldn't hide her smile as she stood at her podium in front of the residents. Her enthusiasm was nothing compared to the pure joy evident in every breath Ronnie took, but he was less noticeable, tucked away within the crowd.

"Morrisey," Nancy addressed everyone after it became clear no one else was coming. "I have a surprise for you." She swept her hands to her left, where Penny had been hiding behind a large potted fern.

Gasps rang out as people moved through their surprise and landed on elation. Penny ran out like a contestant on a game show, taking Nancy's place behind the podium.

"Hey, everyone," she said, wiggling her fingers toward the

residents in a familiar wave. "It was about time for me to visit Meg." At that, she sent me an adoring glance. "But I also thought, wouldn't it be fun to run one more Morrisey Masterpiece Classic while I'm here? It's the perfect time of year, after all."

The gathered residents nodded, anticipation growing among the few who had yet to hear the news.

"Because Penny's here for a limited time, we're going to jump right in today." Nancy clapped her hands together, surveying the crowd. "So, if you're not interested in participating, you're free to leave or come over here to sit with Edna if you'd just like to spectate, and then we'll split up into partners."

A few people stood, making excuses for why they wouldn't be able to take part or stay to watch. One of those was Zoe, who rose with a sigh. "I've got work in an hour, and I'm guessing this will take longer than that."

Grimacing, I confirmed her suspicion. "Sorry."

"No problem," she said. "You and Laurie are going to be a team, anyway."

Laurie slid an arm around my shoulders from where he sat on my other side, but before we could say anything, Winnie Wisteria raised her hand in the row in front of us.

"You're not actually going to let Meg and Laurence be a team? Are you, Nancy?" she asked in her best *let me talk to your manager* tone.

Scoffing, Zoe placed a hand on her hip. "Why not? Because they're a couple? Are you going to stop the married people from being a team? Or the Rosenblooms?" She flicked her fingers toward the sisters in the front row.

Winnie whirled on her, matching her attitude. "It's *not* because they're a couple."

"And the married people aren't a threat because they usually get distracted by their kids," Darius mumbled from his seat next to Winnie.

Hayden Nutters lifted his chin. "Teal and I don't have kids."

"Yeah, but the two of you get sidetracked any time you see a plant," Art said. "If one of the clues leads up to the roof, forget it. You're obsessed with that greenhouse. You won't be able to resist disappearing inside for hours."

Hayden pulled an offended face, but his wife tipped her head and said, "He's got a point."

"Laurence and Nutmeg have actually *never* been allowed to be on a team together," Nancy answered for the group.

"We were always the fastest runners in the building, and they wanted to spread us out so we could run for clues if we were paired with someone who had trouble with the stairs," Laurie explained.

I held up a finger. "I kind of hoped we might change that rule now that we're all grown up, though."

Ronnie Arbury stood. "If you and Laurence are a team, the rest of us might as well not play." He folded his arms like a petulant child.

"That's not—" Laurie started.

But Ronnie wasn't done. "Have you seen the two of you? You practically finish each other's sentences. You act like you're still in the honeymoon phase, even though you've almost been together for a year now. You're a power couple. You'd crush us."

I placed a hand on my heart. "Awww. Ronnie, that's actually really sweet of you to say. Thank you."

Laurie stood. I prepared myself for an impassioned speech about why we should be allowed to compete together. I kept my hand over my heart, waiting to be blown away by a romantic declaration that he wouldn't accept anything less than the honor of being my partner.

"If I can't be with Meg, I want Opal," he said instead.

"Yes!" Opal punched the air from her place near the front, the motion making her long gray braid fling out behind her as her thick-rimmed glasses toppled off her nose. Righting them, she said, "I have no idea what we're doing, but I'm in. Let's do this, kid. Team Laurpal!"

My hand dropped from my chest. Ripley cackled from where she floated nearby.

Laurie glanced down at me and said, "What? They're right. We're too good of a team." He planted a kiss on the top of my head. Leaning close, he whispered, "And Opal's great with puzzles. You're going down, Dawson." There was a competitive gleam in his eye as he stood up straight once more and moved to find his partner.

After that, the crowd devolved into chaos as everyone paired off, chattering excitedly about what the clues might be.

Zoe patted my arm, holding back a grin. "Good luck, buddy." She turned to leave before she could break into laughter, but I heard the chortle as she reached the stairwell.

Ripley swooped into Zoe's now empty chair. "Meg, you've gotta snap out of whatever catatonic state you're in and partner up, or else you're going to be stuck with Ronnie or Wendell."

Panic jolted me into action. She was right. And if Laurie

wanted to play this way, I was going to show him exactly how competitive I could be. Shooting to my feet, I frantically assessed the crowd.

Penny was obviously out, since she was the person who wrote the clues. Iris stood with her, proving she was likely helping with clues as she had in years past. And Nancy was always off-limits, preferring to put her scrapbooking and paper-crafting skills to use creating the clue envelopes rather than participating.

Most of the pairings were no surprise. The Rosenbloom sisters were always a team. Art and Darius could barely go twelve hours without seeing one another, so we all knew they would pair up. Bailey and Cascade stood next to each other, chatting animatedly about their mutual yoga instructor, looking as if spandex was their team uniform, and that they'd coordinated ahead of time. Cascade's black yoga pants and sports bra were the same color as Bailey's braids, and Bailey rocked a tan set of leggings and tank top that matched Cascade's dirty-blonde locks. The Nutters were sticking together, as were the Porters and the Youngs—though the children were already acting up, and it was unlikely they'd be able to stay focused for long.

Ronnie had been trying to get close to Winnie ever since he'd found out she worked at the Third Avenue Theatre last year. He made a beeline for her, sending her running off in the opposite direction. In her retreat, she ran straight into Wendell Underwood. Winnie took one look at her snake-obsessed fourth-floor neighbor, grabbed his hand, and declared him her teammate. The sight made Ronnie stop in his tracks and scan the rest of the group for a different partner.

Alyssa stood near the back of the room, and we locked eyes like hands grasping at a lifeline. In a show of surprising agility for me, I dodged Ronnie and climbed over the chairs to get to her side. She clutched my arm and giggled when we were finally together, our joint relief causing us to lean on one another.

In the end, Ronnie and Julian paired up, something which Ronnie looked none too happy about. The building had forgiven Julian for what he'd pulled last year, but he'd kept to himself ever since as some sort of weird self-imposed punishment.

"Okay, if you've got a partner, come up front to register with Iris and you'll get your first envelope," Nancy's voice cut through the chatter. "Don't open the first clue until everyone has one. And remember, it might be better to go off to a different location to read it, so you don't have other teams following you to the next checkpoint."

The teams lined up behind Nancy's podium, waiting their turn. Those of us near the back began stacking the chairs we'd used for the meeting so they wouldn't be in the way when the teams began moving around for the hunt.

As we waited our turn, Alyssa fidgeted at my side. She must've glanced over her shoulder five times before I followed her line of sight. She was watching the lobby doors.

"You expecting someone?" I asked conversationally.

Stiffening, Alyssa said, "What? Why would you say that?"

"You keep looking at the front doors."

Her neck went taut. "No. I'm fine." After that, she kept her attention focused ahead.

"Okaaay," Ripley said from where she floated next to me. "Someone's a little jumpy."

I widened my eyes in response, knowing I couldn't say anything surrounded by so many people.

"I wonder if this snappy mood has anything to do with the stolen dress." Ripley tapped her lip in thought. "She did mention that the designer was going to be out for blood once he found out she'd lost it."

Ripley had a point, and it made me study my neighbor in more detail. Her normally shiny hair was dull and wrapped up in a messy bun. I'd assumed it was just because it was the weekend, but paired with the dark circles under her eyes and the toothpaste stain on her designer sweatshirt, maybe it was evidence that Alyssa wasn't doing so well. Her ripped jeans were still probably more expensive than one of my paintings, but her toenail polish was chipped in her designer sandals.

Alyssa always looked put together. Something was up.

Before I could ask her how she was doing, however, we stepped up to the front of the line. Iris recorded our pairing on her list as Penny handed us a golden envelope, sealed with a shiny gilt M sticker.

"You must've been up all night," I whispered to my aunt.

She'd ended up staying with Iris, who'd recently purchased a pull-out couch, so I hadn't even needed to worry about sleeping arrangements.

Penny squinted one eye, a sure sign that whatever she was about to say was a lie. "It wasn't bad. The envelopes are all Nancy's creation."

Alyssa and I stepped aside with our clue, waiting as the rest of the group got theirs. Laurie caught my eye from across the lobby, his mouth lifting into a half smile that simultaneously made me want to kiss him and defeat him.

Checking the line to make sure we had time, Laurie said something to Opal before walking toward me. I held up a finger to Alyssa and met him halfway.

"Ripley here?" he whispered against the shell of my ear.

My gaze moved to where she floated just in front of us. "She is."

He shot me a sidelong glance. "But you're not going to use her, right? Since that would be cheating."

Ripley wrinkled her nose in frustration, proving that he had us there.

"Of course not," I said confidently, even though I'd definitely used her help in years past.

Laurie's smile widened. "Good." With that, he took my chin with his thumb and index finger. Tilting my head up, he planted a mind-blowing kiss on my lips before walking away.

"What an evil man," Ripley said in response.

My vision was still a little blurry. "Evil, yes. But still hot."

Laughing, Ripley followed me back to where Alyssa stood. "You know, he'll never be able to tell if I help you," Ripley said.

"I know." I gave a clipped nod. "But I want to prove I can beat him without your help," I whispered.

Saluting me, Ripley stopped short of where my partner stood. "Then I might wander. Good luck!" She vanished.

I gulped in a steadying breath, hoping we wouldn't need it.

"Everyone ready?" Nancy called from the podium now that all the teams had a copy of the first clue. Her question was met with a chorus of yeses. "There are ten teams this year, but we'll stick with our usual format of twelve clues—four in each round. This means no one will be eliminated until after the first two clues. After that, there will be one less envelope at each answer site, until we get to the last one for today, which will decide the eight teams moving on to the next round. So, if you want to be one of those teams, don't be the last to find the answer." Nancy's eyes sparked with excitement as she held up a hand like the person at the start of a race. "Morrisey teams, welcome to this year's Masterpiece Classic. You may begin!"

FIVE

The teams scattered. While time was of the essence, no one wanted to give away the answer by charging toward the next clue. Tailing would get a team disqualified, but that didn't mean everyone wouldn't take note of where other teams were going.

Having taken the envelope, Alyssa peeled off the sticker and slid out the clue as we huddled by the mailboxes. I scooted closer until I was shoulder to shoulder with my partner, and we read the clue together.

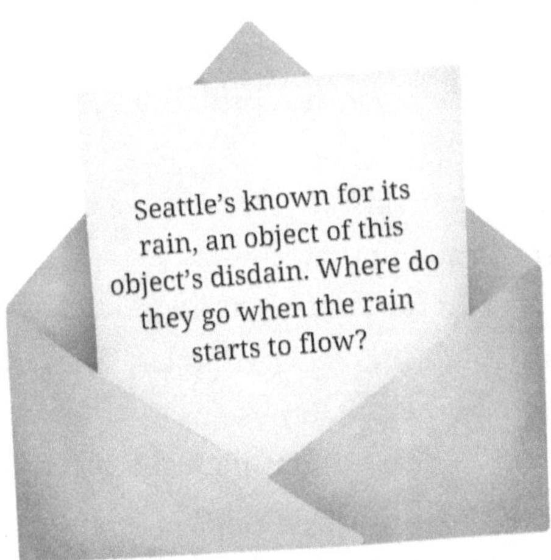

Alyssa and I read over the clue a few times, our lips moving quietly as we digested every word. This first round took place entirely within the Morrisey, so the clue had to be referencing something in the building.

Elbowing Alyssa, I motioned for her to follow me to the stairwell. "I'm not sure what it is yet, but if it's getting rained on, its gotta be on the roof, right?"

Alyssa lit up, and she kept up with the nonchalant pace I'd set. We remained bent over the clue, acting like we were just wandering as we worked out the clue. Laurie, Opal, and the Rosenblooms must've had a similar idea because they were all waiting for the elevator.

"Good luck to Laurie inside that tiny box," I scoffed as we opened the stairwell door.

I wasn't sure if he was in more danger from the rickety elevator or being stuck in a small space with the Rosenbloom sisters, who had a historically hard time keeping their hands to themselves around him, but he was officially on his own.

The moment the door shut behind us, Alyssa and I started sprinting up the steps.

"What hates the rain?" I asked between panted breaths as my lungs burned and our pace slowed.

Alyssa hesitated on the third-floor landing, resting her hands on her thighs as she dragged in air. "Can't be the plants up there. They love the rain."

"The firepit?" I guessed, but immediately corrected myself. "The clue says *they*. It's got to be more than one thing."

We kept moving. Even though no one would get eliminated during this round, the sooner we got the next clue, the more of a head start we would have on the other teams. Below us, the stairwell door clanged open and voices spilled into the space. Children giggled and screeched, the sound bouncing off the walls and reaching us a few floors above.

Glancing at one another, Alyssa and I picked up the pace.

"What changes when the weather turns?" Alyssa asked as we paused on the fifth-floor landing.

Snapping my fingers, I whispered, "The cushions for the outdoor furniture." Checking the clue again, I said, "The next clue must be in the plastic storage shed."

"Oh, good thinking." Alyssa grabbed my arm and pulled me up the last flight of stairs.

The two of us spilled out onto the roof. The group from the elevator had beaten us up there, but they'd split up. The Rosenblooms had gone left, toward Rooftop Rachel. Though the sisters wouldn't be able to see her, the mute ghost always floated in that corner of the roof. They walked right past her as they searched around the greenhouse. Laurie and Opal, however, were loitering by the firepit. They were keeping an eye on the other team, but the moment they spotted us on the roof, they lunged for the storage shed. We shot forward.

"Aha!" Opal called out in victory as Laurie pulled open the shed doors. Ten gold envelopes were taped to the inside.

"Amateur," Alyssa whispered to Opal, jerking her thumb toward the Rosenblooms, who were now headed in this direction after Opal's outburst.

Opal sputtered but couldn't come up with a response.

"I forgot it's Opal's first time," I said as I plucked one of the envelopes from the door. "Good luck with that," I told Laurie before dashing after Alyssa, who was already ringing the call button for the elevator.

"Quick," she said, finger jamming on the door close button as I slipped inside just in time.

I ignored the way the whole elevator bounced as I entered, caring more about our victory than my fear surrounding the contraption. "Ha! Now they'll be forced to wait or take the stairs. Good thinking."

Alyssa beamed proudly. "Thank you." She flapped her hands in front of her, signaling for me to open the clue.

I did, holding it between us as the elevator dropped back down to the lobby.

We sucked in twin breaths.

"The mailbox for 5H," we said at the same time.

Back when the mailboxes had been installed, the contractor hadn't realized that the manager's apartment had a separate mail slot right next to the apartment door. He'd gotten confused and labeled the extra 5H, an apartment that didn't exist. The problem was, the apartment numbers were carved into the brass doors, so it had remained ever since.

The elevator doors dinged open and we shot forward.

"It won't be accessible from this side. Plus, that's way too open." I motioned to the left, and Alyssa followed me through the mechanical room door. From there, we slipped into the mailroom.

These doors were usually locked to residents, but everything was open during the scavenger hunt, save for our individual apartments. Still, it made me feel like we were on the right track.

Sure enough, mailbox 5H was filled with gold envelopes. Alyssa swiped one, and we got out of there as quickly as we could. No one else was in the lobby hallway when we emerged from the mechanical room, but the elevator was on the move, if the creaking, grinding noise coming from the door was any indication.

Alyssa and I slipped back into the stairwell, huddling close once we found the landing clear. Footsteps and voices rang out above us, but we couldn't tell if they were ascending or descending. Alyssa ripped open the clue, our careful movements from earlier gone.

Frowning, we reread the clue before meeting eyes.

"The elevator?" Alyssa suggested. "But we were just in there, and I didn't see a clue anywhere."

"They rarely choose main thoroughfares as locations," I

agreed. "It would be too easy for someone to stumble on a clue or pick one up out of order."

"Cause trouble." Alyssa flexed her fingers as she thought. "What would be a problem if it was wiggly?"

I paced, keeping my voice down as I listed items: "Nancy's podium, a chair, the firepit. Oh, the front door kept getting stuck during those hot days this summer, but that's more of a jam than a wobble."

Alyssa's eyes crinkled into slits as she pondered the clue. "I like the idea of the chairs. Are any of the lobby chairs wobbly?"

Eyes flying open wide, I said, "The couch at the entrance has one leg shorter than the rest." Opal sat there whenever she did her puzzles, and I'd noticed her tottering around like she was sitting on a makeshift rocking chair.

Checking out the small stairwell window, we pushed our way into the lobby hallway. We kept our pace slow, so as not to attract attention, but it didn't matter. Laurie and Opal had beaten us to the front sofa.

Of course, they had. Opal sat on that couch every day.

Laurie spotted me, sending me a playful wink before ushering Opal out of the way, clutching the next clue. Alyssa and I moved to take their place, immediately crouching next to the couch.

I couldn't help but stop to glance at where Laurie had moved, however, hoping to get another glimpse of that handsome smile of his. He obliged by beaming at me from where he and Opal had stopped to read their next clue.

A smack to my arm interrupted my staring. "Hey, stop drooling over your boyfriend and help me look." Alyssa grunted as she dropped her head down, level with the floor, so she could peer underneath the couch.

"Sorry." I shook my head, as if that would do anything to release his hold on me.

"Distracting you is probably part of his plan." Alyssa lifted the left cushion.

"Then we're doomed," I grumbled as I helped her search, running a hand under the cushions.

Competitive Laurie was one of my favorite versions. And even though it was a side of him I'd seen a lot over the years, I'd also been in love with the guy since I could remember, so it was obviously working.

Just then, my fingers grazed a folded piece of card stock stuffed into the corner of the couch. There had to be eight of them, but I only plucked one from the group. "Got it."

By the time we got to our feet and brought the envelope over to the fireplace to look at the last clue in private, Laurie and Opal had moved on. Good. Less distraction.

The final clue envelope was full of loose puzzle pieces. It was clearly a photograph of something in the building, but the pieces were too small to tell what without putting them together.

We scanned our surroundings. No one else had made it to the couch clue yet. There were a few teams searching in front of the building, incorrectly guessing that the first clue had been referencing something out there, but they seemed occupied.

Alyssa and I sank to the floor next to the fireplace and started on the puzzle. It was probably only in twenty pieces, but the colors were so similar, we had to go mostly by the shapes. I placed the last piece, and we craned our necks as we tried to find which direction was up.

"It's one of the trash chutes," I whispered, looking around to make sure we were still alone.

"So, what? They just want us to check every garbage chute in the building?"

My smile grew as I pointed to a patch of slightly darker paint on the wall next to the chute. "No. This has to be from the second floor. Do you remember when Art tried to throw away that shoe rack, and he got it lodged into the opening? It was before I left for the East Coast."

Stifling a giggle, Alyssa said, "Oh! I do remember that. Yes, you're right. That's where he scraped up the wall and tried to cover it with the wrong color paint." She gathered the puzzle pieces back into the envelope, and we strode past the Rosenbloom sisters as they bustled over to the lobby couch.

Laurie and Opal weren't around when we reached the second floor, but given Opal's aptitude for puzzles, and how funny Laurie had thought the shoe rack situation had been at the time, I was under no illusions that they hadn't beaten us.

My suspicions were confirmed as we pulled open the garbage chute and found seven gold envelopes taped to the inside of the door panel.

"They got here first." Alyssa snapped her fingers in defeat. "I was really hoping Opal would slow Laurie down, especially since she's a rookie."

Sighing, I said, "There's no slowing that woman down. She may be spindly, but she's quick." Even though I knew what it would say, I opened the envelope.

We shared a quick high five before heading back downstairs. This time, we wound our way down the stairwell at a leisurely pace.

"So ... how's everything going?" I asked as we walked. When Alyssa frowned in question, I added, "With the whole dress situation. Was that designer mad about the stolen dress?"

"Yeah, he was. It's bad." She cringed as she held the stairwell door open for me. "The whole thing has been a little catastrophic, actually."

I was about to ask her if that was why she'd looked so jumpy earlier, but we rounded the corner to cheers as Penny, Iris, Nancy, Laurie, and Opal greeted us. Edna, there to spectate, clapped.

"Team two!" Nancy waved her hands in the air.

"Well done!" Penny squeezed me into a hug. "Not that I had any doubts," she whispered into my ear before pulling back with a grin.

But I didn't feel like smiling. Not after hearing what Alyssa had said about the designer. What did catastrophic mean? Was she in danger?

Laurie wandered over, hands in his pockets. His mouth tilted into a shy grin that I knew was 100 percent an act. "Sorry we beat you."

Pushing Alyssa's comment out of my mind, I shoved him in the arm and said, "You're not the least bit sorry."

He chuckled, wrapping that same arm around me. "You're right. I'm not. It feels amazing."

"I'm going to have to try this whole distraction technique on *you,* next round." I leaned into him.

"Oh, I'd like to see this. Wanna practice on me now?" He spun me around to face him.

"Sure." I snaked my fingers around his neck, running them over his skin until he shivered. Then I leaned up and kissed him.

Arms wrapping around me, Laurie pulled me closer and returned the kiss.

"Bleh. That's too much PDA for me." The comment sounded so much like something Ripley would say, I almost thought she'd returned.

But then Laurie smirked into the kiss and said, "I can't help it if your partner is irresistible, Alyssa."

She rolled her eyes. "Well, if we're done here, I'm going upstairs. Brad's waiting for me. We've got dinner plans later."

I pulled away from Laurie. "I, uh, need to grab something from my apartment. I'll walk with you."

Catching Laurie's gaze, I widened my eyes, letting him know I was working an angle. He stood up straight, slipping his hands back into his pockets as he watched me skip off after my partner.

Once we were in the stairwell, I waited until we'd passed by a group of scavenger hunters to ask, "Are you sure you shouldn't talk to the police about the dress? I mean, if the designer guy is so mad, maybe they can help find who stole it and take some of the burden off you."

Alyssa considered my words for a few steps, but she finally said, "It has to be me. He doesn't want authorities involved."

What? That was a red flag, and it stopped me in my tracks for a moment. "That's odd. Isn't it?" I took a couple of stairs at a time to catch up.

She held out her hands. "Not really, Meg. These designers are paranoid. They always think people are trying to steal their designs, and they only trust me because I might get them something out of the deal."

"Yeah, but right now the design *is* in someone else's hands. The police would only help. They're certainly not going to take the dress and submit it themselves."

Alyssa let out a humorless laugh. "I know that, and you know that, but try telling it to him." She eyed me in a way that told me to drop it as I held the fifth-floor door open for her. An odd, acrid aroma billowed out to meet us. It stung at my eyes and nose, but wasn't strong enough to be worrisome. In a building this old, sometimes weird smells gathered in the hallways.

"I'm just saying—"

But I didn't get a chance to finish that statement because I ran into Alyssa's back. She'd stopped right in the middle of the hallway.

"What's—"

Again, I didn't get to finish my question. I peered around Alyssa and found what had stopped her in her tracks.

Sitting slumped against the wall next to apartment 5C was a young woman. She had shoulder-length pink hair, and she was wearing a sparkly gold dress. The low neckline of the dress showed off the red marks already bruising around her neck. I opened my mouth to ask if she was okay, but that was when I caught her eyes, open and unseeing.

Alyssa let out a shaky breath. "Well, there's one problem solved."

Incredulous, I reared back and turned to my neighbor. "Lyss, I think that woman's dead."

Swallowing, Alyssa nodded. "Yeah, but she's wearing my missing dress."

Six

My eyes watered, but not from tears of sadness. Whatever hung in the air was irritating my eyes and lungs the longer we stood in it.

"Okay, now we *have* to call the cops." I coughed.

Alyssa shot me a scowl that told me I was being unhelpful. "I know." She swiped at her eyes and pulled her shirt up to cover her nose against the stinging smell.

I patted my jeans and found my phone tucked in my back pocket. "I'll do it." The call itself didn't take long, and did I hear a hint of attitude from the dispatcher when I mentioned the Morrisey? Was it possible that we'd started to get a reputation in the city?

The reality was that this made the third body—well, fourth, if you counted Addy's hundred-year-old skeleton—found in our building. It was a concerning pattern, for sure.

Once I'd hung up with them, I called Laurie.

"Hey, you coming back down?" His voice sounded light. I could picture the grin he probably wore as he joked around with the other residents and celebrated his victory.

Too bad I was about to quash all that.

"Uh ... no. There's a dead woman in the fifth-floor hallway. I've called the police."

There was a pause, and the sounds in the background faded. "Dead?" he asked once he was away from the others. Smart man. "Do we know her?"

"No. I've never seen her before. Neither has Alyssa." At that, I turned my focus on my neighbor, who'd inched closer to the dead woman. She was studying the dress, wincing at the places where it had been ripped along the right side. "You don't recognize her, right, Lyss?" I asked, just to make sure.

Alyssa turned to me in a daze, swinging her head in a no.

"No," I reported to Laurie. "Neither of us do."

"I'm on my way up." I could hear the telltale sounds of the stairwell door and his puffs of breath as he climbed. "See you in a minute."

My fingers clutched at my phone even after I ended the call. I wished Ripley were here with me. Before I knew it, Laurie was in the hallway.

"Whoa." He stumbled back for a second as the odd scent hit him. "Is the smell what killed her?"

I shook my head, pointing to her neck. "Strangled."

Seeing the devastation clear in my features, Laurie closed the distance between us and wrapped me up in his arms. He squeezed tight, resting his head on top of mine as he took in the rest of the scene.

Alyssa glanced over, taken aback by the sight of our embrace. As if seeing me with my boyfriend reminded her that she had one, too, she dragged in air, the quick motion making it hiss between her teeth. "Brad!" Racing to her apartment, Alyssa sidestepped the body so she could open the door.

Laurie and I stood alone in the hallway with the dead woman for a few beats before Alyssa returned with a confused Brad in tow. She held her hand out toward the figure slumped against the wall.

"Look."

Brad peeled the headphones off his ears, letting them settle around his neck. Coughing as he breathed in the mildly spicy air, he swore as he took in the spectacle in front of him. "Is that your missing dress?"

"Yes, and it's completely ruined. Look at the rip along this dart. And the hem's trashed." Alyssa held a hand to her forehead as she catalogued the damage.

While his girlfriend fretted about details that were arguably not important in the grand scheme of things, Brad grew agitated. At first, I thought he was having a reaction to the smell in the air, but his distress seemed directed at the dead woman. He scratched the back of his neck, then glanced behind his back a few times as if he'd felt someone watching and needed to verify that no one was there. After staring at the dead woman, eyes squinting shut like she might be one of those Magic Eye posters that he just needed to look at in a different way, he moved his concentration to the hallway ceiling. His gaze trailed along the wall, searching for ... what? Cameras?

In his thirties, wearing scruffy sweatpants, a stained T-shirt, and with his shaggy brown hair a mess, Brad was exactly the type of guy who might believe in a surveillance conspiracy. And he was just audacious enough to think anyone would want to watch a regular guy like him. But there was something about the way the planes of his throat tightened in a swallow and the fear behind his eyes that told me this was more than paranoia.

Did Alyssa's boyfriend have a reason to be worried?

"Have you seen this woman before, Brad?" I asked, stepping forward out of the comfort of Laurie's arms.

Brad jolted at my question, as if he hadn't realized anyone else was in the hallway. He blinked, then looked back at the pink-haired young woman. "No. I—no." He shook his head decisively, like he thought the two nos he'd already given wouldn't be enough to convince me.

And he was right. They weren't.

"You didn't hear anything?" Laurie picked up the questioning. "Have you been home for long?"

"He hasn't left the apartment all day," Alyssa answered for him, something that rubbed me the wrong way.

Brad interrupted his staring at the dead woman to nod distractedly at Alyssa's statement. "I didn't hear anything."

"There must've been a scuffle." Laurie pointed to the torn dress, the marks on her neck, and finally to the rug that usually sat in the middle of the hallway to soak up any Seattle rain during the wetter seasons. It was skewed, bunching up by Iris's door after being shoved away from Alyssa's.

"I was listening to music," Brad said. "Loud." Another hard swallow.

The sound of footsteps clomping up the stairwell made us all tense and step away to make room. A group of Seattle Police Department officers and crime scene technicians filed in through the stairwell door. I craned my neck, hoping to find Detective Amaya Anthony in the mix. Just as I'd given up, the elevator doors opened, and the detective spilled out, a hand on the wall to steady herself.

"That elevator is terrifying," she said to no one in particular. Straightening and tugging at her suit jacket to reset herself back into professional mode, the detective stepped forward.

When her attention landed on me and Laurie, I could've sworn that the detective's eyes flashed with, dare I say, warmth. Like, maybe we were friends?

"Meg. Laurence. Hello, again." She paired the word *again* with an eye roll. "Can you explain to me what I'm looking at?"

Her team was already kneeling next to the dead woman, checking for signs of life, but from the grim set of their expressions, Alyssa and I were right to assume the worst.

At the same moment the detective asked her question, Ripley appeared next to me. Her eyes were wild as they took in the scene.

"Oh, you're okay." She collapsed forward, resting her hands on her knees. "I saw the police show up, and I couldn't find you anywhere downstairs. Phew."

Laurie must've sensed my hesitation, or maybe he even felt me tense. Either way, we still hadn't answered the detective's question. He obviously thought the information would be best coming from me, because he gave my hand a squeeze.

"We've all been doing a building-wide scavenger hunt for the past hour." I checked my watch to make sure I wasn't lying. "Hour and a half. But when Alyssa and I came back to our floor, we found her here. None of us recognize her." I glared at Brad for a quick moment, wondering if I truly wanted to lump him in with the rest of us. "But we do recognize the dress she's wearing. It was stolen from my neighbor's apartment, 5C, two evenings ago."

"Seriously?" Ripley said, floating over to the deceased woman.

Alyssa, who was standing near her apartment door, wrapped her arms around her middle. Maybe she felt sick. Maybe it was self-protection. Either way, she didn't look happy with me as the detective's focus moved to her.

"This is your dress?" Detective Anthony asked.

"Not exactly. I was borrowing it from a potential client to pitch a new line to my bosses." Alyssa, who always sounded confident in a way I never would be, was visibly shaken. "I'm a buyer at Nordstroms, and this is from a local designer. My apartment was broken into Thursday night, and this was the only thing taken."

Detective Anthony's eyes narrowed, as if her eyelids were giving a visual representation of how much information Alyssa had just shared: a sliver. "Did you file a police report?" She pulled out a notepad, preparing to write down a case number.

"I thought I might be able to find it myself," Alyssa admitted. She lowered her gaze, making the end of the statement come out quieter than the rest.

"Find the dress, or find the person who stole it?" The detective pushed back her shoulders.

"The dress." Alyssa's eyes snapped up, pleading with her. "I promise I wouldn't hurt anyone. I've never seen her before in my life."

"Alyssa's been with me for the past hour and a half," I chimed in, knowing that would help the detective move on, though I had to admit that it was all pretty suspicious.

Amaya Anthony gestured to me. "Thank you, Meg." Her attention shifted to Brad. "And you are?"

"Bradly Ing. I'm Alyssa's boyfriend." He smoothed his T-shirt.

The detective started jotting down notes. "You live here too? In 5C?" She pointed toward the other end of the hall.

"I have my own place in SoDo, but I have roommates, so I spend a lot of time here with Lyss." He cleared his throat. "Alyssa, my girlfriend."

"What's up with this dude, Megs?" Ripley moved to study him and jerked a thumb toward his face. "He's totally sweating. Does he have something to lie about?"

I couldn't answer her at the moment, but I widened my eyes and touched my earlobe to tell her she was on the right track. I just hoped the detective was noticing all the same signs.

"Were you at the scavenger hunt as well?" Detective Anthony asked Brad.

"No. I was here." Brad plucked at his headphones. "Listening to music. I didn't hear anything. I'm sorry."

Taking those notes, Detective Anthony glanced between her notepad and Brad about six times as she wrote. Good. She'd seen the signs too. My shoulders relaxed a smidgen. At that moment, a crime scene tech was able to extract the woman's ID from her wallet. He held it out to Amaya.

"Quinn Garret. Age twenty. Lives in Queen Anne." Her eyes swept across the room. "That ring a bell to any of you?"

We shook our heads, most of us looking at the floor, weighed down by the guilt of not knowing the woman who'd died in our building.

The detective sniffed the air. "Smells like someone used pepper spray too."

Ah, so that was what the spicy scent had been when we'd first entered the hallway. My eyes no longer stung, though, telling me it had dissipated even more as time passed and people opened the stairwell door.

The crime scene team confirmed Amaya's suspicion. "No sign of a bottle on her, but we noticed the smell too. She obviously fought whoever did this to her."

The techs also pulled out one of our building keys from the young woman's purse. We all confirmed what it was while admitting that we had no idea how she could've gotten it. Detective Anthony dismissed us a short while later. Alyssa and Brad disappeared back into her apartment, but I pulled Laurie downstairs. We needed to fill in the rest of the building.

"I'm surprised Nancy's not up here making a fuss after seeing the police rush in," I said through panted breaths as I rushed down the flights. "I should've called her after I talked to you, to warn her. I'm sure she and Penny are terrified."

Laurie stopped, tightening his grip on my hand. "I texted Nance on my way up the stairs after you called. I told her what happened and that there would be police coming in. She said she was going to try to prepare the residents in the lobby, so it didn't turn into pandemonium."

She really liked that word lately. But I couldn't focus too much on Nancy's lack of a thesaurus, because gratitude took over. Turning back toward where he'd stopped between the third and fourth floors, I lunged at him, wrapping my arms tight around his torso since our position on the stairs made our heights so uneven.

"That was a really thoughtful thing to do, Laurence Turner." My words were muffled since my cheek was smooshed against his stomach.

"Laurence?" A laugh rumbled from the base of his chest. "Uh-oh. You'd think I'd done something wrong to evoke my full name."

Peeling myself off him and stepping up a few more stairs so I was on the same level with him, I said, "The very opposite. Thank you." I leaned forward and kissed his cheek.

"What is going on here?" Ripley tapped her ghostly foot as she floated near us.

Cheeks heating, I leaned over the railing to check that we were alone in the stairwell. "Rip's here," I said to him before turning back to her. "I was just telling Laurie that I appreciate his thoughtfulness."

"Even after he abandoned you in the scavenger hunt and then destroyed you?" Ripley scoffed.

I inclined my head in confirmation for Ripley, but spoke to Laurie. "I know you warned Nance, but I'd say she deserves an update. Should we brave the lobby?"

He inhaled, puffing out his chest, then said, "Okay, let's do it."

"Then we need to discuss why Brad just acted so guilty," Ripley mumbled as she followed behind us.

SEVEN

The Morrisey lobby was buzzing.

It wasn't as if I truly believed Nancy would be able to distract the residents long enough for an entire team of police officers and crime scene techs to pour into the building unseen, but I had hoped she might contain them better than this.

We heard the madness before we saw it, but I still wasn't prepared when we stepped out of the hallway by the mailboxes and turned right toward the scavenger hunt headquarters. Ronnie pouted in the corner, glaring at Julian. Bailey and Cascade were screaming at each other. The Rosenblooms were having a similarly loud fight, but theirs involved some light slapping. Art and Darius were sitting on opposite sides of the lobby, refusing to look at one another. And every single child in the room was crying.

The moment everything came into view, it was so alarming that Laurie actually wrapped an arm around me from behind, like a seat belt of safety. I loved him for having the instinct to protect me, but these people were our family. Patting his hand until he let go, I stepped forward.

"Hey. What's going on here?" My voice plowed through the noise, causing everyone to stop.

I know that shouldn't seem like a big deal. Most people can raise their voice when needed. But I'd spent most of my life hiding, making myself as small and quiet as possible. After being branded a weirdo, *Nut Meg,* by my peers in school, for talking to "myself" more than once, I usually opted to say nothing at all. It became part of my personality. I hadn't realized how much moving back to Seattle, living at the Morrisey, and being with Laurie had changed all that until that moment.

I hadn't even hesitated. I hadn't given in to my instinct to shrink back. I hadn't even tried to convince someone else to speak for me. In my peripheral vision, Ripley regarded me with so much pride that it made me want to break into tears.

Penny looked up, doing a double take when she noticed it was me. Her lips parted in surprise, and she watched me warily, like I'd body-snatched her niece.

"Is this about what's happening on the fifth floor?" I asked. My question was directed at Nancy, but I kept my voice loud enough that the rest of the residents could hear.

Nancy, red-faced and reading glasses askew, huffed out a breath. "Unfortunately, this is because of the scavenger hunt," she finally answered, sounding like she'd just ran a marathon. "I got distracted trying to prep for the police showing up and couldn't help put out the fires happening between ... all the remaining teams."

Softening my voice, I took in the room of my neighbors. "You didn't have fun?"

Art spoke up first. "Darius tried to push me down the stairs."

"I did not!" Darius stood and confronted his best friend. "I tripped, and you just happened to be in front of me."

"Why were you two taking the stairs in the first place?" My confusion tugged my eyebrows together. "You always take the elevator."

They glanced around sheepishly. "We were trying to beat Winnie and Wendell," Art confessed.

Surveying the lobby, I couldn't find either of them. "Where are they?" I asked, assuming they'd gone back to their apartments after moving on to the next round.

But Darius said, "They're still on the roof. They haven't made it past the first clue yet."

"We really didn't need to take the stairs." Art closed the distance between him and Darius. "I shouldn't have suggested it. Sorry, friend."

"Me too." Darius held out his hand. "Conversationalists?"

"Conversationalists." Art gripped his hand in a hearty shake.

Ripley let out a squeak and placed her hand over her heart. Love for those two guys surged inside me, too, but there was more to clean up.

"Ronnie?" I turned toward the sour-faced man.

"Julian and I didn't even make it past the first round," he complained. "It's the first time that's ever happened to me."

"Don't put this on me." Julian met Ronnie's ire with indifference. "You're the one who was convinced there was a secret trash chute in the basement."

Ronnie puffed out his chest and turned away, grumbling something about how there could've been.

"Why are the two of *you* fighting?" I asked the Rosenbloom sisters.

Bethy scoffed. "Well, Shirl thought it would be a grand idea to sabotage the other teams by hiding some of the remaining clue envelopes for the first location, even though I told her that was unconstitutional."

"Unconscionable," Laurie corrected.

Bethy clicked her tongue and pointed at him. "That's it."

"Wait." Cascade stepped forward. "That's why those envelopes were stuffed in the garbage can? That was you two?"

"She hid them in the rooftop garbage can?" Ripley deadpanned. "The one without a lid so you can see right inside?" She wheezed out a laugh.

"Not us *two* ... only Shirl," Bethy repeated, stepping away from her sister.

Cascade turned toward her partner. "Bailey, I'm sorry. I thought you were skipping ahead to another clue by taking the one in the trash."

"It's okay." Bailey shrugged. "I would've thought the same."

They pulled one another into a tight hug.

"No wonder Winnie and Wendell have been up on the roof for ages. There aren't any more clues left up there." Nancy shook her head, fatigue slowing the motion.

"And the kids?" I asked, turning toward the crying offspring of the Youngs and the O'Briens. The Porters, nowhere to be seen, had obviously taken their daughter back to their apartment.

"Just tired," Victoria Young said, patting their youngest on the back. "We were just about to go grab an early dinner."

Something settled over the lobby like a communal exhale. Or maybe it was more of an angry fog lifting. When I turned back toward the scavenger hunt headquarters, Nancy and Penny were both staring at me. The women wore very different expressions, however. Nancy's features were relaxed, grateful. She took a moment to fix her glasses now that the yelling and crying had stopped. Penny, on the other hand, regarded me as if she didn't know me.

"Well, someone should probably go up to the roof and let Winnie and Wendell know they can stop searching." Nancy moved past me, squeezing my shoulder affectionately on her way by. Then she stopped, pivoting around to point at Shirley Rosenbloom. "Shirl, don't think you're getting out of talking about that stunt you pulled, by the way. Penny should disqualify you, but I'll let her decide what she wants to do about it."

Shirley studied her feet but sheepishly agreed to take whatever punishment Penny dished out.

"Wait. What happened on the fifth floor?" Edna Feldner asked from her chair behind the podium.

Iris moved over to talk to her.

Once Nancy had left the lobby, Penny wandered over to join me and Laurie. She still eyed me cautiously, but now a tentative smile curled the corners of her mouth.

"That was pretty amazing, what you just did there." Penny tugged on a lock of my hair that had escaped my messy bun. "Where'd my quiet little kiddo go?"

I hunched my shoulders. "She found a place where she wasn't so scared of being loud."

"The same place she grew up?" Penny cocked her head.

I ducked my head in confirmation. "Sometimes you've gotta leave for a while to appreciate what you had."

Penny beamed, her eyes sparkling with the smile. "Your mom was right about this place."

Coughing in surprise, I sputtered out a mostly incoherent, "What?"

Laurie stopped next to me, patting me on the back like I might be choking on something other than just my own spit.

"Your mom loved this building. She's the reason we moved in here in the first place." Penny glanced fondly around the lobby. "We used to walk by it and strategize how we could both live here. The goal was separate apartments, of course." Penny chuckled. "Your mom and I weren't very good roommates."

I hung on every word, eating them up like a starving woman. Penny hardly ever spoke about Mom. Seeing that my birth coincided with her death, it wasn't surprising, but something like this? I wanted to know more.

The eagerness must've been clearly written in my posture, because Penny's eyes flicked between me and Laurie before she said, "Why don't we follow the Youngs' lead and grab some early dinner together? I'll tell you all about it. I'd also love to hear the story about how this happened." She wagged her finger between Laurie and me.

I'd told her everything over the phone, of course, but I couldn't fault her for wanting to hear it in person.

"You free?" I checked with Laurie.

The grin he wore was almost bigger than Penny's had been a moment ago. "As a bird."

While Penny and Laurie discussed where to eat, I turned my concentration to Ripley, who wore the same expression she had at the end of every romantic comedy we'd ever watched together. Her eyes were big and glassy, her chest rose and fell in big expansive breaths, and her head was tipped to one side.

"The three of you are too emotional, and you're starting to rub off on me. I think I'm going to follow that Brad guy and see what's up with him." She waved at me. "Have fun, Megs."

I tugged my ear, our sign for *yes* when I couldn't speak. *I will.* But I watched the place Ripley stood even after she disappeared, heart hurting, wishing she felt comfortable coming with us. It was then that I decided, if Penny was going to open up about Mom, maybe I could get her to talk about my dad as well. It was the least I could do for Ripley.

"The Pink Door, it is," Penny said triumphantly, raising her hands in the air. "I've been craving their lasagna."

Laurie pulled out his phone. "I'll put in a table request now, and they should have something by the time we walk up to the market."

That done, the three of us started walking. Choosing the easier of the topics first, Laurie and I told Penny all about how we got together last fall. Well, not *all* about it. I loved my aunt, but the whole ghost conversation hadn't ever felt like something I was prepared to have with her. Laurie had taken it extremely well, but I knew how special he was. I didn't expect that everyone would accept such an unbelievable thing so easily.

The Pink Door was notoriously busy. Between its location in Post Alley, so close to Pike Place Market, and its reputation for delicious food, it was hard to secure a table on a good day. Summer, when their patio was open, was even harder. While more tables became available, they quickly filled up with tourists and locals alike. Today it helped that we were eating early.

I waited until we'd been seated and Penny was dipping a slice of freshly baked bread into oil and vinegar before pressing her about the other subject we were here to discuss. Bread was one of Penny's favorite food groups, and she was always happiest when she was breaking off pieces and stuffing them into her mouth.

"Pen, I'd love to hear more about the plan you and my mom had to get into the Morrisey." I focused on my own bread, trying not to put too much pressure on my aunt.

"It obviously worked," Laurie added.

She swallowed and took a drink of water. "It did. Sort of." The way her jaw clenched told us all we needed to know about why it wasn't a complete success.

Mom died before she could get an apartment of her own.

Penny wasn't someone who showed a lot of emotion. I only know how much she cried about her sister's death because of Ripley. I'd been a baby, and by the time I was old enough to know what was happening, Penny had accepted her grief as a part of herself. I knew it was still on her mind a lot, though. Her novels often featured a sibling or best friend dying and leaving the main character in a depressive state.

"This was back when your mom and I were in our early twenties, and we worked at that terrible bar in the financial district." Penny gagged. "It almost made me lose all faith in men."

I'd heard about this part, the story having been divulged to me one day during my last few days here before moving to the East Coast. We'd walked by the bar, and Penny had let out a full body shudder. Then, she'd pulled me inside for "old time's sake," telling me some of the tamer stories about the entitled guys who hit on her and my mom as they worked behind the bar.

Laurie laughed into his drink. "Financial bros can do that to a person."

Widening her eyes, Penny agreed. "I was still writing on the side, and the two of us usually got shifts together, so we would walk together from our place near Occidental Square." Penny's lips twitched at the memory. "Every time we passed the Morrisey, we'd sigh and gaze up at the warm yellow lights spilling from the brick-encased windows. She couldn't stop talking about how great of a place it would have been to grow up in, how magical it seemed." Penny took another bite of bread.

That word *magical* felt like a punch to my gut. Penny didn't talk much about my grandparents, but I'd been persistent enough in my questioning that she'd explained how toxic they were. She and my mother had spent the first sixteen years of their lives—well, sixteen for my mom, eighteen for Penny—alternating between being beaten up by their father and watching him do the same to their mother. When their mother refused to leave him, Penny took Mom, helped her emancipate herself, and they moved to Seattle to start a new life.

My grandfather had been why Penny had kept my existence out of Mom's obituary or any news stories about the accident. She'd pleaded with the reporters, telling them we could all be in danger if her father tried to come back into our lives. As it turned out, Penny hadn't needed to worry. Even after news of my mom's death was released, Penny didn't hear from her parents, and she was happy to keep it that way.

Clearing the emotion from her throat, Penny continued her story. "When we saw a studio open up on the fifth floor, we knew we had to jump at it. I'd just sold my first novel, so I had enough for a down payment. Even though it wasn't ideal, I told her we could share the space. It would probably only be for a few years until a bigger apartment opened up. But she had a friend, a girl we worked with at the bar, who had an extra room for rent in a different building, so Charlotte lived with her for about six years. I quit the bar and started writing full time, but I watched out for a space to become available in the building for your mom. She was saving as much as she could, stashing away her tips. The moment another apartment became available, I let her know, but her circumstances had changed." Penny stopped to take a sip of water to cover the frustration she'd obviously felt at the time. "That's when she told me she was pregnant. She'd been dating your father for about six months at that point and was pretty sure he was going to ask her to move in with him once she told him about you, so she passed on the studio at the Morrisey." Any lightness behind Penny's blue eyes went out, leaving behind hard ice.

While I'd never heard this particular tale, I knew enough to guess that this was when Mom's story—and mine, by extension—turned tragic. Sensing the same, Laurie reached under the table and took my hand, lacing his fingers with mine.

"Char came over one night not long after that, in tears.

He'd broken up with her." Penny pursed her lips like she wanted to spit, like all the bread in the world couldn't take the bad taste out of her mouth. "The other apartment had already been picked up, and I didn't want her to be alone with a baby, so as soon as her lease was up, I moved her in with me. It was tight, as you know." Penny smiled at me, remembering the eighteen years we'd lived together in the same space. "But we made it work. We kept an eye out for another apartment to open up in the building, but nothing did in the months before the accident. And then ... it was too late." Trailing a finger through the crumbs of bread on her plate, Penny looked up, her features pulled into an apology. "That wasn't supposed to turn into such a sad story."

Reaching across the table, I took her hand. "It's okay. I like hearing about her, even though it's sad." I took a breath before saying, "My dad was one of the financial bros from the bar, wasn't he?"

A plan formed in my mind. If we could track down the friend Mom had lived with, the one who worked at the bar with her, she might be able to give us the name of my dad, especially if Mom had met him while she was at work.

Penny pulled her hand away. "Meg, I told you before, he's not worth your time."

My heart ached, and I suddenly wished I *had* told Penny about Ripley. If I'd been open with my aunt about my ability to see ghosts, she'd know that this wasn't for me. I didn't need to know my father. The information I sought was all for Ripley's benefit, to help her figure out why she was still here. To give her a chance to move on.

"Is that why you flew out here?" I asked, hating the edge to my voice. "To monitor me because Iris told you I've been asking about my dad?"

Indecision flashed over Penny's face before she admitted, "You caught me, kid."

"Really?" I asked, having a hard time keeping the exasperation from my tone. "You flew four thousand miles just to stop me from finding out who he is?"

"Meg," Penny said with a sigh. "Once she told him she was pregnant and his response was to end things, she only ever wanted two things. The first was for your father to never be a part of your life. And the second was for you to grow up in the Morrisey. I even pushed back about your father, asking over and over if she was sure. She implored me not to question her. So, I stopped. Your mom knew enough about bad men to understand what she was dealing with. If she wanted him to have nothing to do with you, it must've been because he wasn't the type of person you would be safe around." Penny stabbed a piece of bread into the oil and vinegar. "I was unaware at the time, but that was her dying wish, and I'm going to do everything I can to keep the promise I made to her not to let him in your life after he made his decision all those years ago."

A part of me wondered why, if he was such a bad guy, she'd even wanted to move in with him in the first place, but I knew people changed. Sometimes they hid their true self away long enough to trick people into getting close.

There really wasn't any arguing with Penny's logic. Even Laurie seemed to agree that this felt like a vow we had to honor. He squeezed my hand under the table.

I didn't know what to say, but our food came, saving me from figuring anything out at that moment. We concentrated on eating, and I mentally shut the door I'd been keeping open in my mind about my dad. It was time to let him go.

EIGHT

The defeated energy I dragged back into my apartment was a stark contrast to Ripley's enthusiasm when Laurie and I returned from our early dinner with Penny.

"Hey!" She raced forward, eyes wide with excitement. "How was it?"

It was as if her own positive vibes had created a happy halo around her, and she couldn't recognize my less-than-thrilled body language until she got closer. But once she did, she balked.

"Whoa. What happened to you?" She revised her question.

Laurie followed me over to the couch, where we both collapsed.

"Penny told us some stuff about my mom," I answered.

Forehead wrinkling for a split second, during which he thought I'd been talking to him, Laurie's eyebrows kicked up with understanding. "Oh, Ripley's here." Now that he knew I wasn't talking to him, he rested his head back on the couch and closed his eyes.

Ripley didn't pry. She just moved closer. I turned my body to face her, seeing that Laurie was checked out.

I repeated everything Penny spilled at dinner.

"She really said it was your mom's dying wish?" Ripley grimaced.

I pinched the bridge of my nose as I gave her a tired nod. It was all I felt I could do at that moment.

"It was *bad*, Ripley," Laurie chimed in.

When I checked, his eyes were still closed.

"I feel like it drained all the emotional energy from my body," he added, letting his arms rise a few inches and fall limply back onto the couch.

"Oh." The word was so small that it made me glance over to make sure the quiet sound had actually come from my loud best friend. Her mouth was still in an O shape and her attention flitted around the apartment.

"Oh, what?"

She met my eyes, but quickly shook her head. "No. Never mind. You two are tired. That sounds like it was a lot. You should rest."

"Ripley." Her name was a dozen scoldings in one. "Spill it."

Floating off toward the door, she doubled back. "Welllllll, it's just that I found out where Brad works, and I thought the three of us could go there tonight."

That piqued my interest. "Where?" Feeling Laurie shift behind me on the couch, I amended the question to add more information. "Where does Brad work?"

"He kept talking to Alyssa about how he had to go to work tonight. He was driving me crazy because I thought I was going to have to follow him, but then he said the name of the club."

"Club?"

She nodded. "He works at Skin's Café."

Anise, who must've been sleeping on my bed, padded down the loft ladder and trotted over to us. After rubbing up against my leg, she jumped onto Laurie's lap and settled in for more sleep.

"Skin's Café?" I repeated for Laurie's sake.

"That gritty venue out by the market?" Laurie curled his lip as if he'd just touched something inexplicably sticky. "Only really niche bands play there."

Ripley blew out a one-note laugh. "He has no idea."

"Rip, isn't that the place where we saw that band who wore astronaut helmets?" I wrinkled my nose.

"It is," Ripley said with a reminiscent chuckle. "I wandered over there earlier, and it looks like the bands playing tonight are Bargain Basement and Tres Patos. The first describes themselves as acid metal, which I didn't know was a thing, and the second says they play intergalactic punk music."

After relaying the information to Laurie, I patted him on the thigh. "I think we should go. Can you rally?"

He made a show of pulling in a deep breath and letting it go before answering. "I wouldn't miss it. Intergalactic acid punk metal nights are my favorite."

Ripley punched the air in triumph. "Yes! Who knows? We might find new music to love."

"Sure," I giggled. "Laurie's a big fan of metal. Maybe he's been missing out on a whole subsection of the genre by not listening to acid metal."

"Right. These Basement guys might turn out to be my new favorite band," he agreed.

Checking the time, we went to take Leo on a nice long walk before we had to leave for the shows. After that, we split up to get ready.

"What do I wear that says 'intergalactic'?" I chewed on my lip as I assessed my closet.

Ripley bounced her shoulders. "It's Seattle. Just wear black and you'll be fine."

Choosing my nicest jeans—one of the few pairs that didn't have paint on them—and a black T-shirt, I got the thumbs-up from Ripley. Laurie went with the same casual aesthetic, and we laughed the moment we saw one another in the lobby.

"Twins." He plucked at his black shirt.

"Now, where are the two of you off to?" Opal peered at us through her giant glasses. She sat cross-legged on the wobbly couch, teetering back and forth as she worked on a crossword puzzle.

Art and Darius, also sitting near the entryway, turned to look.

"We're going to a show up by the market," Laurie told them, taking my hand in his.

Opal twiddled her fingers in the air. "Have fun, kids."

"We'll wait up for you," Art called just as we stepped through the front door.

I hesitated. "Oh, no." I moved to turn back, but Laurie squeezed my hand, pulling me outside with him before I could protest. "They shouldn't wait up for us," I argued once we'd stopped in front of the Morrisey.

But he just chuckled. "You know them. They'd be up that late, anyway. Telling people who walk by that they're waiting for us will make them feel good."

Smiling up at him, I said, "Okay. I can see your point."

The walk up the hill was lovely, giving us a peek at the water each time we crossed a street. At the market, we took a right and an immediate left. Skin's Café was across the street from the Moore Theatre, a gorgeous Seattle landmark and a venue that saw much more mainstream headliners. But our destination was a small building that I'd originally thought was uninhabited, thanks to the large pieces of painted plywood covering the front windows and the wrought-iron gate blocking the entrance. The fact that there wasn't any signage on the outside had initially felt like a warning sign, but now it seemed like Laurie and I knew a secret everyone walking by on the street didn't.

As we opened the gate and stopped at the door to show the bouncer our IDs, I hoped the secret was a good one, and not something we'd regret.

I immediately did, however, once the scent of sweaty bodies and old warehouse reached my nostrils. Much like the outside, the interior of Skin's wasn't much to see. This was mostly because we couldn't see it. Everything was painted black, and the only lights in the room were either focused on the stage or of the neon variety. The room was a big rectangle, with the stage sitting on the other end of the room and a funky bar to our right. There were probably about a hundred people inside. Not the biggest crowd I'd seen at one of these smaller venues, but definitely larger than the guys who wore astronaut helmets had pulled.

Laurie and I each ordered a drink and then moved around the space to find Ripley. With the neon lights on the stage, it wasn't a hard task. Light reflected off spirits in a way that made them shimmer, glow even. Moonlight was the strongest. Incandescent bulbs had a much weaker effect, and LEDs had almost none. Neons, though? They lit ghosts up like Christmas trees.

"Okay, maybe the black was a bad idea," Ripley said with a cackle as we approached. "I can barely see you."

Glancing down, I giggled and told Laurie. Our black shirts and dark jeans blended in with the equally dark floors and walls. Conversely, everyone else wore things that were bright, glowing, made of colorful flannel, or that included sparkles.

He examined the space. "So, this is what it's like to feel old and out of touch."

"Ripley fits in." I motioned to her fishnet stockings, cut-offs, black Nirvana T-shirt, and loose flannel.

She placed her hands under her chin like she was posing for a Glamour Shot—a terrifying part of the nineties she'd described to me in great detail. Dropping the act, she shook her head. "I've searched everywhere for Brad, but I can't find him. Unless they're waiting on another bartender, he's not behind the bar. You guys saw the bouncer, and he's not doing the sound." She gestured to a bored-looking man sitting behind a soundboard at the back of the pit.

But before Laurie or I could even mention going off to check the rest of the venue, the houselights dimmed, and the audience clapped and screamed with excitement.

"Please welcome Bargain Basement to the Skin stage!" a disembodied voice called over the speakers.

Laurie and I gagged.

"Skin stage?" Laurie shivered.

"Why would they call it that?" I turned to see Ripley's reaction, but she was staring at the stage as if she'd seen a ghost. Her arm slowly lifted, and she pointed.

"Oh." I breathed out the word as I noticed what she had. Tugging on Laurie's arm, I gestured to the band. More importantly, to Brad, who was taking his seat behind a large drum set.

"Brad's a drummer?" Laurie asked, but if he said anything else, I couldn't hear it over the music. We moved to the left of the stage, hanging out by the wall so we had some space to ourselves, away from the mass of bodies crowded toward the stage.

Acid metal turned out to be a lot like other metal, but it had a lot more distortion, and it was much slower. Laurie went through every emotion possible as he listened. He was so entertaining to watch, actually, that Ripley and I had a hard time paying attention to the band. Laurie started out confused, then became hopeful, and quickly grew mad. Then he moved into acceptance, experienced joy and sadness, only to settle on curiosity.

"What do you think? Adding them to your list of favorite bands anytime soon?" I asked once they'd played their last song.

Laurie scratched his temple. "I mean, no. But Brad's actually pretty good. The biggest disappointment was that metal's usually all about face-meltingly fast drums, and the slower tempo meant he was half-asleep during the songs."

"I noticed that too," Ripley said, winging an elbow toward me. "Look, they're coming out to a merch table. Let's go hover."

The merch table was near the front of the building on the side we were already standing on, so we didn't have to go far. At this distance, I could see the band members better than I'd been able to from the stage. All three had some level of unfortunate hygiene on display. One of them had greasy dark hair that didn't seem to have been washed this month. Another had a buzzed head of hair. Being shorter didn't make the hair better, though. That guy kept scratching at his scalp as if something was very wrong with his skin. And then there was Brad, sporting the messy, floppy hair I'd come to know so well from seeing him around the fifth floor. His real crime, however, was his beard. It was untrimmed and likely holding any number of food particles.

We lingered about a yard away, acting as if we were just there to get a break from the audience. One guy purchased a T-shirt that looked a lot like the guys in the band had painted it themselves. But he was the only person who even approached the merch table.

After a while, Laurie felt so bad for them that he shook his head and said, "This is too sad. I'm going to buy a shirt." But before he could move, Brad stood up, his hand moving to his pocket where he pulled out a phone.

"I've gotta take this." Brad ducked his head in an apology before leaving the table and moving toward the entrance to take the call outside.

"On it." Ripley followed him, knowing we would draw too much attention if we tried to listen in on his conversation.

Little did we know, there was another conversation that we would be able to eavesdrop on in Brad's absence.

A nasally scoff rang out from the merch table and the greasy-haired guy said, "Figures he'd leave us to run the table alone. He probably doesn't even have a call."

Buzzed Guy said, "Or it was the pink-haired chick, and he doesn't even care about hiding what he's doing anymore."

At the words *pink-haired chick,* my heart stopped. Or maybe I stopped breathing. My eyes clamped on to Laurie's, and he squeezed my hand.

"Can you believe he thinks we're stupid enough not to notice that he's sneaking around with her?" Greasy propped his dirty Converse high-top up on the merch table, officially giving up on anyone coming to buy anything from them.

"Shhh. Here he comes." Buzzed Guy elbowed Greasy, and he dropped his foot from where it had been resting.

Ripley wagged her head as she rejoined us. "Nothing. It was his mom. She was calling to see if he was coming to dinner tomorrow."

I motioned toward the door where we'd entered. Laurie didn't fight me on leaving. Ripley didn't, either, but once we were outside and past the people smoking just beyond the club, she moved in front of me and put a hand on her ghostly hip.

"Are we just giving up?"

I glanced around us to make sure no one was within earshot. "While you were with Brad, we heard his bandmates complaining behind his back."

"They said he'd been seeing a *pink-haired chick.*" Laurie picked up the story, widening his eyes for emphasis.

Ripley's mouth hung open. After a second, she punched the air. "I *knew* he knew the dead woman!"

"Yes, you called it," I whispered, hooking my arm through Laurie's as we started back toward home. Ripley followed, floating next to me as we walked.

"And if he was cheating on Alyssa with Quinn, the pink-haired woman..." Ripley began, but she screwed up her face. "I don't understand how that leads to Brad killing her while she's wearing Alyssa's dress."

Sighing, I admitted it didn't make sense to me either. "Maybe Brad told Quinn he would break up with Alyssa, but he was dragging his feet, so Quinn forced his hand by breaking into her apartment, stealing her stuff, and then showing up at her place to confront her in person?"

"Sounds plausible." Laurie pulled me closer to him as we passed by another club on First that had a long line snaking out the front door and onto the sidewalk.

"Bleh." Ripley stuck out her tongue. "Brad's been with Alyssa, who's in her thirties. What's he doing dating a twenty-year-old?"

I sent her a scowl, like, *Do I really need to explain that to you?*

She put her hands up. "Nope. Never mind. I answered my own question."

We pulled up, waiting at a light to cross the street.

"Do we tell Detective Anthony?" Laurie asked, not having been privy to Ripley's and my conversation about how gross some guys could be about younger women.

"I think we should," I said. "We heard it with our own ears." When Laurie cocked his head at me, like that was a weird thing to say, I added, "Usually I can't tell her everything I know because I learned it through Ripley or another ghost, and I don't have a plausible reason to know that information." I opened my hands. "But this is perfectly normal."

Ripley nodded. "Good, and I'll keep following Brad, since he seems to be our guy." She clapped her hands together as the light changed. "Watch out, Brad. We're coming for you."

NINE

Ripley wasn't around much for the next few days as she followed Brad around.

"Watching this guy is like a full-time job," she complained Wednesday evening as I did my hair and makeup for an evening out.

Zoe had gotten me a last-minute reservation at The Cooler, and I was taking Penny with me. Even more exciting was that I didn't have anything hanging over my head during my time with my aunt this time around. Having an ulterior motive whenever I talked to Penny lately had become exhausting. But Ripley and I had come to a mutual decision that we couldn't push Penny about my dad anymore.

"The man isn't as lazy as we assumed," Ripley continued talking about Brad, her eyes narrowing with discernment as I applied eyeliner. She'd been the one to teach me how, and I could practically see her running through her list of tips as I swept the charcoal liquid along my lash line. She must've approved of the result, because she dove back into what she was saying without skipping a beat. "He might be in sweatpants most of the time, but he really is working most of the day. Well, I mean, I can't *see* him when he's at his house, but I can hear him practicing the drums. When he's at Alyssa's, he's either listening to music or watching tutorial videos online about different drum techniques."

A muscle twitched in my cheek, a physical manifestation of the disappointment I felt in myself for making such an uneducated, impulsive judgment about the guy. No. I shouldn't feel bad. This was a murder investigation, and there was a distinct possibility that he deserved my judgment.

"You *do* remember why you're following Brad, right?" I flicked mascara over my lashes, holding her gaze in the mirror. I pointed the wand at her. "He's a murder suspect, Rip. Don't go getting all gooey on me because he's a musician, aka your kryptonite."

She rolled her eyes. "Puhlease. I've seen this guy get a Cheeto stuck in his beard for most of the day. I'm *not* getting *gooey*." Ripley swatted at the mascara wand, her hand passing right through it. "I'm just saying that he's busy and unpredictable. I can't figure out his schedule. The moment I think he's staying put, he'll jump up to go somewhere. Sometimes it's to grab more snacks from the store. Other times he's stopping by the music store. And in the three days I've been following him, he and his band have already practiced twice."

"You'd think they'd be better with that many rehearsals," I said, to which Ripley widened her eyes in agreement. "So, he's a full-time musician?" I wondered aloud, the math not quite adding up.

But Ripley nodded. "That's not as impressive as you think,"

she added when my lips parted in surprise. "He lives in a mostly dilapidated house in Georgetown with, from what I can tell, about ten other people. I don't think he pays all that much for rent."

"He lives with that many people, and they don't mind that he plays the drums at all hours of the day?"

"Based on the sound, he has an electric set for practicing. Much quieter, but I can still hear him hitting the pads. He keeps his real drum set at his friend's creepy house, in the garage where they practice," Ripley explained. "You wouldn't want to sneak into either house so I can gain access, would you? Being stuck outside is killing my information gathering."

"Oh, because you made both places sound so inviting?" I flinched, remembering her use of the words *dilapidated* and *creepy*. "I mean, if you really need me to, I can try."

"No. It's okay. I'll manage. Well, I'll leave you to your evening with Penny. Is Laurie coming?"

I shook my head. "He's having dinner with Gavin."

Ripley and I had gotten to know Laurie's college friend during our investigation into the Underground last summer. And even though we'd briefly thought he was a murderer, he was a nice guy and a good friend to Laurie.

"Oh, good for them. Well, have fun." The earnestness behind her eyes made my chest tighten.

"You could come with, you know?"

She fixed me with a small smile. "Yeah, but it'll be good for it to be just you and Penny. Plus, I really *should* keep an eye on Brad."

"Okay. You know where we'll be if you change your mind."

"Thanks, Megs." She blew me a kiss. "Love you."

"Love you," I called as she disappeared, jumping at the almost immediate knock on the door.

Frowning, I capped my mascara and peered through my peephole. Penny stood on the other side.

"Hey!" I greeted her as I swung open the door and stepped back. "I'm almost ready."

My aunt must've been missing the big city after living in the Scottish countryside. Not only was she wearing the highest heels I'd seen her brave in years, her dress would've had me tugging at the hem all night, worried it was too short. But Penny was confident, and she strode inside without a shred of self-consciousness.

"Did I hear you talking to someone just now?" She peered around my apartment.

"Anise." I jabbed a thumb at the sleeping cat, curled on the back of the couch.

At the sound of her name, she picked up her head and fluttered her eyelids sleepily in our direction.

"She likes it when I talk to her," I added unnecessarily.

Luckily, I had the cutest cat in the universe, and her adorableness pulled my aunt in like a tractor beam, erasing any worries or doubts from Penny's mind about who I'd been talking to as she snuggled into the cat's black fur and kissed her head.

Ducking back into the bathroom to run a brush over my curls to loosen them up, I clicked off the light and grabbed my purse and a jacket from the hook by the door. "Ready?"

"Ready." Penny ran her fingers through her own hair, as if checking that it didn't need one last brush as well.

Hers was a shade more auburn than my brown hair, but it

was so similarly styled that I worried we'd look like we were trying to twin. I wore a cropped top and high-waisted trousers—from Alyssa, of course—so at least we were different in that regard.

Our reservation wasn't for another thirty minutes, and the speakeasy was just around the corner, but Penny and I understood time management when it came to the Morrisey. Getting down to the lobby? That would take a few minutes. Getting *through* the lobby? It could take as long as twenty, depending on how chatty the Conversationalists were feeling tonight.

Spoiler alert: they were always chatty, hence the nickname they'd given themselves.

As expected, our outfits and the timing of our departure garnered much interest from the residents hanging out in the lobby.

"You two look gorgeous!" Opal kicked her legs out from under her on the couch as if she might race over to inspect us closer up. Her eyes always looked huge, given the giant nature of her green-rimmed circular glasses, but they must've doubled in size as she took us in.

Further adding to our twin status, Penny and I curtsied at the compliment, and I was sure the pink blush to her cheeks was mirrored on my own, given the heat creeping over my skin.

"Where are you off to at this hour?" Art asked, checking his watch.

We may have been in a bustling city, where nightlife was abundant, and you could find something to do at any hour of the evening, but our building was populated by a lot of retired folks and young parents. Leaving after "dinnertime" was an infrequent occurrence.

"Zoe got us a reservation at The Cooler." The pure giddiness behind my aunt's statement told me she'd definitely had a hard time finding any nightlife in her rural Scottish village.

She and a friend had taken a week to explore Edinburgh earlier that year, but it was clear that going out to shows, meeting friends for drinks, or hitting an impromptu sports game, because there were last-minute tickets available, were not part of my aunt's routine anymore.

We were about to break off toward the door when Opal inquired about both our outfits. My admission that I'd borrowed my whole look from Alyssa prompted the Conversationalists to ask if there had been any breakthroughs in the murder investigation.

"Not that we've heard." Penny turned to me as if realizing I was the more likely of the two of us to have the information they wanted. But I didn't know any more than she did, so I mirrored her gesture and moved the conversation on to a more pleasant subject.

Penny checked her watch a few moments later, as we pushed our way through the Morrisey's front door and stepped out onto the bustling street. "Ten minutes. Not too bad." She hooked her arm through mine as we started toward the other end of the block.

Getting into The Cooler was a process that involved passing through the seedy bar above, picking up the phone in the back of the space, saying the name our reservation was under, and then walking through the door to an old walk-in fridge. It only added to Penny's delight in our outing.

"This makes me miss the city," she said as we crept down the staircase into the speakeasy.

I chuckled, knowing full well not to get my hopes up about her moving back. Penny had spent decades living in the heart of the city, and she'd been more than ready to trade crowded streets and constant noise for the peace and beauty of the Highlands.

If anything could've tempted her, though, it was the one-of-a-kind cocktail Zoe created based on a few questions about what each person preferred, in both taste and type of alcohol.

Penny was charmed by the space, Zoe, and the remaining flapper-girl paintings I'd created to hang in the speakeasy. I'd sold a few, but the majority still hung on the walls. The series I'd done was inspired by a 1920s' ghost named Addy, and her intense connection to my cat. They were still some of my favorite pieces I'd ever created. Visiting them was like spending time with old friends.

We had just ordered our second cocktails when Ripley showed up. Happiness surged through me, thinking she'd finally decided to spend the evening with us. But those feelings immediately flattened when I got a better look at my best friend. Her spine was rigid and her expression tight.

"I'm going to use the restroom," I told Penny. "I'll be right back."

She nodded, shimmying her shoulders as she drank the last bit of her first cocktail.

Slipping past other customers and their quiet conversations, I lifted my chin in greeting as I passed by Blake Stimac, the manager of the speakeasy, and Zoe's long-lost cousin. While Zoe's search for her own father had been a dead-end last year—literally, the man had passed away when she was a little girl—she'd found out she had a large extended family. In the time since, she'd made a point to connect with them. Other than working for her cousins, she'd taken part in a handful of family holidays.

Blake waved, overly friendly to me after I'd helped save his life last year, something that conveniently outweighed the fact that I'd been trying to prove he and his brother were murderers. The reminder that I had yet another murder to solve, and that Ripley might have information about it, made me scamper past Blake and into the hallway where the bathroom was located.

Thankfully, the space was unoccupied. It was close enough to the bar that I had to be careful, so I kept my voice low as Ripley appeared beside me, next to the sink.

"What's up?" I asked, locking the door behind me.

Her face arranged itself into a wince, as if I might've grabbed her arm and held on too hard. "I hate to pull you away from Penny, but it's an emergency."

I drew in a quick breath.

"A case emergency," Ripley quickly clarified, holding up a hand. "I followed Brad to band practice tonight, but he stormed out about halfway through. I couldn't hear what they fought about, but he stomped around his car for a few minutes before calling someone on the phone. His big head blocked the screen, so I couldn't see who it was, but he said he needed to meet with them."

"It could be Alyssa," I whispered.

"I thought of that too. They made plans to meet at ten, and he was going to send a location."

"That's in just over an hour." I glanced back toward the speakeasy.

Ripley didn't miss the movement. "You stay here, for now.

I'll follow him to see where he goes, but I'll let you know if there are any updates."

As much as I ached to go with her, tonight was supposed to be about me and Penny. "Thanks, Rip. Let me know what you find out."

She gave me a salute and vanished. I washed my hands, because it didn't feel right to leave without doing so, and rejoined my aunt.

"Sooo," Penny said, dragging out the word as I sat down. "I know about you and Laurie, but how's everything else going for you out here?"

"Great." I released a slow exhale. "You were right."

Penny beamed. "Tell me again, in great detail, what I was right about." She rested her chin on her palm.

"About moving back to Seattle," I admitted, even though I'd already told her as much. "About the Morrisey being just what I needed." Emotion made my words feel stuck in my throat for a beat. "Mom was right; it really is magical."

Penny's smile only grew at my mention of Mom. "She saw things no one else did."

My heart stopped. Was Penny telling me that Mom could see ghosts too? No, the possibility was too wild. I couldn't help the quick squint my eyes adopted, however, and Penny took it as a question.

"She was always aware of her surroundings in a way I've never encountered since. I blame it on our father, that she had to keep an eye on him to make sure he wasn't about to blow. And you'd think it would've meant that she only saw the negatives in every situation, but she didn't. She saw everything— good and bad."

I took a sip of my drink, needing time to catch up. Wait. That made it sound like my mom had merely been observant, a trauma response from growing up with an abusive parent, not that she shared my clairvoyant gifts. My excitement ebbed.

We talked more about Mom. The conversation made my heart feel warm, though it could've been the alcohol from my cocktail. I asked Penny about Scotland, and she dove into such a detailed description of her life there, I felt like I was experiencing it myself. I suppose that was why she was a writer. We paid for our drinks, thanked Zoe, and left so she could use our table for another reservation.

"Thank you, kid." Aunt Penny placed a hand on my cheek as we stopped on the street outside the bar. "That was so much fun." She let out an enormous yawn, the motion swallowing most of her final word before she turned toward home.

But I stayed where I stood.

Penny shot me a sidelong glance. "You coming?"

"I think I might stay out, actually." I pointed north. "A friend of mine is up by the market, and I thought I might go join her."

"Sure. Sure! Your aging aunt is going to hit the hay, but by all means..." Penny's smile glinted in the light of the nearby streetlights.

Snorting at her characterization of herself, I nodded, and we began walking. I stayed with her until we reached the Morrisey, but then I twiddled my fingers and kept going. Once I'd crossed Cherry Street, my mouth twisted into a frown. I may have said my friend was at the market, but I didn't actually know where Ripley was. It was almost ten, and she still hadn't told me where Brad was meeting the mystery person.

It was incredibly hopeful of me to assume they might be at Skin's again, but that was the only place I could think of, so that's where I headed. I texted Laurie while I walked.

> Done with drinks with Penny. Where'd you and Gavin end up? Hope you're having a good time.

I'd just about made it to the art museum before my phone buzzed with a response.

> We're walking back from the International District. Went to a great noodle spot. Want to meet somewhere?

I was just typing out an answer when Ripley appeared in front of me.

Her shoulders sagged forward in exasperation. "*There* you are. I looked everywhere for you. I had to go beyond the tether just so it would bring me back to you."

"Ripley!" I shoved my phone against my ear so it would seem like I was talking on the phone. "Sorry. I got antsy, and I didn't know where you were, so I was just wandering."

After thinking about it, going back to Skin's didn't make much sense, so I didn't particularly want to admit that's what I'd been doing.

"Did you find out where Brad's meeting the mystery person?"

"I did." Her eyes glimmered, matching the way her spirit glowed slightly in the combination of moonlight, streetlights, and the traffic lights of the intersection I still stood on the corner of. "Sorry, he moved around for a bit, and I didn't want to lose him, but he finally settled on a place. I wanted to tell you, but I have to hurry back. It's almost ten."

"Can I come with?" I called out, my question like a hand grasping the arm of someone who was about to leave.

"Uh, sure, but it's at that little brewery in SoDo. Seapine?" She looked at her wrist as if she had a watch that worked. "I doubt you'd make it."

"SoDo?" The local nickname for the southern downtown area starting at the sports stadiums and extending to Georgetown was a groan as it left my lips. "But I just…" I pointed toward the hill I'd been walking up, halfway to the market.

Ripley snapped her fingers. "I've gotta go. For real. Don't worry about coming. I'll fill you in on who he's meeting. It's probably just Alyssa." And that was all she said before disappearing.

I paced with indecision for the next few moments. Pivoting so I faced south, I stopped myself. That brewery was miles away. It would take me close to an hour if I walked, less if I ran, but let's be honest… It wasn't worth it. By the time I got there, Brad and his guest would likely be gone. Ripley would fill me in.

Pivoting back toward the market, I watched the light I'd missed a few times now, waiting for the pedestrian walk sign. With a shake of my head, however, I realized I had only been walking this way because I thought Brad might be up here. Turning again, I started down the hill toward home.

But that was when I spotted the scooter.

TEN

Electric bikes and scooters were everywhere in the city. Like, literally *everywhere*. People just left them wherever they wanted when they were done renting them— blocking the sidewalk, in front of our building, sometimes even in the middle of the street, though that was definitely frowned upon. I'd even seen one bobbing toward the shore of Elliott Bay before.

Laurie and I were usually of the mind that they were too scary to ride through the crowded streets during the day. Maybe we'd seen too many people wipe out to fool ourselves about their safety.

At ten o'clock at night, when the streets weren't so full of traffic, and the sidewalks weren't packed with pedestrians, they were a much more reasonable option. I didn't have a helmet on me, but I could be safe. Right?

Racing over to the scooter, I pulled up the app and scanned the QR code on the handlebar before remembering I'd been in the middle of texting Laurie back when Ripley had shown up.

Scootering to SoDo. Wanna join?

While I waited for him to respond, I finished up the rental process. My scooter chimed at me in greeting just as my phone buzzed with an incoming text.

I'm in. I'll grab one in front of the Morrisey. Is that where you are?

I didn't really want to explain what I was doing north of our building, so I was vague in my response.

I will be in a few minutes. I'll swing by and meet you.

Once I'd sent the text, I turned toward the scooter, toed the kickstand out of the way, and got on. Waiting for a car to pass, I pulled onto the road. The light in front of me turned red, and I slowed.

The brakes made a terrible grinding noise, and the wheels stuttered, making the scooter wobble and swerve. Crying out in panic, I gripped the handlebars even harder and got myself back under control in time to screech to a halt just before the light.

"Well, that was terrifying," I grumbled as I waited.

Once the light changed, I accelerated down the hill again. The next few lights remained green, thank goodness, so I didn't have to deal with slowing. Laurie stood next to a scooter of his own as I drove onto the sidewalk next to the Morrisey. I sped past him.

"Hey, speed racer," he called, the sound reaching my ears on the wind as I zoomed past him.

Turning the scooter in a circle, I doubled back toward

Laurie. "Sorry, can't slow down. This thing has death brakes," I said as I passed him again.

"Get a different one." His words shook with laughter, and he gestured to the many scooters parked in front of our building.

I huffed, waiting until I'd circled around a second time. "And abandon Scoots?"

"You named your dysfunctional scooter?" Laurie was behind me this time, and we moved off the sidewalk and back onto First Avenue, heading south.

"He's my steed, and I'll stick by him no matter what," I called back to Laurie as we started picking up speed.

The cool night air swept over my cheeks, holding the faintest scent of the waterfront. The buildings were a blur as we zoomed by, and it seemed like we'd be at our destination in no time at all. And for a few minutes, I totally felt that way.

Then, out of nowhere, Ripley appeared right in front of me, directly in the way of Scoots.

"Bah!" I screamed, cringing as I plowed right through her spirit. Icy cold rushed down my back. I wriggled in discomfort as I hit the brakes. They groaned, screeched, shuddered, and I finally eked to a stop, the last wobble forcing me to jump onto the curb.

Laurie, who was behind me, stopped too.

"What gives?" I sneered at the space where Ripley's spirit hovered, which also happened to be where a bouncer stood outside a cowgirl-themed bar.

The intimidating man canted his head forward, shifting his shoulders so his arm muscles bulged even more. "What did you say to me?"

"Nope," Laurie said, scooting between me and the man. "Let's move." He jerked his thumb toward the other side of the street.

"Uh. I wasn't talking to you," I called, laughing nervously and scooting away—arguably the least cool way to leave a confrontation.

Once we'd gotten a block away from the angry man, and there was no one else on the street nearby, Laurie and I stopped.

"Okay, what's going on?" I faced Ripley.

Ripley scoffed. "If you're going to the brewery, Brad's not there anymore. He's on his way back to Alyssa's."

"Brad's coming this way?" I asked, craning my neck.

Laurie looked for him too.

"In a cab." Ripley appraised us with tired disdain. "Not on a scooter. He's not *cool* like the two of you." She stifled a laugh.

"Oh, in a car," I whispered, just for Laurie.

He nodded and focused on the building I was staring at, where he had to assume I was talking to my dead best friend. Have I mentioned that I have the most amazing boyfriend?

Thinking of how amazing Laurie was reminded me that he had no idea what was going on. Taking a moment, I filled him in on what Ripley had overheard, and why she was following Brad in the first place.

"Okay, so the meeting's over. What happened?" I asked once Laurie was officially caught up. My right hand circled in the air in front of me, telling her she needed to get moving on the explanation.

Ripley pulled in a breath she didn't need—you know, because of the whole *not having lungs* thing. "Get this. He was meeting with..."

I leaned forward, my scooter almost toppling forward onto the sidewalk as I bent too far. "He was meeting with..." I repeated for Laurie, and also to urge Ripley to finish.

"A pink-haired woman." Her eyes were as wide as her smile.

I jolted. "A pink-haired woman?"

Laurie's lips twitched downward. "What?" he asked in disbelief.

"I *know*," Ripley said. "I was freaked out, too, thinking I was seeing a ghost ... or he was ... but it wasn't Quinn Garret. This was a different pink-haired woman. The hair color is where the similarities between them end. *This* pink-haired woman's name is Ray, and she's the bassist for a band called Foxy Stud Muffin. And, unlike his current band, it sounds like this one actually makes money. They've got a gig at the Showbox at the end of the month and want him to practice with them to make sure he's a good fit."

I recalibrated as I repeated the information for Laurie. "So... Wait... He's not cheating on Alyssa?"

Ripley's head swung back and forth. "I don't think so. But he was really jumpy, looking behind his back until he could find a seat that faced the door so he could see everyone who entered. He apologized to her and said that he hadn't told his band that he was leaving yet, so he was a little paranoid. This didn't appear to be their first time meeting either. I think Ray's been courting Brad for a while."

"What made him change his mind about joining their band?" I asked, hoping that gave Laurie enough information.

"He's been trying to get Bargain Basement to take things more seriously for a while, but they're all about playing around and taking small gigs at venues they deem worthy." Ripley fixed me with an incredulous look. "They referred to performing at places like the Moore and Nuemos as *selling out*."

I told Laurie what she'd said.

"I'm guessing a similar conversation happened at their practice earlier, and that's why Brad stormed out, calling Ray to let her know he was finally going to take her up on her offer," Laurie said, distilling everything.

Ripley touched her index finger to the tip of her nose. I glanced at Laurie and nodded to show him he'd been on the right track.

"Do you think the fact that he was so nervous about his current band finding out that he's been talking to Ray might be enough to explain his odd behavior the night we found Quinn's body in the fifth-floor hallway?" I asked, grasping for a reason.

But Ripley said, "He *did* tell Ray that it would be nice when he finally came clean about this to his band because he didn't like sneaking around, but I think it's more likely that he just mistook Quinn for Ray when he first saw her in the hall that day. I fell for it too. At first glance, they look pretty similar. I bet it just freaked him out."

"I guess that makes sense," I said after filling Laurie in on Ripley's theory. "Which means Brad's not our killer." My statement hung in the night air.

"Right," Laurie and Ripley said at the same time, the word holding the same amount of discouragement.

It wasn't like any of us wanted Alyssa's boyfriend to be guilty of strangling the young woman in our building, but...

"Without him, the dress designer Alyssa was so afraid of is the only other suspect that makes any sense," I voiced what I knew we were all thinking.

Again in unison, Ripley and Laurie bobbed their heads in agreement.

Looking down at Scoots, I emptied my lungs in a sad sigh. "Well, I guess we should just head home, then."

"Yeah, Detective Anthony has the name of the designer. I'm sure she's already looking into him." Laurie swung his scooter around, facing it back toward the Morrisey.

"See you at home." Ripley blew a kiss before disappearing.

Following Laurie's lead, I turned Scoots toward home. He was right. The seasoned detective knew everything we did. There was no need for us to get involved any more than we already had.

ELEVEN

"The universe is seriously playing a joke on me," I said as I listened to a voicemail I'd missed the next morning.

Ripley glanced up from where she was people watching at the window overlooking the street. "Huh?"

I pointed at my phone. "I missed a call when I was in the shower just now."

"Yeah, I heard it buzzing." She didn't even turn around.

"It was Detective Anthony." I paused there for emotional impact.

Ripley spun toward me.

Now that I had her full concentration, I told her the rest. "She wants me to come to the station to talk to her about the Quinn Garret murder." I let my eyebrows lift for emphasis. "The moment I decide I'm going to let her handle it, she ropes me back in."

Ripley blinked once, twice. "What? Wait. Why?"

"I have no clue." I pulled my shoulders up to my ears before letting them drop.

"Not according to Amaya," Ripley said with a huff of laughter at her own punny joke. "She must think you know something if she's calling you in."

"I guess we'll find out." I braided my hair and made sure I was presentable before leaving for the Seattle Police Department building on Fifth Avenue.

In most of the other cases I'd been involved with, I'd been a potential suspect at one point or another. This felt different. While I was apprehensive about the cryptic message the detective had left, and lack of information I had going into this meeting, I wasn't worried that she counted me as one of her suspects. In fact, for once, I was reasonably sure no one at the Morrisey was in danger of being on that list.

Sighing out any remaining reservations, I reached for the door handle and stepped through to the bustling lobby of the SPD headquarters. As always, the building smelled like too many things at once—some good, others bad. The burnt coffee smell was mitigated by someone's floral perfume. Body odor was balanced out by some pleasant fresh rain potpourri scent coming from the restrooms.

"I'm here to see Detective Anthony," I said as pleasantly as I could to the man behind the reception desk, an Officer Hendrickson.

When he looked up, I fixed him with my biggest, most I'm-not-a-criminal smile, refraining from adding, "Not for arresting reasons."

But it appeared that Hendrickson hadn't been hired yesterday, and he was well-versed in the myriad of reasons a person might visit the police station. He neither openly judged me, nor did he tell me he knew I was one of the good guys—like, let's face it, I really wanted him to do. He asked an officer passing by to walk me back. I didn't mention that I knew the way, figuring that wouldn't help my I'm-not-a-criminal image.

Ripley wandered in front of me, nodding in appreciation at a few changes they'd made to the bullpen since we'd visited last. One of the more notable differences was that they'd changed out the type of water cooler that sat in the corner. Now, it was a water cooler *and* warmer, and it looked like it would be much more difficult to push over.

"Well, I guess splash-and-search is no longer an option," she grumbled as we approached Detective Anthony's desk.

That was fine with me. I'd never felt good about the one time we'd gotten so desperate we had to resort to Ripley knocking over the water dispenser to create a distraction so I could search the detective's files.

Speaking of Amaya, she sat behind her desk, eyes poring over documents in folders open in front of her. Detective Anthony always looked put together, even the time I'd seen her wearing clothes other than her standard work suit. Today, however, she'd put even more effort into her appearance. Instead of one of her gray suits, she wore a sharp black one, and while her hair was always pulled back, she'd slicked the sides to make sure not a hair was out of place.

"Meg. Hey." She stood, nodding in thanks to the officer who'd escorted me. Hand outstretched toward the chairs next to her, Amaya said, "Have a seat."

I watched her warily, wondering what exactly had prompted this visit. All signs pointed away from me being in trouble, though, so I tried to loosen my shoulders as I sat back in the plastic chair facing her desk.

While I waited for the detective to explain why she'd asked me there, Ripley wandered behind the desk, scanning the notes with a discerning eye.

"I really appreciate you coming in," Detective Anthony said. She tugged at her suit jacket. "I had planned to come to you, but I've got a big meeting today and wasn't sure I could make the trek."

Ah, so the big meeting was likely the reason for the step-up in her wardrobe.

"Sure. No problem," I said, unsure how else to answer. *Was it a problem?* I didn't know yet.

Threading her fingers together, she leaned forward. "I'm going to be candid with you. I've got a meeting with my captain today, and she wants to hear about my progress on this strangler case." She released a tight breath. "I'm at a dead end, and I wanted to check with you to see if you had any leads."

Brown eyes bright with hope, the detective waited for my response.

"Me?" I sputtered.

"You?" Ripley stopped her perusal to gawk at me.

"Meg," Amaya said, "you've managed to figure out who the killer is in the last three cases linked with your building. You know that building and the people in it better than anyone. You also have an inability to stay out of official investigations." Any sharpness in her tone softened as she realized scolding me probably wasn't the best way to gain my support. "Look, I'm not too proud to ask for help, and I definitely need it in this instance." Her fingers massaged her right temple.

Pride welled inside my chest. She wanted my help? She was asking me what I knew?

"That's actually pretty cool of her," Ripley said, regarding the detective with a new respect.

My happiness was short-lived, however. "I don't really know anything," I said, grimacing as I let the admission slip out.

Detective Anthony's expression fell. "Oh. Right. That's okay."

"What about the Brad stuff?" Ripley snapped her fingers. "You could tell her about that."

Swallowing, I straightened my posture. "The only thing I've been able to figure out was why Brad, Alyssa's boyfriend, was acting so odd that evening when we found Quinn's body."

Amaya tilted her head in question, proving she'd caught his awkward behavior as well. She chuckled a little as she listened to me explain Brad's reasoning behind doing a double take when he saw the dead woman's pink hair.

"All because their hair was the same color?" The detective rolled her eyes.

"I think he's living in a very paranoid state," I said in his defense, but added, "which is funny because his band totally knows. That's how I found out about this in the first place. I heard them talking about him meeting up with a pink-haired woman behind their backs. Well, behind *someone's* back. At first, I thought they were worried that he was cheating on Alyssa with Quinn, but when I saw him meeting with a woman with pink-hair last night, and listened in, I learned the truth about their relationship."

Amaya tossed me a confused glance, leading me to realize that I'd never given her that much insight into how I'd gotten information in the past. Apparently, all she had to do was put a little trust in me, and I would babble away about anything she wanted to know.

Finally, she asked, "You were able to overhear his conversation with the pink-haired bass player without him noticing you were there?"

Gulping back the worry that cropped up anytime we strayed close to the topic of my ghostly ability, I simply said, "I can be very stealthy." My voice sounded croaky and unsure.

The detective pinned me with a shrewd stare for a moment. "Who do you think could've killed Quinn now that you've decided it's not Brad?"

I didn't love the way she said, "you've decided." It pointed out my amateur status. Pushing past that momentary blip, I squared my shoulders. "I haven't had a lot of time to think about it, but the designer of the dress makes the most sense to check into next."

"You would think so, wouldn't you?" The way the detective mumbled the question made me wonder who was giving her pushback on that topic. Unlike her last observation, any criticism veiled inside this one didn't seem to be directed at me.

She flipped open a folder, glancing over the first page inside. Ripley leaned forward to read what it said.

Before she could open her mouth to tell me, though, Amaya said, "His name is Dirk Evans. He's got a boutique off Occidental Square. Dirk Evans Design."

At just as much of a loss for words as I was, Ripley opened her hands. "That's him," she confirmed.

Finally, I found my voice. "Why are you telling me?"

Amaya coughed before saying, "He's been pretty evasive

with anyone we've sent in to question him. My superiors think there's nothing there, but I've got a feeling there's something else going on." She fixed me with a wary look. "I didn't know if you'd want to use that stealth ability of yours to question him."

"You're asking me to get involved?" My eyes blew wide open.

The detective flinched. "Of course not. Not officially. But three previous cases have shown me that there's no stopping you if you have a hunch." At that, she sat back.

"She must be majorly out of leads if she's coming to you," Ripley scoffed in disbelief.

I had to agree.

But that didn't mean my answer was going to change. Standing, I held the detective's gaze.

"I'll let you know what I can find out."

TWELVE

Being the overachiever I was, I swung by the Dirk Evans Design boutique on my way home from the police station. I walked there in a fog of both disbelief and excitement. The feeling was likely exacerbated by the way Ripley swirled around me as I walked, repeating, "I cannot believe that just happened."

Now that I was an "approved" unofficial investigator, one tasked with a mission by an actual detective, I figured doors would simply open for me.

But the door to the boutique remained locked, even after I shook it a few times.

"Bummer." Ripley pointed to a sign taped to the inside of the glass.

Fashion emergency. Will reopen Saturday at noon.

I bounced my eyebrows. "What do you think qualifies as a fashion emergency?" I whispered to her, making sure there weren't other people within earshot to hear me talking to myself.

"I don't know," Ripley scoffed. "Possibly losing a dress that represents a life-changing contract, finding it on a young woman, and accidentally killing her to get it back." She eyed me as if telling me to catch up.

"Right." I winced. "But he didn't even take the dress." I turned back toward home.

"What was he supposed to do? Kill her and then snatch the dress off her corpse?" Ripley pulled a disgusted expression at the thought.

"Well, whatever he did, we have to wait until Saturday to find out."

Saturday, however, was also when the second round of the Morrisey Masterpiece Classic was taking place. Because it was set to start at noon, I figured I could finish the scavenger hunt and still make it to the design boutique with plenty of time. After all, Dirk Evans was coming off of a fashion emergency. I might not get his full attention if I showed up right when he opened after two or more days off.

At least, that was what I was telling myself to ease my guilt about prioritizing a silly building scavenger hunt over a murder investigation. But I wasn't about to let Laurie and Opal—I refused to call them Laurpal—win the second round as well as the first.

I told Laurie as much as we walked down to the lobby together a few minutes before noon.

"Whoa," he said with a chuckle, catching my eye. "Threatening is a good look on you, Dawson."

Ripley released a delighted laugh. "You're lucky he thinks you're hot. That was pretty terrifying."

Okay. Maybe I'd whispered my vow to destroy him and his partner creepily over his shoulder as he walked in front of me. Same difference.

"You know what's an even better look?" I asked, taking advantage of the way my threats had stopped him in his tracks to slip around him and grab the stairwell door first. "Leaving you in my dust, like I'm about to do in this scavenger hunt."

His mouth hung open as I stepped into the lobby, closing the door without holding it for him.

"Is he following?" I whispered to Ripley as I walked away, not wanting to give him the satisfaction of glancing back.

Ripley guffawed. "The same way Leo follows the two of you around. Honestly, I'm not sure if you just scared him or made him fall even more in love with you. Oh, incoming." She darted to the side just as footsteps sounded behind me, and Laurie's arms wrapped around my waist, lifting me up.

I squealed out a happy scream. "Hey, this has to be illegal. Manhandling the other team is grounds for disqualification." I tapped on his arms half-heartedly, not truly wanting him to let me go.

"If you don't tell about this, I won't tell them about the threats you just made to me in the stairwell," he whispered in my ear before setting me down.

I turned to face him. "Oh please. I threatened to beat you, not kill you."

"You sure about that?" His eyes glittered with enjoyment from the game we were playing.

Laurie and I had always been competitive. We'd always thrived on making up weird contests. It was a necessity when we were the only two kids in this building.

When I didn't answer, he surveyed the lobby hallway, making sure we were alone before saying, "Ripley, if you're here, I hope you remember the rules. No helping."

She crossed her arms and tapped her foot.

"Of course she remembers. Getting help from her is like having to look things up on a phone," I told him, eyeing the phone in his pocket. "Make sure *you* remember the rules around that as well."

The rules were, officially, that contestants could use whatever means necessary to find out the answers to the clues. We could check our phones, ask other locals as long as they weren't Morrisey residents, and even consult books. But Laurie and I had different rules. We'd decided back when we were teenagers that using any of those things to help us would count as a disqualification for our team. We knew this city just as well as we knew our building. If we didn't need help from the internet to solve the Morrisey clues in the first round, we shouldn't need it during the other two.

Laurie huffed. "Please. I'm the one who came up with the no-phone rule. I'm not about to break it."

"Well, neither am I." I leaned in close to glare at him like I was a boxer about to enter the ring with him and was trying to intimidate the guy.

Smirking at my display of hostility, Laurie leaned down and kissed me.

"Hey," I sputtered, then hissed out a disgruntled, "Not fair."

He smirked at me—looking way hotter than I wanted to admit walking away—and made his way down the hall toward the meeting area.

Ripley shook her head at us, but grinned all the same as she gave me a wave before disappearing. We'd decided her time would be best used hanging out at the boutique to see if she could glean anything about Dirk Evans before I could get there. She might not be able to go inside until I did, but she could watch the designer through the windows.

The stairwell door opened, letting out a final stream of residents.

"Hey! You ready?" Alyssa came up behind me, hooking her arm through mine.

"Ready." I set my shoulders, and we walked forward. As we did, I eyed my partner out of my periphery. "You seem to be doing better. Everything settle down with the designer?"

Alyssa let out a dry laugh. "Not really. But I think he's used up his most threatening lines and doesn't know what else to say anymore. Plus, he was on a road trip to pick up a special purchase of fabric he got from some woman online, so that gave me a few days of peace."

So *that* was Dirk's fashion emergency.

We filed into the meeting area, noting there weren't seats this time. We'd likely be grabbing our clues and heading out, so it wasn't necessary to set everything up. Just as with last Saturday, Penny stood at the front of the space with Nancy. But this time, Iris and Edna weren't anywhere to be seen.

"I'd bet you Iris and Edna are stationed out in Pioneer Square to hand out clues," I whispered to Alyssa.

We'd learned our lesson during the second annual Morrisey Masterpiece Classic. Penny thought it would be fine to hide the stack of clues on the windowsill of the building she'd used as a location. But some man had come by and stolen the lot before the first team even had the chance to find the building, and there was chaos and confusion until Penny was called in to help, having to tell everyone the clue verbally since they'd all been snatched up.

Ever since, Penny had stationed people who weren't competing nearby to hand out the next clue. She was careful not to place them too out in the open, however, so people couldn't just get lucky by spotting them on the sidewalk and rush over to gather a clue they didn't quite earn.

"Okay, everyone. It's about time to start." Nancy checked her watch and then glanced at Penny. When she received a thumbs-up from my aunt, she added, "You know the rules."

At that, Laurie looked over at me. I nodded somberly, fighting the quirk of a lip that wanted to come out at his serious expression.

"Then come get your clues!" Nancy wafted her hands toward herself, beckoning us forward. "Remember, don't open them until every team has one, and I give you the okay."

Based on the mean mugging, whispered threats, and high fives going on between teams as we all crowded toward Nancy and Penny, Laurie and I weren't the only ones feeling the competitive spirit. It also looked like Penny had let the Rosenblooms advance to this stage with a warning, because they grabbed an envelope along with the rest of the teams.

Alyssa took ours, and we rushed off toward the front doors, crouched over the golden envelope like it was the ring and we were Gollum. We waited just inside the doors, however, until everyone got theirs. Teams joined us close to the doors, knowing we'd be heading out into Pioneer Square, anyway. Some wandered toward the end of the lobby, opting for the back entrance. It wasn't a bad idea. The front door often bottlenecked.

But Alyssa and I were positioned perfectly. On the other side of the door, however, were Laurie and Opal. The four of us locked eyes just as Penny called out, "Okay. Open those envelopes!"

Alyssa's fingers ripped at the sticker, and she pulled the clue out with shaking fingers. Unlike the first round, instead of sentences, this clue was just three letters.

"The post office?" Opal blurted out before she could stop herself. She slapped a hand over her mouth in embarrassment and sent a sheepish look up at Laurie. "Sorry."

"Don't worry about it," he said, leading her outside while watching me and Alyssa warily.

"But it's *not* the post office," I whispered to Alyssa as we followed them through the front door and out into the September sunshine. "That's USPS."

Alyssa snapped her fingers. "Right. So, is there a UPS store around here? Is that really the location?"

"Seems too easy. Doesn't it?" I narrowed my eyes as we stopped near the Pioneer Square totem pole to think.

Bright as the sun was shining, the temperature had started to drop lately, and the leaves of the massive oak trees filling the small park outside our building were turning from bright summery green to a combination of yellow, orange, and red.

"Is there something else locally that might fit that acronym?" Alyssa screwed up her lips as she thought. "Underneath Pioneer Square?" she asked excitedly, each word coming out with more fervor as she committed to the answer.

But her enthusiasm wasn't catching. "There's the original Underground Tour, which would be UT. Or Beneath the Streets, but that's BTS," I said, naming a newer underground tour company that had started up since I'd returned from my time on the East Coast. "I think it might really have something to do with the shipping people."

"Should we—"

"I've got it!" I didn't even let Alyssa finish. Lowering my voice, since there were teams all around us huddled over their clue and discussing options, I said, "The Waterfall Garden." I widened my eyes.

Alyssa took a gulp of air. "You're right. I always forget about that place."

We wandered south, acting as if we were unsure where we were going. No need to alert a bunch of other residents to our destination.

Once we'd crossed James and Yesler, we booked it down the alley next to Merchant's Cafe. At Main Street, we took a hard left and jogged toward the metal bars that enclosed the garden and the sound of rushing water. We passed by a sign at the entrance that explained that this had been the location of the first headquarters building of the United Parcel Service of America.

"Do you think the security guards will have the clues?" I asked once we were inside, gesturing to the two men standing in the corner farthest from the water feature to make sure no one vandalized the park.

"They're not holding anything," Alyssa said with a nervous chuckle. "And they definitely don't look friendly."

Just then, Laurie and Opal raced in from the entrance on Second Avenue, spotting us immediately. After shooting me a handsome grin, Laurie examined the garden. We both turned our attention to the lower level at the same time.

Laurie was closer to a set of stairs leading down toward the water, right next to the falls. I, however, had to rush around and down a long ramp from this side. By the time I navigated my way around the bistro tables and potted plants, he was standing over Edna Feldner, who was sitting at one of the small tables, feet propped up on a chair, snoring. Her eyes were closed and her mouth was wide open.

She clutched a stack of seven golden envelopes.

Laurie put a gentle hand on Edna's arm just as Alyssa and Opal joined us. He lightly patted our elderly neighbor's arm, giving her shoulder a slight jostle as he said, "Edna. Wake up."

The waterfall, however, was pretty loud, and it took Opal stepping over and clapping in front of the woman's face to get her to jolt awake.

"Oh! I'm sorry." Her eyes dropped to her lap, making sure she still had the envelopes she'd been tasked with watching. "The sound of that water just lulled me right to sleep."

I glanced up at the buildings on either side of the courtyard created by the waterfall garden. As much as I loved my home at the Morrisey, I'd always thought the apartments that looked over this garden were probably some of the most peaceful in the city, having the rushing sound of water anytime the garden was open.

Edna moved her feet off the other chair and handed us each an envelope. "Good luck, kiddos," she said, even though Opal was in her eighties, definitely not a *kiddo*.

Other Morrisey teams began filing into the park, telling us it was time to go. Breaking off to our separate entrances, I waited until we were on the street again to open our envelope. This time, we just got a visual. It was of three quarters.

"Seventy-five cents?" I said aloud.

As I did so, Alyssa and I looked at one another and said, "State Street Hotel" in unison.

We rushed forward, toward First Avenue, knowing the vintage sign well. We walked by the thing all the time, and its neon lights advertising **Rooms 75c**. Rounding the corner of

Main and First at a jog, we kept up the pace as we traveled another block north. We were waiting to cross, when I spotted Laurie and Opal rushing toward us from the other direction.

The light turned green, and we beat them to the sign. I didn't see Iris anywhere nearby, but there was a restaurant right under the sign. Hearing Laurie and Opal on our heels, I pulled Alyssa into the restaurant.

It was a cute place Laurie and I had been to a few times before. We loved the brick walls and funky décor. Because it was dark inside, it took my eyes a moment to adjust, but once they did, they locked on to the woman behind the bar who was smiling at us.

"You wouldn't happen to be looking for one of these?" she asked, sliding a golden envelope toward us on the polished wood bar top.

"Thank you," Alyssa and I said, snatching the thing up just as Opal and Laurie approached for theirs.

The next clue was easy.

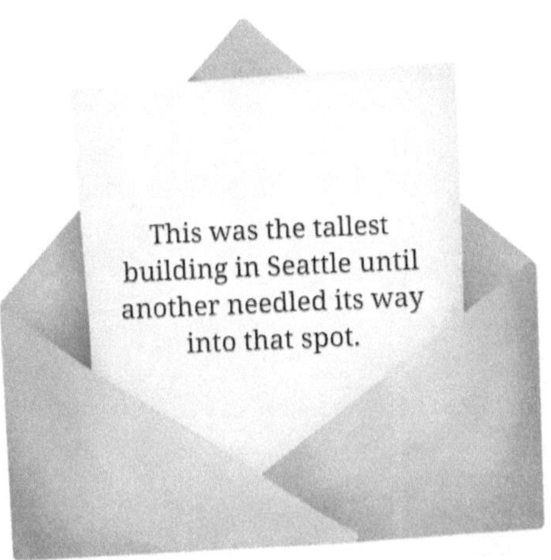

Alyssa and I didn't even need to say the name of the tower aloud as we took a right out of the restaurant and headed for Smith Tower. It was one of the more prominent sights in the Pioneer Square skyline, after all. But I'd also paid to go to the observatory many times, and had heard all about how the Smith Tower was the tallest in the city until the Space Needle was built in the 1960s.

The security guy standing out front had our envelopes, only five this time, which was a relief since I neither wanted to pay for a ticket nor travel to the observatory on the thirty-fifth floor.

"Our last one of this round," Alyssa said as I peeled open the envelope and slid out the piece of card stock that held the clue.

"Nighttime security provided by a unicorn?" I read, confusion lacing my tone.

We started walking, looking back just in time to see Laurie and Opal get their own envelope. Behind them, I could see the Rosenblooms making their way up to the tower security guard. Art and Darius weren't too far behind them.

Knowing Pioneer Square didn't extend much beyond Cherry Street, we took a left, heading back toward the Morrisey and the waterfront as we thought. It was just as we rounded the corner of the Morrisey that I locked eyes with a building across the street.

Magic Mouse Toys. The toy shop was a Pioneer Square staple. Whoever closed for the evening usually put a toy on top of an overturned shopping basket, blocking the front door as if it were guarding from intruders. The past few months, it had been a plush unicorn.

"It's the toy shop," I said, taking off at a run. Alyssa followed behind.

Seeing no one I recognized outside, I entered the shop, glancing around at the bright, colorful array of toys. Golden envelopes were going to be harder to find in here than they had been in the restaurant. But then I felt the salesperson's attention fall on me, and I focused on what sat next to them on the checkout counter. A stuffed unicorn guarded a small pile of four golden envelopes.

We thanked the worker, and the unicorn, grabbing our envelope and opening it to confirm there wasn't a special, extra clue this round.

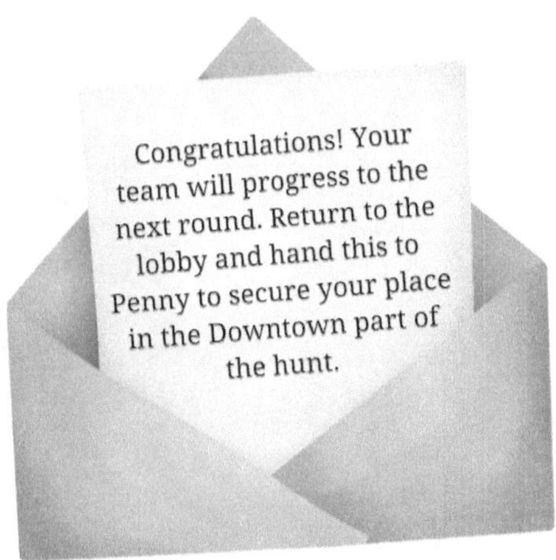

Alyssa and I high-fived. Our place in the final round secured, we returned to the Morrisey.

After Penny and Nancy congratulated us in person, Alyssa

left to go back to her apartment, but I plopped onto the wobbly couch to wait for Laurie to return.

"Winning sure is sweet," I told him when he sat next to me.

"Yes, I know the feeling, from when I won the last round, remember?" Placing a hand on my leg, he said, "Ready to go interrogate a fashion designer?"

Still riding high from my win, I felt like I could do anything. "Bring it on."

THIRTEEN

irk Evans Design was located in an updated building just off Occidental Square. The square was an open area where they often set up outdoor markets, held concerts, and had other gatherings throughout the year. The neon business sign in the boutique's front window displaying his name was in a trendy, handwritten script—maybe even Dirk's own signature.

Ripley paced in front of the store, eyes lighting up as she noticed us approach. *"Finally.* He's been in the back, like, the whole time, so I haven't been able to see or hear a thing." Appraising me, she said, "You won, didn't you?"

I beamed. "Yes, we came in first." I shot a playful smirk in Laurie's direction.

He was just about to say something in response—probably a super-flattering compliment about how smart and capable and beautiful I was—when his phone began buzzing with an incoming call. Checking the screen, he said, "It's Dad. I should take this."

Eyes wide, I asked, "It's tile install day, right?"

He crossed his fingers. "Yeah, and I hope this isn't a call telling me they've changed their minds *again*." Laurie motioned toward the boutique. "You and Ripley go in without me. I'll be right there."

While he answered his call, I opened the door to the boutique and stepped inside. I braced myself as I entered, like I did whenever entering any clothing store. The possibility that there might be mannequins, one of my greater fears, always put me on edge. But the store was surprisingly stark, and there wasn't a single mannequin in sight.

I must've still been jumpy, however, because I jolted as a small bell dinged behind me when the door closed. Once I'd gotten over my surprise, I continued to look around the space. Not only were there no mannequins, there were no people inside at all.

I looked to Ripley, who said, "I told you. He's been in the back for hours."

The store smelled like it had been recently renovated. The aroma of fresh paint still hung in the air, and the floors appeared to be newly installed. Definitely not holding any of the creaky, scratched, or worn qualities of original floors like the ones we had in the Morrisey. Honestly, they might not have even been made of real wood. The old brick inlaid along the walls *was* real, as was the plaster sticking to sizeable areas. It created a cool, artsy feel that reminded me of the restaurant we'd visited earlier on the scavenger hunt. I loved funky décor like that.

That was where any funkiness ended, however. Everything else within the space felt curated, intentional in a way that made me scared to touch any of it. The clothes were all in different shades of earth tones, and they were flowy in that effortless way rich people dress when they're on yachts or summering in Barcelona.

There were only a few duplicates of each style instead of the dozen size options I was used to seeing at larger retail stores. Each piece was one of a kind or one of a handful in that style.

"The guy loves a neutral tone." Ripley whistled as she took in the space.

That was for sure. Even the colors he had included didn't seem particularly colorful. The only green was a heathery sage color. Red? More like sandstone or salmon. The yellow was the color of turmeric, and I could've sworn the blue was mostly gray. Other than that, it was tans, grays, browns, and whites.

Near the back of the space, by the two changing rooms, a dress form stood on a small pedestal. Dirk's most recent creation was taking shape on the form, pins still sticking out of it and only certain pieces sewn in place.

"I'm going to check to see if he's even here," Ripley said, moving toward the back now that she had the freedom to roam inside.

I touched my ear, turning around to walk back toward the door and check the hours. Maybe he wasn't even open, and I'd just wandered inside when I wasn't welcome. But the sign on the door said we were within the listed business hours, so...

I was usually a quiet person. As someone who'd grown up not always knowing who was alive and who wasn't, I kept to myself, made myself small so people wouldn't notice me. In this circumstance, I needed to do the opposite.

Striding across the shop, I made sure my sandals made a

scuffing sound each time I stepped. I cleared my throat. I even hummed.

Finally, a man stepped out from the back room. Ripley followed, wearing an exasperated expression, as if she'd had to convince him to show his face. He was probably not too much older than I was, honestly. From his fancy boat shoes, cropped pants, and brocade jacket, I made a leap and assumed he was the designer.

Beaming at him, I waited for us to instantly connect. Nothing to see here, just two artists, kindred spirits. Well, except for the whole *he's a suspect in a murder investigation* thing. But it wasn't as if I were really going to become his best friend. I just needed him to think I was so I could get some information out of him, the information he'd been, so far, unwilling to share with Detective Anthony or any of the officers she'd sent in to speak with him.

The reality, or problem, was that Dirk did *not* instantly connect with me.

In fact, he glanced at my jumpsuit—the one I'd picked especially for today because it was my *coolest,* most *artsy* piece of clothing—and sneered. Sneered! Defensiveness for the woman I'd bought it from at a stall in Pike Place Market swelled inside me.

I tugged at the fabric self-consciously. I supposed it was rather different from anything he carried. But I'd worn it after seeing that golden sequin dress Quinn had on when she'd been killed. That thing had totally been funky and fun. Was I in the wrong shop?

Just then, Dirk's interest moved from me. "Perfection," he

whispered just as the bell on the door dinged and Laurie entered.

Ripley and I shared a wide-eyed stare of disbelief. Not because Laurie wasn't stunning. He was, but he was also just wearing basketball shorts and a T-shirt. My floral jumpsuit had to qualify as better fashion than that.

Feeling the man's concentration on him, Laurie glanced at me, worry flashing in his eyes. I didn't blame the poor guy. If I thought Dirk's look of disdain about my outfit was discomfiting, it was nothing compared to the unsettling nature of his apparent admiration.

"Sir, you are *just* who I've been looking for to model my newest line." Dirk raced forward.

Laurie sidestepped the man to stand by me. He surveyed his own outfit, obviously sharing in my assessment that shorts and a T-shirt did not a fashionable outfit make.

"Do you already have representation?" Dirk asked quickly in a tone that sounded like he hoped that wasn't the case.

Shaking his head, but still at a loss for words, Laurie put a hand on my shoulder to steady himself.

"Oh." Dirk's countenance hardened. "I see. I probably have to talk to your agent, huh?" He sighed, holding out his hand. "Okay. Give me their card."

Wetting his lips, Laurie said, "I'm sorry. I'm not a model."

Dirk's eyes widened, and the look on his face was positively feral with delight. "Not *yet*. But I can help you change that. You have amazing bone structure."

"He really does." Ripley pursed her lips as she studied Laurie, along with Dirk and me.

I touched my ear in agreement.

But the attention suddenly became too much for sweet Laurie and he snapped. Stepping behind me, he said, "I'm not a model, nor do I have any interest in becoming one."

Dirk brushed off his comment like it was a piece of lint on one of his perfect garments. "Psh. *Everyone* wants to be a model. Who wouldn't? I'm giving you the opportunity of a lifetime here. And I'll pay you well. Don't worry."

The way he added that last sentence gave me the distinct impression that we actually should worry a little. I was wondering if Laurie agreeing to model might win us some goodwill, and some questions answered pertaining to the case.

But before I could even let that play out in my mind, Laurie stiffened. "I said no. End of discussion. Now, if you're interested in helping us, you could talk to my girlfriend, who is the reason we came here today."

"Ooooh," Ripley stretched the word out, giving voice to the surprise I felt.

Laurie was never short with people like that. This guy must've really gotten under his skin. And even though Laurie's declaration shut the door on the possibility of getting close to Dirk through modeling talks, I respected his choice to say no.

Bristling slightly, the man said, "Well, if you change your mind, my name's Dirk Evans. I'm the designer." He gestured to the sign at the front of the store. Then he turned toward me. "Now, what did you need help with?" The sneer was back.

Even though his attention was what I'd wanted since I walked in, now that I had it, I felt distinctly caught off guard. "I, uh, well ... do you have any ... more fitted items?"

There had to be another collection, maybe even this new

one he'd brought up to Laurie, that more closely resembled the dress I'd seen on Quinn Garret.

Dirk's nostrils flared, and I felt like I wasn't explaining myself very well, so I dug back through my memories of what Alyssa had said about the dress. "Anything with darts?" I added.

At that, Dirk went red. If he'd been a cartoon, I think steam might've poured out of his ears. "Darts?" He spat out the word. "Darling, I drape. I don't *do* darts."

Laurie, who'd been standing behind me, stepped up next to me at that. His jaw was set. "We must've gotten you confused with a different designer." He ground out the sentence.

"Whoa, don't get on Laurie's bad side today," Ripley muttered, watching him with pride as he stood up for me. "Or Meg's."

Dirk made slits of his eyes. "Must've."

But as much as Laurie seemed bent on burning any bridge we had with this guy—to the ground—I had more questions.

Placing a hand on Laurie's arm, I waited for my pounding heart to settle and took a metaphorical leap.

"It's probably my fault. I'm not explaining this very well. I came by last Saturday afternoon, but you were closed. Something about a fashion emergency." I squinted one eye as if I was trying to recall the exact time but couldn't, so I shook my head. "Anyway, there was a dress in the front window, but it's not there anymore, and I was wondering if you still had it."

I was banking on a lot here. My first leap was venturing that the "fashion emergency" sign was something Dirk used whenever he needed to close. But the biggest reach was assuming he'd been closed last Saturday during the window Quinn had been killed.

Air burned in my lungs from the breath I held as I waited for his reaction.

"Oh, right." His expression softened. "I'm sorry about that. I had a"—he belted out a note of laughter as he tipped his head —"well, it was an emergency, but it's all taken care of now." Twiddling his fingers, he examined the shop. "Is this the dress you're talking about?" Dirk skirted over to a rack where a single dress hung on a hook in the wall.

It was white and looked a lot like the kind of dress a bride might change into for her reception so she could dance without worrying about a long train or a large tulle skirt.

Nodding, because I couldn't speak while I worked through my surprise that my stunt had worked at all, I stepped forward. I needed to come up with a reason not to try on this dress now that I'd made it sound like I'd waited a whole week to come back for it.

"Yes, that's the one." I smiled, letting it visibly drop as I turned to him. "I was hoping you might have it in a different color, though."

Dirk's ire was back in an instant. A muscle in his jaw ticked as his eyes flicked from me, to Laurie, and back again. "This. Is. One of a kind." He ground out the phrase.

"She was only asking." Laurie's support came in the form of his retort and a hand on my waist.

"*Just asking*," Dirk repeated in a mocking tone that sounded like a child. "Everyone's always just asking, just wanting something different, just ... just ... get out!" He pointed toward the door as his anger reached some sort of peak.

"Whoa, this guy's fuse is nonexistent," Ripley observed

aloud as I threaded my fingers through Laurie's and pulled him out of the boutique.

The three of us stood outside in a daze for a moment before Laurie began walking. "I don't want to chance that he'll come out and yell at us again," he explained as we crossed the street, returning to the waterfall garden we'd visited earlier during the scavenger hunt.

Sitting at one of the tables, Laurie finally relaxed.

"That was..." Ripley floated beside me.

"Yeah." I puffed out my cheeks.

But Laurie must've still been hanging on to some anger, because he flexed his fingers out and then into a fist. "I'm so sorry I lost my cool in there, Meg. That was all my fault. I should've just said yes to modeling for him, and we would've had the perfect reason to go back and ask him more questions."

I let my hand rest over his clenched fist, his fingers loosening at my touch. "Don't blame yourself for a moment. I don't. He was awful, and we got the information we needed, anyway."

"Because you were able to save the mess I'd made." Laurie blew out a thin breath.

"Yeah, quick thinking there, Megs." Ripley nodded her approval.

The planes of Laurie's handsome face hardened. "It's just the way he was looking at you when I entered, like you weren't good enough to be there, and then the way he bossed me around. I couldn't stop myself from shutting him down imme-diately." A dry laugh escaped him. "And that's after a particu-larly frustrating conversation with my dad, so..."

"Not the tiles." I gasped.

Laurie's hands went up in defense. "No. They stuck with

their choice and the install went fine. But Dad was calling to tell me that the kitchen remodel has made them want to do both bathrooms, and they think they know enough now to do the work themselves."

I closed my eyes and cringed, knowing the brunt of that would definitely fall on Laurie, since a lot of *this* renovation had, and that was with professional help. "I'm so sorry. I can see why that put you in a bad mood, heading into that conversation."

"And that guy didn't help," Laurie said. "He was awful. I'd say that man is definitely unhinged enough to get so angry about a missing dress that he strangled a woman."

"Definitely," Ripley added.

"Yeah, and he was closed during the time Quinn was killed to fix a problem that's been taken care of now? That's suspicious." I jerked my head in a swift arc. "There's something bugging me, though. Did you hear what he said about darts?"

Laurie set his mouth in a stern line, proving he hadn't.

Ripley pretended to pat my hand. "Laurie was feeling a little protective in that moment. I'm not sure what got through."

"He said he doesn't do darts," I repeated his words. "He drapes, which is evident in the pieces in his boutique. But that dress, the one Quinn was wearing when she died, that one had them. I remember Alyssa saying it had been ripped along one of the darts."

"You don't think the dress was his?" Laurie lowered his brows in concern.

"It sure didn't look like anything he had in that shop." I stood. "I think we need to have another talk with Detective Anthony."

From the waterfall park, it was a short walk. The detective usually worked weekends, so it wasn't a surprise to find her at her desk when an officer led us back.

"What can I help you two with?" She glanced at us as she closed a folder and gave us her full focus.

"Well, we just got back from talking to Dirk Evans," I told her.

"More like Jerk Evans," Laurie added with a grunt.

Ripley threw her head back and laughed. "Angry Laurie is my new favorite." Proving that she trusted the detective to tell us what we needed to know, my ghostly friend wasn't even snooping around the desk, preferring to float next to me.

Detective Anthony rolled her eyes. "Let me guess. He wouldn't talk to you either?"

"He barely gave me the time of day," I told her. "Laurie? He wanted to recruit him to model his new line." After hesitating to let Amaya react to that statement, I added, "But we were able to find out that his shop was closed during the afternoon last Saturday." I repeated his exact wording to her.

Amaya slumped back in her chair. "Bleh." When she saw my surprised expression, she sat forward again. "Sorry, that's great information. More than I could get out of the guy. It's just, I was hoping he'd have an airtight alibi so I wouldn't have to talk to him anymore." She chuckled. "After questioning him once, I share in Laurence's assessment." Tapping the paper in front of her with a pen, she said, "I'll bring him in. Maybe an interrogation room will get him to come clean about what he was doing last weekend. Thank you."

"There's one more thing." I held up a finger. When I knew I had Amaya's attention, I told her about his slipup with the darts and his comment about draping. "Is it possible that we have the wrong designer? I really don't think he designed the dress Quinn died in."

Chewing on her lip, Detective Anthony reached for one of the files on her desk and flipped through the pages. She pulled out a piece of paper and scanned it before shaking her head. "The tag inside the dress said so, and your neighbor Alyssa confirmed he was the designer she was trying to get a contract for with her company." A spark of something lit behind the detective's eyes. "But I'll look into the possibility that he stole the design as well. That could be a motive in and of itself."

Fourteen

Before we left the police station, Detective Anthony gave me her cell number, and it took everything I had not to jump up and down. I officially had a direct line to the detective.

Once I'd gotten my celebrating under control, Laurie and I started for home. Now that Amaya had all the information we did, any of our earlier urgency dissipated. We plodded along at an unnaturally slow gait for us. Ripley floated next to me, not even bothering to pretend she was walking.

Normally, we would speed by businesses, not taking the time to glance inside. But our slower pace allowed me time to peer through windows and study the businesses up here. It may have only been a few blocks from our apartment building, but it wasn't an area we frequented.

Which was why I had to do a double take when I recognized my aunt, standing inside a coffee shop.

Fingers tightening around Laurie's arm, I pulled him to a

stop with me and gestured inside. "Why is Penny here?" I whispered to him, as if he might know.

"Maybe she's here to write." He bobbed his head to see past the glare on the windows.

Ripley and I shook our heads in tandem, but I answered for the both of us. "No way. If she was going to get any writing done while she was here, she'd go to the place across the street from the Morrisey or the library." Those had been her two favorite places to write. If she wasn't in our apartment, that was.

"You're right. She doesn't even have her laptop with her," Laurie said. "Want to go inside?"

My heartbeat quickened. I definitely did. I'm not sure why, but her choice of this coffee shop instead of our favorite one felt like an important consideration. It made it seem like she was trying not to be seen, especially by me.

"Yes, but do you think we can stay hidden? I want to watch her. See why she's here." My concentration strayed to Ripley, who held her hand flat in a salute, understanding what I was asking her to do.

Laurie must've guessed I was speaking to Ripley, because he moved toward the door without answering. He opened it for me, then ushered me inside and immediately to the left where a small table was open right near the window. It was tucked away enough that Penny wouldn't automatically see us unless she was looking in this direction.

She stood in line and was next up to order. Over the chatter of the customers, and the cacophony of sounds from the baristas, I couldn't hear what she ordered, but she counted off the drinks on her fingers.

"She just ordered two drinks," I whispered to Laurie,

holding up a newspaper someone left at the table as Penny paid and glanced our way.

Laurie looked down, his back to the line. "You think she's here meeting someone?"

"She must be." I peeked out from my ink-and-paper hiding place to see her waiting for her drinks at the counter.

Ripley crouched next to me. She didn't need to hide, but the place was crowded, and she didn't want anyone to walk through her. "The question is who?" she whispered.

Was there a small part of me that wanted it to be my dad? Of course. What else did Penny have to be secretive about?

My first clue that it probably wasn't my dad was when the barista set three drinks in front of my aunt at the pickup counter.

"Three drinks?" I whispered. "So, she's meeting two other people?"

Ripley moved to follow her. "I'll go—"

"Rip?"

My ghostly best friend and I adopted rigid postures at the same time, as a woman in her twenties rushed forward. She looked ... well, a lot like me, if I was being honest. But while we had similar long, brown hair, pale skin, and hazel eyes, her eyes were rimmed in thick black eyeliner, her hair was parted on the side so it draped over her face, and her lipstick was a dark shade of red that leaned to purple. Her nineties' grunge aesthetic matched Ripley's to a T.

Oh, and she was obviously a ghost. I might not have noticed her transparency at first glance, but standing next to Ripley, who appeared solid anytime she was near me, it was clear that this was a spirit.

"Jade?" Ripley's response was mostly a gasp. Her eyes went wide, and she jerked her head back in surprise.

Jade? I scrambled through my memories, wondering if Ripley had ever mentioned someone by that name. Nothing came to mind, but my best friend obviously knew this person well. They couldn't hug because of the whole being-ghosts thing, but they raced toward one another, grinning.

Between the new ghost, the crowded coffee shop, and the added noise of the baristas grinding beans, steaming milk, and calling out orders, I was officially overwhelmed. Laurie's voice pulled me back to our task.

"Do you recognize them?" he asked.

My attention flicked to him. Unaware of the odd reunion happening between the spirits nearby, he'd watched my aunt walk the three coffees to a table at the back of the shop. Smart woman. If she'd been sitting back there when we'd walked by, we wouldn't have ever seen her. She set the drinks in front of a man and a woman before sliding into the seat across from them.

"I don't recognize any of them," I murmured, shooting another questioning glance at this Jade person Ripley was talking to.

She noticed. Jade's heavy-lidded gaze thinned as she caught me staring. Her merlot-colored lip curled. "What's her problem?"

Ripley's gaze snapped back to me. If she could blush, I was sure she would've gone red, based on how flustered she appeared. "Oh! That's my ... Meg. Don't worry about her. She's cool."

"Cool?" Jade's eyebrows tipped up as she snorted in a definite rebuke. "You hang with a living person?"

Checking over her shoulder, Ripley motioned for Jade to move outside so they could talk, away from me. The motion felt like a knife to my heart, and I inhaled like the pain had been physical.

"Hey, everything okay?" Laurie's hand landed on mine.

I met his familiar eyes and softened at the concern I found there. "Yeah, I—Ripley just met some ghost she knows. She's outside now." I hoped he didn't notice the slight break in my words as I admitted as much. I couldn't help but stare at Ripley while she beheld Jade with a level of adoration reserved for idols or, in my case, big sisters. It was how I was sure I used to look at Ripley when I was growing up.

"So that means we're on our own to figure out who these two are?" Laurie craned his neck, trying to see the table Penny and her mystery guests were seated at.

"We are." Raking my teeth over my bottom lip, I made a decision. "Stay here. I'll see if I can get closer and hear what they're saying." I held up my finger and stood.

The next few minutes were filled with me pretending to read the menu, but still staying out of Penny's line of sight so I could get a closer view of these two strangers. It wasn't my best work. I stepped on a woman's foot, ran straight into not one but two men, and almost knocked over a whole container of clean silverware on their sideboard.

After all that, I still didn't recognize the two people Penny was meeting with, nor could I hear anything they were saying. They looked to be a little older than me, and had similarly colored blonde hair and blue eyes that made me think they might be siblings.

My siblings? I wondered for a gut-wrenching moment,

remembering Penny mentioning kids, plural, when she'd been holed up in the mailroom, talking to Iris about my dad. *Did I have a half brother and half sister out there just wandering around in the world and I didn't know it?*

Seeing Ripley catching up with the ghost outside, like they were long-lost relatives, didn't help me process the possibility.

Returning to Laurie, I sat down with a huff. "I can't get close enough to hear." Angling myself so I was next to his direct line of sight to them, I said, "Do you think they look like me at all?"

Adding reason number quadrillion to the list of why I loved this man, he spent about a minute squinting at me and then looking at the people in question before saying, "The only person you look like over there is Penny. Why?"

I grimaced, not sure why saying it aloud made me feel silly. "I got a weird feeling that she's hiding this meeting because maybe it was about my dad, or because those are my half siblings."

Laurie's hand settled over mine. His brown eyes were soft when I finally mustered the courage to look at him. "Meg, I love you. But those two random people look nothing like you." He held back a smile. "Also, the meeting doesn't seem to be going well, so I'm not sure if you would even want to claim them as family."

He was right. Penny's posture was stiff with frustration, and the other two were stuck in a loop of clenching their jaws and shaking their heads.

Chuckling, I let out a cathartic breath. "I know. I know. I'm just not used to this weird dynamic with Penny. I'm so used to her trusting me, and us not having any secrets." I pouted.

But Laurie wasn't having any of it. "No secrets? You've literally been keeping a huge secret from her your whole life."

Sucking air through my teeth, I said, "You are not wrong there, my friend. Okay. Point taken. I need to give Penny a break."

"Give me a break about what?" My aunt stood next to our table, hand on her hip. She wore an expression I'd only seen a few times, when I'd really done something bad.

"Penny!" I stood, almost toppling our small table.

Laurie grabbed on to the thing, steadying it as I faced my aunt. Glancing back at the table she'd been sitting at, I realized the two other people had left while Laurie and I had been talking. A quick check on Ripley proved she and her ghostly friend were gone too. The coffee shop swirled around me in my unsettled state.

"How'd you... Well, I didn't know you—" I stumbled over my words until I stopped myself out of service to everyone present.

Penny laughed. "How'd I notice you and Laurie over here spying on me?" She jabbed a thumb over her shoulder. "You just about took out three people and a sideboard a few minutes ago. And Laurence is a head taller than half the people in here." Her tone was flat, her features serious.

I collapsed back into my chair. "Sorry. We *were* spying. I saw you here and thought you were hiding something because you never come to this coffee shop."

At that comment, Penny was the one who looked embarrassed. She sank onto the third chair around our table and played with the cardboard sleeve on her coffee cup. "Well, in that respect, you weren't wrong." Penny glanced over her shoulder toward the table where she'd had her brief meeting.

I tensed, waiting for my aunt to change the subject or tell me it was none of my business. But she didn't.

"Those were Casey Kincaid's kids," she finally said with an exhale. "I was meeting with them about the Morrisey."

Laurie and I blinked at one another in surprise before turning our focus back on my aunt.

"And? Why'd they want to meet with you?" I leaned forward. "You don't even live at the Morrisey anymore."

Penny shook her head. "I asked if they'd see me." She wouldn't meet my eyes.

"I'm guessing things didn't go how you hoped," Laurie said.

Her lips thinned into a grim line as she finally looked at me. "They're selling the Morrisey."

The words were a stab to my gut. It was a pain that only increased when I heard her next words.

"The highest bidder right now is some conglomerate known for coming in, grabbing up these old buildings, buying everyone out who lives there, and gutting the inside so they can completely redo everything and turn them into luxury apartments." Penny flicked her fingers toward Elliott Bay. "They've done it to a bunch of those buildings on the waterfront now that the viaduct is gone."

It hurt to breathe. After Nancy's announcement last week, I'd known this was a possibility, but it hadn't felt real. And then Penny had shown up, and we'd gotten distracted by the death in the building and the Morrisey Masterpiece Cl—

"That's why you agreed to do the scavenger hunt. Isn't it?" I drew in a thoughtful breath. "You were trying to distract us."

Penny flinched. "I thought it would be a nice way to bring the building together before everyone's ripped apart."

Laurie rubbed a hand over his face. "Wait. So, it's a sure thing?"

"I thought I could convince them to hold on to the building," Penny said. "But the moment I sat down with them, they told me they weren't sure why I was here because they weren't going to change their minds." Penny swallowed. "That's when I panicked and told them I would get us drinks. I needed time to think of a plan, but it didn't matter. They were set on their decision."

Even though I knew it was coming, her words still made me deflate, any hope leaking out of my posture.

"That's why I flew out here the moment I heard Casey died," Penny explained. "It's the whole reason he and I broke up back in the day. I can't remember how we got on the topic. I think I was making up a will because I had you to think of now, but he mentioned that he'd left the building to his kids in his will." She groaned. "His kids were awful even back then. He constantly complained about how spoiled they were and how their mother only cared about him for his money, and that's why he'd left her, but she'd managed to pass down that trait to their kids."

I watched her. "So, you didn't fly out here because you thought I was looking into my dad?" My mind flipped back to the conversation in the mailroom with Iris I'd overheard, along with the other Morrisey residents who'd had their ears pressed up against the mailboxes. She'd been talking about a father and children. It hadn't been *my* father. It had been Casey and his kids. "You were filling Iris in on the drama inside the mailroom."

Penny pushed her fingers into her temple. "Yes, which I cannot believe I did. I've only been gone two years, but I completely forgot how nosy everyone is. I'm disappointed in myself that I didn't think that through better. It's partially why I jumped at Ronnie's suggestion about the scavenger hunt."

We sat there in silence for a moment.

"Sorry, kids." The corner of her lip quirked up, but the motion was sad. "I wish I could've gotten you a different outcome."

"Thanks for trying." Laurie's large shoulders moved up and down in an enormous sigh. "When do you think Nancy will tell the rest of the building?"

"The Kincaid kids still have yet to accept the offer." She gritted her teeth for a moment before continuing. "I think they want the three top bidders to fight it out for a while so they might get more. But I'd say they'll probably decide within the next week or two. Nancy will have to tell everyone then. I don't blame her for putting it off until it's absolutely necessary, though."

Tears filled my eyes, and I swiped them away. As much as I didn't know how I'd survive without seeing my Morrisey family every day, I'd be okay. Even Laurie, who depended on the lenient rules about dogs so he could have Leo live with him, would be able to find another place that would take a pit bull.

Our neighbors, however?

Where could Art and Darius go that would allow them to bring their personal armchairs down into the lobby so they could be the Conversationalists? Opal had just gotten back into the building after spending decades at another building that she hated. Would Winnie be able to find a place close to the Third Avenue Theatre? And would Hayden's new building allow him to have a greenhouse on the roof? Wherever I went wouldn't have a fifth floor of all girls where we shared clothes and hid keys in light fixtures.

And it wouldn't be where I'd grown up. It wouldn't be the building my mom thought was so magical that she'd known I had to grow up there.

FIFTEEN

I didn't see Ripley until later that evening. Instead of appearing at my side in the apartment, like she usually did, she slipped through the door, almost like she'd "walked" up the stairs.

At first, I almost wondered if I was looking in a mirror. Her posture was hunched forward, defeat weighing her down. She looked like I felt.

After going our separate ways from Penny, who'd wanted to wander the city a little before she had to come back to the Morrisey and face everyone, Laurie and I returned home. And even though taking Leo on walks with Laurie was one of my favorite things, I just couldn't muster the strength to join them. So, I'd been rotting away on the couch, watching a reality show where people spent most of their time arguing with one another. It felt like the only other option for me if I could no longer live with my Morrisey family.

I was *really* leaning into my sadness.

Normal Ripley would've had something to say about my choice of television. We used reality television like the government used color-coded warning systems. Baking shows? Those were fine all the time. Code green. Matchmaking shows? There might be some underlying sadness, but things were generally good if we were watching one of those. Code yellow. The incredibly dramatic ones, where conflict lurks around every corner—along with manufactured tension? Something was majorly wrong. That level was the equivalent to code red.

But Ripley didn't mention a thing. She just slumped onto the couch next to me and wouldn't meet my eyes.

"I'm so sorry about today," she whispered after a few beats.

I didn't know what to say. I wanted to ask about my ghostly nineties' doppelgänger, but I feared all my insecurities surrounding how she'd reacted to me would be on display.

"I shouldn't have left you to listen to Penny's conversation alone," Ripley continued. "I was just so caught off guard. I haven't seen Jade since I was ... eleven?" She squinted at the ceiling, but shook her head. "Seeing that she'd died, too, right around the same age I had, it messed with me more than I thought it would."

I finally found my voice. "You were friends?"

"Foster sisters. She was six years older than me, and I thought she was *so* cool."

Ah, so I'd recognized her look of big-sister reverence correctly.

"It was an awful house, the worst I'd lived in, and Jade looked out for me. She's the reason I got so into grunge." Ripley plucked at the flannel she wore. "I wanted to be just like her in every way, even more so once I left that house and moved in with my foster family."

While Ripley had always been in the foster system, she only referred to one of the families she'd lived with as her "foster family." From what she'd told me, not all the houses she'd stayed in were bad, but her last family made her feel like she was a part of something, accepted for the first time.

"I knew the survival rate for foster kids was lower, but..." She swallowed hard. "Meg, I think she might be why I'm still here. I think Jade could be my unfinished business."

Surprise wrapped around me, the conviction in her words making me feel automatically terrible for my earlier jealousy. "Really?"

"She mentioned she was working at a bakery up by the market when she died, but has no idea how she died or why she's still here." Ripley's eyes sparked as they met mine. "I think we should help her."

"You don't think you're here because of my dad anymore?"

She shrugged. "I don't know what I think. But we've hit a pretty definite wall with him, so why not look into this lead?"

"Sure. Whatever you need, Rip." My voice was small.

Ripley turned toward me. "Back to my apology."

"You don't need to—" I started.

But she cut me off. "I do. Jade or not, I shouldn't have left you when you were trying to figure out who those people were. I felt so bad that I followed them once they left the coffee shop."

My spine straightened. So that was why she'd disappeared.

"I know who they are and why they were meeting with Penny." Her lips twisted downward.

Seeing my best friend try to psych herself up to tell me terrible news was too painful. "So do I." I flapped my hand toward the television. "Why do you think I'm watching this?"

Understanding lifted her posture, and I realized she'd walked into this scene assuming she'd been the cause for my bad mood. She'd thought I'd been disappointed in her, and that was why I was moping.

"Penny spotted us," I explained. "She came over and told us everything."

Ripley pushed out a breath she didn't need. It was purely an emotional response. "Did she tell you there are three bidders?"

"Yeah, but either way, I don't think it looks good for us." I let my hand smooth over Anise's soft fur. "Penny seemed to think the only way we were safe was if the kids held on to the building. She was trying to convince them what a good investment it was. If they want to sell, I'm sure they're looking at a company who will want to kick us out and remodel."

Tapping her mouth with the pad of her finger, Ripley said, "I'm not so sure about that. The company coming in second in the bidding war sounds different. The Kincaid kids were talking about how the owner had some kind of personal connection to the building and wanted it preserved." Another sigh escaped her. "But I think he was coming in, like, fifty grand short of the other offer, so..."

A groan pealed out of me, and I let my head fall back onto the couch cushion. "It doesn't even feel real. I just got the Morrisey back. How can I possibly say goodbye?"

Ripley didn't tell me everything was going to be okay. She wasn't one for platitudes. "It's going to suck. Plain and simple."

I could've sat there and complained about it even more, but my phone buzzed with a text from Laurie.

> Just got back from our walk. You want company or do you need more time to yourself?

My heart hurt.

"That man is too sweet for his own good," Ripley said. A small chuckle escaped her. "Except around Dirk the jerk. That was actually pretty entertaining to see him lose his temper."

It felt good to laugh. "It really was." Moving the kitten next to Ripley, I stood and stretched. "Okay, enough wallowing. I should go." A small smile pursed my lips. "Who knows how much longer I'll be able to just walk downstairs and see him?"

I wasn't worried that we wouldn't last as a couple if we didn't live in the same building, or anything. It was just that I'd started picturing our future together, here, and letting go of that felt like having a piece of me ripped out of my body.

Turning on the show once more for Ripley, I stopped before leaving. "I'm glad you got to see Jade again. I'm glad you had someone to look out for you. I know how important that is."

"Love you, Megs." She held my gaze, tearing up.

I swiped at my eyes. "Love you, too, Ripley."

Slipping out of my apartment, the only thing I wanted was to be able to get down to Laurie's place without having to see anyone else from the building. Not only was I in an emotional mood, but seeing them and not telling them about the impending news felt like a betrayal of epic proportions.

Alyssa was walking onto the fifth floor right as I closed my door behind me.

"Hey, partner," she said with a tired smile.

I returned the gesture. "Hey." Then I braced myself to get sucked into a conversation.

Alyssa was beyond extroverted. She loved people. I wasn't ever surprised when I found her sitting with the Conversationalists in the lobby, despite being decades younger, just to chat and people watch.

So, when she passed right by me without another word, something snapped inside my brain. Suddenly, I was the one who needed to start a conversation just to make sure something wasn't wrong.

"Lyss?"

She stopped and turned, eyebrow raised. A few shopping bags bounced at her side, proving she'd been doing a little retail therapy while I'd been moping.

"I visited Dirk Evans' boutique today. Do you really think he designed that dress?"

That brought her out of whatever fog she'd been in. She stepped back in my direction. "It's a departure from his regular style, right?"

I widened my eyes. "A complete departure. He even told me he doesn't *do* darts, and I was thinking, uh, you did on the dress Quinn was wearing when she died. But I didn't say anything, of course. He didn't know I knew about the dress," I added, so she wouldn't worry.

Alyssa didn't appear to be worried. She simply scoffed. "I was surprised he pulled it off, to be honest." Jerking her head toward her apartment, she gestured for me to follow her inside.

I did, but I shot a quick text reply to Laurie, letting him know I'd be down in a few minutes, as Alyssa unlocked her door. She set down her bags and plopped onto her couch. After moving a blouse that had been crumpled there and draping it next to her, she patted the cushion, inviting me over.

"Dirk is new to the Seattle fashion scene. He started in California and just moved up here last year." She held her hand against her mouth as if what she was about to say was a secret. "He sold his house in the Bay Area for a fortune and was able to lease that awesome space and an apartment in the same building."

It wasn't an uncommon story. While Seattle prices were pretty astronomical compared to a lot of other cities, California—especially the Bay Area—was one location that had us beat in outrageous real estate prices. Selling a home down there usually meant that they had their pick of places up here. We got a number of Californian transplants up in Washington for that reason.

"Anyway," Alyssa continued, "he's been really aggressive about inviting buyers to his store and trying to get on our good sides. I'd been in his boutique a few times, but nothing ever stood out to me." Her hands clasped together. "Except the last time I went in, and I saw *that* dress." There was a sparkle in her eye that would've been more fitting during a story about how she and Brad met and fell in love, but I wasn't about to judge the woman for her passions. "He was still in the middle of designing it, but it caught my eye, and I told him if he finished it, I would try to sell it for him."

"Did he mention why he decided to make something so outside of his normal style?"

Alyssa bobbed her head. "He was frustrated that his stuff wasn't taking off as much as he thought it should. So, he told me he wanted to try something really formfitting, completely opposite of what he'd been doing. I think he was a little annoyed that I was so drawn to it, like he wanted to create it and have people hate it, so he could truly blame his lack of success on us instead of his designs."

"You weren't worried about the dress not matching anything else in his collection?" I tucked a leg underneath me, getting more comfortable as I realized this conversation might take longer than I thought.

"Not for this kind of contract. It wouldn't have been for a full collection, just the one garment," she explained. "But we sometimes sign a designer for an entire line if their one-off sells well enough. I wasn't really thinking in that direction, though. I was just excited to get my hands on this dress. I've been coveting it for years."

"Years?" I blurted out the question. "I thought you said Dirk was a newer designer, and he didn't have this started until the last time you went in."

Embarrassment flashed across Alyssa's features. She looked at her hands for a moment, then fiddled with the blouse now strewn over the back of the couch next to her. "Yeah... This is the part I'm not proud of. The design Dirk created is really close to another local designer's work. Jerome Arundel is Seattle fashion royalty, but he doesn't mass-produce anything. He prefers to create unique pieces. In fact, the only design I've seen him go back to more than once is that dress, though he always changes something about it, so it's not an exact replica. I've approached him so many times about purchasing one, to no avail. When I saw the dress in Dirk's boutique, I knew he based it on Jerome's work, but I got selfish, and couldn't see past the dollar signs." She held up a hand to stop me, even though I wasn't going to say a thing. "I *know*. I've learned my lesson. Before it went missing, I'd convinced myself that it was different enough from Jerome's design that we wouldn't be in trouble, but once it was gone, and Dirk talked about making another one, I told him the deal was off. I couldn't go through with it."

Swallowing, I took it all in. "And he was mad about that?"

"Extremely."

That explained why she'd been so jumpy the days following the disappearance of the dress. She'd been on the lookout to make sure Dirk wasn't coming to get her.

Alyssa puffed out her cheeks. "It's a good thing I pulled out of the deal, though, because I think the guy might've actually stolen from Jerome."

"What made you think that?"

"The moment I told him the dress had been taken, he freaked out, talking about how we needed to monitor social media to make sure it didn't show up anywhere. He was really worried about other people seeing the dress. Which can only mean a few things."

"One of which is that he stole the design and was trying to secure the contract before the actual designer of the dress found out."

Alyssa tapped her nose twice before pointing to me.

Sighing, I thought through what that meant for the case. It didn't change much since Detective Anthony already suspected Dirk. I told Alyssa as much.

"Well, that's a relief to hear." Alyssa stood, moving to her kitchen and reminding me it was closing in on dinnertime.

"It also gives us another suspect to investigate," I explained.

Alyssa cocked her head as she opened her fridge.

"The other designer you mentioned. If he saw someone wearing his dress, he could've gotten mad enough to try to question her about where she got it. Remember how the techs said they thought she'd used pepper spray. What if she felt threatened enough that she sprayed him?"

That theory elicited a shrug from Alyssa, but she didn't look convinced. "Doesn't really sound like Jerome, but maybe. Are you hungry? I've got some veggies and hummus."

"Thanks, but I was on my way to Laurie's when I ran into you," I said, standing as well and turning toward the door.

"Oh, right." Alyssa released a quick laugh. "See you around, partner," she called from where she stood in front of her open fridge.

I left her apartment, jogging down the flight of stairs to the fourth floor. Knocking on Laurie's door, Leo's three warning barks made me grin. The dog was sitting in his crate when the door swung open. Laurie gathered me into his arms and hugged me tight, pulling me inside so he could shut the door. He rested his cheek on the top of my head, making me wonder if the embrace was more for me or him. I tightened my arms around him, regardless.

"Did the walk help clear your mind?" I asked, having a small amount of regret that I hadn't gone with him and Leo.

"I think so. Are you feeling any better?"

Exhaling through my nose, I shook my head. "But I did find something to distract myself, at least."

Pulling back, Laurie met my eyes. "And what's that?"

"I'm late coming down because I was talking to Alyssa. I think we've got an additional motive for Dirk and a new suspect in this case."

Laurie motioned for me to have a seat, freeing Leo from his stay position so he could pile onto the couch with us, and I told him everything I'd just learned from Alyssa.

Sixteen

"If it *was* Jerome who killed Quinn, that solves the problem of why the killer didn't take the dress," Laurie said after listening to my story about the allegedly stolen dress design.

"Other than not wanting to undress a woman he'd just killed?" I shot him a sidelong glance.

Laurie waved a hand to dismiss my theory. "Sure, but it makes even more sense if it wasn't technically his dress. What if Jerome saw Quinn wearing a dress, one that was obviously his design but that he hadn't made, and he followed her, asking her where she'd gotten it? I don't know how Quinn ended up in our building, or got the dress to begin with, but she could've been attempting to get away from Jerome, and when she got him with pepper spray, he might've snapped and strangled her."

"Fleeing the scene before we could catch him," I added. It made sense.

My fingers drew circles in Leo's fur as we talked, his head

resting on my lap. But at that, I pulled out my phone and typed in Jerome's name.

"He's got a studio in Lower Queen Anne, but it says it's by appointment only. Should I see if he'll meet with us?" I pulled my shoulders up toward my ears.

"Let's do it." Laurie snapped his fingers. "You could say you've got a gallery coming up, and you're looking for someone to design an outfit for the showing."

I grinned. "Great idea." But my smile quickly morphed into a wince. "I'm never going to be able to afford that. Did you see Dirk's prices? And he has a retail store. I can't imagine what Jerome's custom designs cost."

Laurie ran his tongue over his lips as he thought. "Maybe you can pretend to be a snob about it. After you hear what he has planned, and we get the information we need, you tell him it's just not your style?"

"Ah, yes. That sounds like me." I used a haughty tone as I added, "Your ideas are too poor for what I'm looking for. Definitely not the other way around."

I clicked on the appointment link all the same, filling out the information and hitting send.

"I guess now all we can do is wait."

It took Jerome two days to get back to me, and by that time, the only opening he had left in the week was on Friday afternoon. Laurie finished his work for the day early so he could come with me.

I wore my paint-covered overalls and the Scotland tank top

Penny had brought me. Trying to dress-to-impress the last time I'd met a fashion designer had backfired spectacularly. So, why fake it? I was an artist, and I was looking for a gallery outfit. At least I would fit the part.

As Pioneer Square residents, we didn't get out to the Seattle Center as much as we should've. Though it was only about ten blocks past the Pike Place Market, the walk always felt like it took forever.

"I'm kind of wishing we'd taken scooters," I said between panted breaths. "Or the bus, at least."

We'd opted to walk since it was so nice out, but I was regretting that choice now that we were approaching our destination.

Laurie's laughter was low and quick. "Hello, Mr. Arundel. We're here to try on your bespoke fashions. Do you mind if we get sweat on everything?"

Flinching at the reality of his joke, I said, "I hope he won't be too put off by it."

"Well, we're about to find out." Laurie came to a stop in front of the address that had come up online when we'd searched for his studio.

It was an industrial building with a large garage door that had windows in it to let in light. **Arundel Designs** was painted in an understated serif font just on the door, and I pulled it open before I could talk myself out of it.

The place smelled like a fabric store, something that made sense when we stepped around the entryway and into the large warehouse space and found it stacked with bolts of fabric of every variety.

Laurie's hand closed around my arm in warning just as I glimpsed a few dress forms to our left, next to the garage doors.

I patted his hand, telling him it was okay. Dress forms were fine, eliciting none of the fearful responses I got around mannequins. It must be the heads that really freaked me out, then. Or maybe it was the arms.

The non-terrifying dress forms wore clothing in various states of progress. Each outfit was unique and interesting, using completely different color palettes, materials, and design aesthetics.

If Dirk's boutique represented someone with one specific style, Jerome was obviously a designer who liked to dabble.

As an artist, I knew there were benefits to both. Having a defined style made it easier for customers to recognize your work, and it created a sense of safety in those who purchased from you, knowing you would always produce work of similar quality and style. As a dabbler myself, I knew it meant I never got bored with my work because I was always changing, pushing my previous limits. It also gave me a way to reach different customer bases and appeal to a variety of sensibilities.

I hated that I automatically felt a connection with Jerome after merely setting foot in his studio. We were here to investigate him as a suspect in a murder, after all. I wasn't here to make friends.

But that seemed like it was going to be tough as a man walked out of the back room, half a cookie hanging from his mouth. Alyssa hadn't been kidding when she'd said he'd been part of the fashion scene in this city for decades. Jerome looked like a shorter Denzel Washington, and had to be in his fifties, at least.

Again, respect swelled in me at that realization. It was difficult to remain both esteemed and pertinent for a few years, let alone decades.

Eyes widening as he spotted us, Jerome covered his mouth, popping the rest of the cookie into his mouth.

"Sorry," he said through a full mouth, chewing hard so he could swallow. "My granddaughter is in Girl Scouts, and I've developed a small addiction to the cookies." Swatting his crumb-covered fingers against his pants, he held out his hand. "You must be Megan. The artist? Here for your appointment?" His attention swept up from me to Laurie.

I grinned, taking his hand and shaking it. "You can call me Meg. This is my boyfriend, Laurence."

Laurie, whose hand had been resting on my hip, stepped up behind me, getting even closer. From the way his fingers pulsed, squeezing my side, I knew it was because he loved hearing me introduce him as my boyfriend. But to Jerome, I wondered if the motion came off as possessive.

Jerome's smile only widened, though, and his gaze flicked over us. "My goodness. Don't the two of you make the cutest couple?"

My hand instinctively went to my heart. "Thank you."

Jerome snapped his fingers and called out toward the back room he'd just come from. "Atlas, get in here so you can see the scrumptious artist we get to dress today and her perfect boyfriend."

That was it. The man could strangle me right here, and I think I'd still like him.

My resolve melted into a puddle. I'd never, in my life, been called scrumptious before, but it was now the only word I wanted anyone to use to describe me.

A man closer to our age jogged out from the back. His brown hair was floppy and on the longer side, and he wore a white T-shirt and jeans. His skin was pale and eyes puffy, like he didn't get enough sleep—or maybe didn't drink enough water—and his earlobes hung low, proving he'd gauged his ears but didn't have any plugs in at the moment. Compared to Jerome's impeccable appearance, Atlas looked like a bit of a mess.

His expression lit up as he took us in. "Oh, I think the ideas you drafted for her will be perfect." Atlas flattened his palms against each other and brought them to his lips as he studied me. "A cool summer palette for sure." The soft, thoughtful way the man spoke didn't quite match his rough appearance.

Jerome made an "Mmmm" sound in the back of his throat, and locked eyes with me. "We like to play a game of guessing the color palette of each of our customers, based purely on the vibes they give off in their emails to us, or how they sound on the phone." He chuckled. "A bit of color theory for you. We both guessed summer for you. Atlas thought you'd be on the cool side." Jerome winked at me, as if saying, "Don't worry. That's a good thing."

"Meg, you can come through here and have a seat," Atlas said, jerking his head to the right.

The next time Laurie's hand clamped tighter on me, it was out of protection, but as if Jerome could read our minds, he added, "Laurence, you can go as well. We didn't know there would be two of you, so you'll have to excuse us for a moment while we gather another glass."

Glass? Laurie and I exchanged a confused look before following Atlas through the space between two shelves full of fabric and into a sitting area with cozy chairs and a coffee table.

"This is our consultation area." Atlas gestured for us to have a seat. "Jerome likes to keep his works-in-progress up front."

I plopped onto the love seat, a knobby Kelly-green piece so soft I couldn't stop my hands as they smoothed over the oddly textured fabric.

Laurie settled next to me. "He's not worried someone will copy his designs if he leaves them in front of the windows like that?"

I stopped myself from staring adoringly at Laurie. What a smart way to fit in that question.

There was a moment of hesitation, but Atlas shook his head. "Jerome's not worried about stuff like that. He's too unique. Another designer would be hard-pressed to copy him. I've never seen anyone use darts like him. Even I can't recreate them. Sit tight. I'll be right back with another glass of water."

His words sat with me as he disappeared. Atlas was obviously wrong. Someone *had* copied one of Jerome's dresses. Something still didn't sit right with me, though. If even his apprentice couldn't recreate the same darts, how had Dirk, a man who admitted to never using them, recreated Jerome's design?

As I thought, Jerome wandered over, wearing glasses now and clutching a notebook to his chest. He sat just as Atlas arrived with another glass and began filling them with water from a pitcher. After our long walk here, water sounded amazing, and Laurie and I each grabbed for the glasses as he handed them over.

"Okay, Meg. So, you're an artist, and you're hoping to purchase an outfit for a gallery opening. Can you tell me a little about your art?" Jerome flipped open the notebook and clicked a pen, ready to take notes.

Swallowing my mouthful of water, I tried to remember the story Laurie and I had concocted. "I, um ... I'm just in the beginning stages of... That's to say, I just wanted to do a little research around. Look at different local designers in the area first before I make my decision." Bringing my glass to my lips, I took another sip of water. "If that's okay."

Jerome dipped his chin seriously. "Absolutely. You want to make sure you find the right fit."

A sigh of relief escaped me. Oh, good. For a moment there, it felt like me buying a bespoke outfit from them was a foregone conclusion just because I'd shown up.

"Apologies for our eagerness." Jerome placed a hand on his chest. "We like to treat everyone who enters like they're special, but there's no pressure for you to commit until I've designed something for you." He breathed a laugh through his nose. "Then, you know, it's kind of important that you pay for it."

His calm demeanor wore off on me, and I leaned back into the chair. "I wasn't sure about your pricing. I couldn't find anything on your website and ... well, I'm just an artist starting out and trying to make a name for myself, so I don't have a huge budget."

There. At least I'd been honest and gotten it out there. He was less likely to be surprised when I had to turn him down later. Laurie's arm snaked around my shoulders in support.

Sending a quick glance over at his assistant, Jerome said, "That's a little more difficult to answer, which is why we don't post it online."

I tensed, waiting for him to explain that taste costs money

and then quote me an amount that was more than my entire monthly budget.

"We believe in a sliding scale of payment," Jerome said instead.

My surprise must've been clear because his lips twitched into a smile, and he set down the pen he'd been holding.

"If you let me know what your budget is, I can tailor the project to work within those means," he explained. "Atlas is very good at sourcing fabrics, and we can make design choices that are less intricate if you'd like something that doesn't cost as much."

Atlas, who was also taking his own notes, nodded. "We believe fashion's more about the emotional connection people have to it rather than just a price tag."

"Oh." That was really amazing, actually.

When he picked his pen back up and stared at me expectantly, I realized he was waiting for me to tell him my budget. I named the embarrassingly low price I could afford to pay for something like this. Jerome didn't even flinch. He just jotted the amount down on his notepad.

"I think we can work with that." Circling his pen in the air, he said, "And what about your art? Can you tell me about that?"

I proceeded to stumble through a terrifyingly confusing explanation of who I was as an artist that left me feeling like I didn't know who I was at all. Flashbacks from my mentor telling me I didn't have what it takes to make it in the world of art resurfaced in my mind, making me feel sweaty and panicked all over again. He'd hated that I could never succinctly describe my style.

But Jerome pursed his lips and said, "Ah, a creative mind never rests in one place. It sounds like you've got a whimsical multimedia approach to looking at everyday items in a different way."

I could only gape at him. "Yeah. That's—exactly."

Laurie squeezed my shoulder, smiling over at me.

"Tell me what you've worn in the past to your gallery exhibits," Jerome said.

Heat washed over my cheeks as I described my trusty black dress *and* the section of the hem that my cat had clawed up during her wild kitten days. "I used to have nicer clothes when I worked for galleries in Chicago and New York, but I left the East Coast in a bit of a depressed state and ended up leaving most of those pieces behind with my friends out there."

"Too much emotional baggage attached," Jerome said. "I understand." At that, he punctuated the end of his notes with a dramatic period before reading over everything again and saying, "Perfect. I think we can definitely create an outfit for you. I'm thinking something unexpected to show that neither you nor your art fit inside a neat box, but the look has to be professional as well, so potential buyers know you're serious and worth every penny you charge."

Tears crowded in my eyes at being so wholly understood. I could only nod, not trusting my voice. My fingers shook as I gulped down more of my water.

Jerome gave me a sidelong glance. "Unless, of course, you'd like to shop around a little more before we commit to a design?"

"No, this is perfect," I assured him. "I mostly said that because I didn't know if I'd be able to afford your work."

The man chuckled. "I thought that might be the case."

With that, he stood. "Atlas will take your measurements and the deposit from you up front. Then he'll let you know when we have an initial sketch ready for you to approve."

"Oh, I don't think I need to approve any sketch." I pressed my lips together self consciously when he peered at me in question. "Is it weird that I trust you and just want to be surprised when I see it for the first time?"

"Not at all." Jerome beamed. "I've had a few clients request the same. And if that's the case, I'm thinking"—he squinted one eye—"a week should suffice."

"That sounds great," I said, shaking his hand again when he held it out to me.

"I'm excited to work with you, Meg."

I was too. Honestly. And while I couldn't see Jerome hurting anyone, I knew I had to use the time I had with Atlas to do a little digging. The measurements were a quick process, so it wasn't until I was paying the deposit that I had a chance to ask a question.

"I'll call you when the preliminary design is ready for you to view," Atlas said before telling me my deposit total.

Grabbing my wallet and pulling out my card, I gave him a curious look. "I noticed the website mentions Jerome doesn't take appointments on Saturdays. Is there a reason for that?"

Laurie fidgeted next to me, revealing that he thought it was a silly question that might blow our chances of learning anything helpful from Atlas. I knew it was a risk. Most people took the weekend off from work. But it was the only way I could see to slip in a question about Jerome's alibi.

Atlas bobbed his head absentmindedly as he ran my card.

"He watches his granddaughter every Saturday. Well, Sunday, too, if he doesn't have any appointments."

"Every Saturday?" I asked, eyes wide.

"Hasn't missed a single one since I started working here three years ago." Atlas handed back my card.

"All day?" I asked. From the quirk of his eyebrow, I could tell he thought the question was odd, so I added, "It's just ... wow. I didn't have that kind of grandfather, so it's just wild to me to know they exist." I fanned my eyes to show that it was so sweet, it made me want to cry.

"Jerome's special." He swallowed thickly, like the thought was getting him worked up too. "He usually gets Hope on Friday nights, they have movie night and pizza, and then he brings her back to her mom on Sunday morning. I think he'd even keep her longer, but Hope's mom wants time with her on the weekend as well."

With that, our transaction was finished. Atlas must have had more work to do, given the way his focus flicked around the studio. Laurie and I said our goodbyes and walked out into the sunny afternoon. We walked a block before stopping and looking at one another.

"It's not Jerome." I cut the air with my hand.

"Can't be," Laurie agreed.

We exhaled in unison, glad we both felt so sure. He was my new favorite person, and I really didn't want the designer making my outfit to be a murderer.

SEVENTEEN

Laurie walked into my apartment the next day just as I was finishing up with a phone call.

"Yes, that's right, Detective Anthony," I said, cluing him in on who I was talking to. "His assistant said he spends Friday night through Sunday morning with his granddaughter." I paused as I listened. "Mmmhmm. Yeah, the studio's near the Seattle Center. That's the address we went to. Sounds good. Thank you for returning my call. Talk to you later."

I ended the call, happy to have that off my back. I'd called the detective yesterday once we'd returned from our visit to Jerome's studio, but I'd gotten her voicemail.

"She's going to check into Jerome's alibi and bring the dress from evidence to see if it really is his same design." Brushing my palms against one another, I said, "Now I can put all my energy behind beating you and Opal in the final round of the Morrisey Masterpiece Classic."

He cracked his knuckles. "You can try, but I've spent the

morning stretching and brushing up on my Seattle facts. It doesn't hurt that my partner was present for a bunch of the city's history."

That wasn't a dig at Opal's age; she'd told us many wild stories about being involved in plenty of historical events over the decades.

Alyssa and I *didn't* have that advantage; he was right. "But my partner and I can both run," I said.

While Opal bounded around the building on her birdlike legs, trekking up the Seattle hills could get tiring, especially at a faster pace than a walk.

Laurie snorted. "I'll carry her if I have to."

I laughed, but he definitely could. Her thick glasses were probably the heaviest thing about her.

He moved toward the door, seeing that we were closing in on noon, and the rest of the teams would be convening in the lobby soon.

But I reached out and tugged on his arm, stopping him. "Before we go out there, I've been thinking about the building."

My reminder of us losing our home sent Laurie's lips downward into a frown.

"It was something Atlas said yesterday about emotional connection being more important than money." When Laurie inclined his head to tell me he remembered that as well, I added, "And it got me thinking about how Ripley mentioned hearing the Kincaid kids talk about the company with the second-highest bid having a personal connection to the building."

"Yeah, but Ripley also said they were short by a lot of money," Laurie said, obviously not seeing where I was going with this. "I mean, fifty thousand probably isn't a huge amount to anyone purchasing a building, but there has to be a reason he's not bidding higher."

"What if we could combine forces with him?" My fingers clamped down on Laurie's arm. "We could call a meeting with the guy and see if he'd agree to work with us. If all of us here at the Morrisey pooled our money together, we could add it to what he's already willing to spend and help him exceed the competitor's offer."

Laurie used his free hand to massage the back of his neck. "Do you think the building could raise that much?"

"If we could each come up with two thousand, that would be almost fifty, which is how much Ripley said the second bidder was below the other offer. Some people might be able to give more, and that could make the difference." I tensed as the idea took hold.

It would be a little tight for me, and I'd have to dip into savings, but I could do it.

Laurie's smile returned. "It would be worth looking into."

I bit my lip, holding back the full force of my grin. "Good. Because that's where Ripley is. I sent her to find out the name of the company coming in second place, and I'm going to ask them to come talk to us about partnering in the purchase of the Morrisey."

Hope multiplied in my heart, taking a weight off that had been pressing down since the moment we'd learned the truth from Penny. And while I didn't know for sure that this would save our building, having a plan felt better than the resignation I'd experienced when it seemed there was no way around our fate.

With that settled, Laurie and I made the trip down to the

lobby, practicing our trash-talking as we made our way down the stairs. While we'd had a few arguments over the course of our relationship so far, we got along really well for the most part. It was fun to pretend to hate one another, to create tension where there really wasn't any.

The truth was, I'd be just as excited for Laurie to win as I would be if it was me.

We split apart in the lobby, finding our partners already downstairs. While there were only four teams remaining, most of the building had come out to see us off. After the building round, Penny usually gave out copies of the clues once the competitors left, giving the rest of the residents a chance to guess about which locations we would visit in the city. It helped them fill the time until we returned.

Penny stood behind Nancy's podium. Iris and Edna were missing again, telling me they were likely already stationed at locations throughout downtown to help with the clues.

"Okay, everyone. We're ready to start," Penny announced. "Today's the last day of the Morrisey Masterpiece Classic."

From across the lobby, Laurie met my gaze with a sad, knowing glance. Penny didn't say *forever*, but there was a dip in her tone that implied as much—at least to those of us who knew the truth. Nancy, being one of those people, looked down at her feet. The rest of the residents cheered.

"Our finalist teams are ... Shirl and Bethy Rosenbloom." Penny held out her hands toward the sisters while the crowd cheered for them. "The Conversationalists," she said, gesturing to Art and Darius, who got their own round of applause. "Team Laurpal," she said with a bright laugh, waiting for everyone to cheer them on. "And, finally, Meg and Alyssa."

Penny joined in on the clapping now, smiling at the lot of us. "Remember," she said in warning, "even once you have the winning envelope, you have to return here to collect your prize."

The prize was a cheesy trophy the Youngs had donated from their eldest's soccer days. It had been chaotically repurposed for our competition with the addition of a new plaque and a few glued-on pieces of memorabilia, but it meant the world to all of us.

Nancy moved through the groups of finalists, passing out our golden envelopes. Once each team had one, she returned to her podium and looked at Penny, who called out, "Let the scavenger hunt begin!"

Ripping open our envelope, I followed Alyssa toward the front door. We knew the clues would direct us outside, so we might as well start in that direction. The other three teams followed behind us. I pulled off to the side of the building so we could study the first clue. It had some writing and a picture glued to the clue.

"Jam and tea?" Alyssa said, but shook her head. "*JAMS* and tea. And the letters are capitalized, just like UPS was last week."

"What's JAMS?" I wondered aloud. "They obviously serve tea and have"—I craned my neck to get a better look at the picture—"some kind of window into a storage room?"

Alyssa bounced on her toes and waved her hands with excitement. "I know what this is. I know what this is!" Her eyes glittered with intensity as they met mine. "Brad and I took a walking tour with some friends from out of town. It was all about the International District and the history behind what happened after World War II with the Japanese internment camps. There's that hotel that has the museum inside it." She flapped the clue in front of her. "JAMS must be ... the Japanese American Museum of Seattle."

"*Hotel on the Corner of Bitter and Sweet,*" I whispered the title of the novel by Jamie Ford. "That's right. I remember reading about how the Panama Hotel stored the luggage of people who were taken away to the internment camps. Some never came to claim it."

We stood in sadness for a moment as we thought about that dark part of our history. But time was of the essence, so we started moving.

"So what's the tea?" I asked as we jogged across the street toward the hill leading up into the International District.

"The Panama Hotel has a café. They serve tea. It's just a few blocks up on Main Street," Alyssa said.

"JAMS and tea." I smiled as it all clicked.

When I looked back, Laurie was striding in the same direction as we were. I didn't see Opal anywhere. It was possible he was leaving her behind so she didn't have to sprint with us. But it wasn't long after, while the three of us were waiting at a light, that a veritable gang of Morrisey residents came up behind us on scooters. Art and Darius were in the background. Opal, gray braid flapping in the wind, led the charge.

Mortal enemies during this competition or not, Laurie and I weren't above sharing an amused grin at the sight.

But then the light changed, and the three of us on foot charged across the street. Because of how steep the hill was, and the relatively low power the scooters had, the scooter gang wasn't going much faster than we were as we got to the steeper part of the hill up toward the International District.

Sweat gathered on my brow and neck as my jog became a walk, the incline making each breath strain in and out of me. Alyssa looked over at me in gratitude, slowing as well. Laurie quickly pulled ahead, his long legs giving him an advantage. There was a glimmer in his eye as he glanced back at us.

But any happiness drained from his face as he concentrated on something behind us. Opal's scooter had stopped moving. She was frowning at the display, tapping at the screen. He doubled back to help his partner just as Art and Darius finally overtook her.

Alyssa and I kept going. We were just coming to the Panama Hotel when a taxi pulled in front of the building. Shirl and Bethy spilled out, rushing inside. Sharing a look of determination, Alyssa and I jogged the last few yards and got inside just as the sisters were receiving their envelope from the girl behind the tea counter in the café.

I bounded forward, lining up behind them to grab ours. Penny must've asked the girl to hand them out for her since Iris and Edna were nowhere to be seen. That meant they were likely waiting for us at one of the next few spots.

We followed the Rosenbloom sisters out onto the sidewalk to open our envelopes. Just as we stepped outside, Art and Darius arrived on their scooters, setting their kickstands before rushing inside. I searched the hill for Opal and Laurie. They were about a block away, Opal riding piggyback. But as they reached the next street, they noticed the Rosenblooms and the scooters.

Laurie came to a stop. Opal tapped his arm and he let her down. Laurie met my eyes and bowed his head. He knew they were out.

A small nugget of sadness lodged itself into my throat for a moment at the knowledge he was out of the competition. But Alyssa was already ripping open our envelope. She elbowed me as she slipped out the next clue.

Alyssa and I scowled at the clue as we began walking north.

"University 107. Is that a building on campus?" I glanced around as we walked, trying to get my bearings.

We weren't too far from Seattle University. If we went north for a few more blocks and then started up First Hill, we could get there in twenty minutes—that was, if we walked fast. And those were some of the steepest hills in the area.

"They usually give university buildings names, not numbers, right?" Alyssa's pouty expression likely had more to do with the thought of hiking up that hill than wandering the campus in search of the building in question.

It didn't make sense, so I moved on to the next idea. "What if it's written like that to confuse us?" When Alyssa stared at me in question, I said, "What if it's an address—107 University Street? That would be pretty close to the waterfront, I'd bet."

We came to a stop at the edge of Jefferson, waiting for a car to pass.

"Jesus Christ Made Seattle Under Protest," Alyssa whispered, reciting the mnemonic locals used to remember the street names downtown.

Starting where we were standing, moving north, there were two J streets, two C streets, two M streets, and so on until you we reached Pine, and the end of the Pike Place Market.

"Jefferson, James, Cherry, Columbia, Marion, Madison, Spring, Seneca, University." Alyssa stopped there, having been counting off the streets on her fingers to see how many more blocks we had to travel.

Both studying her fingers, we picked up our pace.

"I think this could be it," I said. "The art museum's right in that area. I wonder if that's where it is."

We didn't have time to second-guess ourselves. If the Rosenblooms were taking cabs, and the Conversationalists were on scooters, we had to use whatever lead we might have to get there before them. I just hoped we were right.

EIGHTEEN

The blocks went fairly quickly. We used the time waiting for lights to change to catch our breath. The one reprieve was that a few substantial clouds had moved in front of the sun, so it wasn't nearly as hot as it had been on our trip up to the Panama Hotel.

Once we reached University Street, we hooked a left and walked toward the waterfront, stopping every block to check the address numbers on the buildings.

"Maybe it's not the art museum," Alyssa said as we stood on the other side of the street, in the shadow of the large man hammering outside the museum. She pointed to a postcard shop that had the numbers 109 printed above its door. Eyes alight, she moved on to the next store down, a psychic.

"One oh five?" I asked, my tone dropping with disappointment.

Alyssa held up a finger and jogged down to the end of the block, where a popular cocktail bar sat on the corner. She peered across the way toward the art museum, but didn't seem to be able to see the numbers from there because she pulled out her phone.

I refrained from telling her not to use the phone, per Laurie's rule. Now that he was out of the competition, I wasn't above using a little help to beat the other teams.

"Those two have larger numbers and First Avenue addresses," she explained as she reached me again, showing me her phone. "And when I type in 107 University Street, it comes up with this spot." She pointed right where we stood, between the print shop and the psychic.

I raked my teeth across my bottom lip as I thought. "So it's not an address. We could be wrong about it being on University. Is there anything else with 107 around here?"

At that moment, we both looked across the street toward the Harbor Steps, a grouping of stairs, water features, and places for people to sit that connected the waterfront to downtown and the market. Apartment complexes, restaurants, and retail shops lined the tiered, urban plaza.

"How many stairs make up the Harbor Steps?" I asked Alyssa, who was already typing the question into her phone.

Her eyes widened as she double-checked her screen. She turned her phone toward me with a wide smile, the answer to her search inquiry sitting at the top of the list: 107.

As if the streetlights were on our side, the one in front of us changed at that moment, giving us the okay to cross the street. We raced forward, stopping to look around for either Iris, Edna, or a stack of golden envelopes. There would only be two this time, and the anticipation made my heartbeat kick up another level.

But even though we split up and walked down either side of

the steps when they diverged to make room for a water feature, we'd found nothing to prove this was the correct answer to our second clue for the day. Sharing a confused glance at the bottom of the steps, we started back up.

"Maybe we missed something," I mumbled to myself, trying to look at my surroundings with a more discerning eye this time.

"There!" Alyssa pointed to Art and Darius standing off to the side of the steps, taking a golden envelope from Iris. They spotted us and turned around, opening their clue so we couldn't see their faces.

I laughed with delight as we closed the space between us, reaching her in time to see a second envelope in her hand. We weren't too late.

"Aw, man," Shirl complained as she and Bethy raced down the steps just as Iris handed us her last envelope.

Iris confirmed their suspicion by holding up her empty hands and wiggling her fingers. "Sorry."

Bethy snorted. "Well, it's not like it's going to matter who won in a few months, anyway."

"What? Why?" The exclamations came from behind us. I cringed as I turned to see Art and Darius staring in disbelief at the Rosenbloom sisters.

From the redness creeping over her cheeks, Bethy hadn't seen the Conversationalists standing there. "Oh, uh, no reason."

But Art wasn't buying it. "Tell us the truth, Bethy. Please."

"Fine." Bethy exhaled. "We're going to have to move out," she admitted. "Shirl and I noticed Nancy's been acting really weird lately, and we went to ask her what was wrong."

"She's like a sister to us," Shirl added, unnecessarily.

But Bethy nodded. "We know when she's keeping a secret. Anyway, she admitted to us that the Kincaid kids had contacted her and were going to sell the Morrisey to some apartment complex conglomerate. They're going to buy out our apartments, gut the place, and make a bunch of hoity-toity condos."

Darius staggered backwards, Bethy's words hitting him like an arrow to the heart. But it was Art who clutched at his chest. I thought they were just being dramatic, but then Art wheezed, his countenance turning a concerning shade of gray.

"I can't breathe. I-I think I'm having a heart attack," he whispered before collapsing onto the steps.

The next few minutes were a blur. A high-pitched ringing started in my ears the second Art went down. His terrified eyes were all I could see as I raced forward.

"I'm calling an ambulance," Alyssa said. The rest of her words melded into the cacophony of noise as she spoke with a dispatcher.

If I hadn't already been on the verge of tears, watching Darius fall to his knees next to his best friend and place his hands gently on either side of Art's face would have done it. He patted Art's cheeks as he called out, "Art, buddy. You've gotta stay with me. Please."

The Rosenbloom sisters erupted into wails so loud, I spent a split second thinking the ambulance had arrived in record time. Shirl paced, loudly grieving while Bethy sobbed out admissions of guilt. "I'm so sorry. I shouldn't have said anything."

I placed a hand on Darius's shoulder for a moment as I arrived at Art's side. Despite his claims that he couldn't breathe,

Art's chest was moving up and down in big, fluid movements. And even though he'd collapsed, his eyes were still open.

"Darius, has this happened before?" I asked, trying to remember what I should do in a situation like this. "Does he have any medication he can take to help with his heart?"

Darius didn't answer me. Art had moved from clutching at his chest to gripping one of Darius's hands. I glanced around for help.

Alyssa was still on the phone, talking to the dispatcher, but she nodded at me to let me know they were on their way. Iris was working to detain the Rosenblooms, moving them away from the scene so they didn't cause Art any more stress.

I snapped my fingers in front of him. "Darius, I know this is scary, but you have to focus. Does Art take medication for his heart?"

Finally meeting my eyes, Darius blinked. "No. He's never had heart issues before."

Unsure whether that was better or worse for this situation, I thought through the last time I'd taken CPR training. Had it been back in high school? Oh, gosh. But everything about CPR had to do with stopped hearts and people who were unconscious. Art's heart still appeared to be working, and he was awake. He was breathing hard, looked sickly pale, and had a sweaty sheen to his skin, but he was awake.

Luckily, I didn't have to figure it out. The paramedics arrived, and I had to step away. Darius was much more focused once they started asking him questions, and he answered them quickly as they examined Art, got him onto a stretcher so they could lift him up the stairs to the ambulance waiting on First.

"We can take one person," a first responder said to our group.

Darius stepped forward. "Me. I'll go with him." As if any of us would argue with him, he glanced back toward our group. "I'll keep you all updated. I promise."

We called out words of support that felt flat and insufficient.

And just as soon as it happened, they were gone. A small crowd had gathered on the stairs, but it dispersed as they saw the problem had been taken care of. Alyssa and I walked over to where Iris was consoling the Rosenblooms.

"He's in the best hands possible," Iris assured them. "Darius will let us know when we can go see him."

My heart ached at Iris's words. I knew she was remaining positive for the guilt-ridden Rosenbloom sisters, but the fact that she was being optimistic made me consider the other option. What if Art wasn't okay? What if that was the last time I ever saw him?

Meeting my teary eyes, Iris said, "I'm going to call a ride, and go back to the Morrisey with these two. Do you want me to see if I can get something big enough for all of us?"

I turned to Alyssa, but she looked just as shell-shocked as I felt. "I think I'd like to walk," I said. When Alyssa signaled that she'd go with me, I added, "We'll meet you at home." My voice broke around the final word.

The Morrisey was our home, sure, but it only felt that way because of the people. *They* were my home. They were my family. My chest ached, and I almost clutched at it like Art had, understanding how painful it must have been for him, while knowing I was only experiencing sadness and not a medical emergency.

Iris walked the sisters down the stairs toward the waterfront, knowing it would be easiest to catch a ride there. Alyssa and I trudged up the remainder of the steps to First Avenue, heading south toward our building.

Slightly shorter than me, Alyssa wrapped her arm around my waist and leaned her head on my shoulder. I slung my arm around her in return, resting my head on hers as we moved through the busy Saturday streets. Walking side by side as we were was entirely impractical, and we got many agitated glares from pedestrians as they moved around us. But we didn't separate.

Alyssa had only moved into the building a few years before I'd left for college. But even though we hadn't shared decades together like I had with most of the other residents in the building, she and I had become fast friends. She was like a big sister to me, and had always made me feel understood, even though we were so different. Her offers to lend clothes never came from a place of judgment. I think she just liked to share something that brought her so much joy.

"Talk to me about something happy," Alyssa said as we waited for a light to give us the okay to cross a street.

My lips twitched, as if testing out whether they'd be able to lift into a smile again. "I ordered a custom outfit from Jerome Arundel, and I'm really excited to see how it turns out."

Alyssa's head jerked slightly, and I could feel her eyes on me, but she looked forward again as our light turned. "He's an amazing designer. And, not a killer?" She added the last part tentatively.

"I don't think so. The detective is looking into his alibi, but it sounds like he's cleared."

A small bit of tension left Alyssa's posture. "That's good. That's definitely happy news."

We walked on, and a short while later, our building came into view. I was pretty sure Iris and the Rosenblooms would beat us there, but I dragged my feet a little as we approached, not wanting to be the ones to break the bad news to everyone.

I didn't have to worry, though. Iris and Penny stood among a crowd of residents as Alyssa and I entered. Penny rushed over, pulling me into a tight hug while the rest of the residents crowded around Alyssa.

Suddenly, Penny pulled away from me and addressed the group gathered in the lobby. "Can someone walk up to the Arctic Building on Third to get Edna and tell her the scavenger hunt is over?"

Bailey and Cascade offered, saying they needed to get some exercise despite looking like they'd just returned from a workout class.

Once they were gone, Penny turned back to me.

"The walruses were the third clue," she whispered, squeezing my arm.

Recognition settled over me. That *was* a good clue. The Arctic Building was a local favorite, with the carved walruses lined up along its exterior walls. But I didn't have time to think about the architectural clue because Laurie walked over and wrapped me in his arms.

I sank into him. "That was scary," I told him, not even bothering to pull my face from his chest as I spoke, not caring that my words would be muffled. He stroked a hand over my back and led me over to the chairs everyone had set up for when we returned from the scavenger hunt, helping me sit down.

The rest of the residents followed, and soon we were all seated. Nancy took her place behind her podium.

"Okay," she said with a long, shaky exhale. "In times like these, I like to make plans. So, I say, let's make up a visitation schedule for Art when he's well enough to have guests."

"And he'll probably need meals once he gets back home from the hospital," Winnie called out.

Everyone agreed and began making up a schedule, but I couldn't help but wonder if Art would even make it long enough for any of this to become necessary.

NINETEEN

Actually, it turned out that my worst-case-scenario worries were the unnecessary thing.

We'd only just started putting together a visitation schedule when Darius called Nancy. She held up a hand to quiet the group, listening intently after answering the phone.

"He's coming home?" Her words rang through the silent lobby. Hand on her heart, Nancy exhaled so forcefully, her glasses teetered where they sat on the tip of her nose. "Thank goodness." She stopped to listen, making small noises of confirmation every once in a while. "Okay, we'll see you soon."

The moment she hung up the call, questions erupted from the crowd.

"Quiet. Quiet." She held her hands up to stop the noise. It didn't take any more than that. Everyone went silent. "It was a panic attack, not a heart attack. He's okay and is coming home once he gets discharged."

I sat back in my chair, the fatigue of the day finally clawing through the adrenaline from the past hour. Laurie hooked an arm around me, and I leaned into him, letting my eyes close in relief.

The Rosenblooms, however, wailed louder at the news, their release taking a much louder manifestation.

"We're so sorry," Bethy said through tight, gasping breaths in between sobs.

Penny went to console them. "It's okay. We know you weren't trying to hurt anyone. But it is a good lesson to all of us to watch what we say in this small community."

"So, it's true? They're selling the building?" Winnie Wisteria asked, her voice quiet. The small questions so uncharacteristic coming from her large personality.

Pain skated across Nancy's expression, and she swallowed. "They are," she finally said, lowering her chin and her gaze, like it was too hard to look at us.

I glanced up at Laurie, hoping he could read the question in my eyes about whether I should tell them about my plan to contact the second-highest bidder.

He shook his head, whispering, "Wait until we're sure."

He was right. It wasn't worth getting their hopes up if the company didn't agree to our idea. I tucked away my hope, longing for Ripley to show up soon. There was so much to share with her.

Despite the fact that we knew the Harborview emergency room could be busy, and it might take a while for them to discharge Art, those who didn't have anywhere else to be remained in the lobby to wait for him. We moved the chairs from their meeting rows and formed a big circle of residents, so we could chat and share stories.

Nancy had just finished retelling the story about the time

Art had tried to fit that shoe rack down the garbage chute, and I was wiping happy tears from my eyes. It felt good to laugh.

And then everyone's laughter turned into cries of joy as we glanced over to the front door to find Darius leading Art inside. The man in question stopped just inside the lobby and raised both hands over his head, his grin contagious.

Instead of moving to him and creating a mob, we waved him and Darius over, pulling a couple of chairs into the middle of our circle for them.

Once he was seated, Art placed a hand on his chest. "Thank you for caring so much. It was just a panic attack. The old ticker's still working just fine." His eyes locked with Nancy, a frown overtaking his features. "D-does everyone know?"

Nancy gave a clipped nod.

Art's eyes were full of pain as they moved back over the gathered residents. "Well, Morrisey, it looks like our run might be over."

Despite the momentary reprieve as we celebrated the return of Art and Darius, sadness descended over us once more, spreading across the lobby.

"But..." Art held up a finger, a sly smile curling across his face. "I say, if we're going out, let's go out with a bang."

Applause rose around him. Even Laurie and I joined in, though I definitely wanted to hear what constituted a *bang* in his mind before agreeing to anything.

Art turned toward Penny. "Madam Masterpiece Classic, what do you say to one more round? Everyone's back in, and it's everyone for themselves. Winner takes all."

A delighted laugh bubbled out of Penny, and she grinned as the idea took hold.

"Do you think you've got one more epic clue for us?" Art asked.

Based on the look on her face, Penny did. "I have the perfect clue, actually."

"It can't be the Arctic Building and the walruses," Edna called out, much louder than was strictly necessary, telling us all that her hearing aid must be acting up. "Everyone already knows that's where I was waiting."

Penny chuckled. "I promise it won't be, Edna. I've got something else in mind."

Chatter rose around the group as everyone shared whether they planned to participate or stay put here.

"We've all had a long day." Penny held up her hands, scanning the entire group but landing on Art when she said, "Especially you. Why don't we take the rest of the day off to relax, and we can reconvene tomorrow at noon?"

Cheers communicated the residents' agreement, and everyone rose to stack their chairs and stop by Art to give him hugs, kisses, and well-wishes.

But just as I added my chair to the stack, Ripley appeared in front of me. "What happened? Who won?" She smiled as she searched for who held the trophy.

I jerked my head toward the stairwell.

"Uh, okay. I'll meet you upstairs." She disappeared.

That wasn't exactly what I'd had in mind, but I supposed the stairwell would be crowded with people in a matter of minutes. What I had to tell her would take a lot longer than that.

"I'm going up to my place," I told Laurie, finding him

among the crowd. I widened my eyes for effect. "Ripley's back," I whispered.

"Oh," he said, rubbing his hands together. "Well, let's go."

I hooked my arm through his and pulled him along with me as I walked to the stairwell. Ripley was in an agitated state by the time we arrived.

"Before you tell me about the scavenger hunt, I have news." Ripley stopped where she was, letting us get settled on the stools by my kitchen counter.

"Okay, hit us with the news," I said, unable to wait. "Did you find out who the second bidder is?"

Ripley's smile was so wide, I swear I could see her molars. "I did. It's a Seattle-based company called Pacific Investment, and their CEO is named Wyatt Vandermeer. He's definitely the one with the personal connection. I followed him for a bit today, and I heard him talk about the building. I'd say you'd have a better chance emailing him rather than calling. He doesn't particularly like talking on the phone, and grumbled a lot about how each call he received could've easily been an email."

Biting at my lip to mitigate the sheer size of the grin that tried to overtake my expression, I told Laurie what she'd said. While I was talking, I grabbed my laptop to look up his information and started to craft an email. "I'm trying not to get too excited," I said as I typed, using Laurie and Ripley's real-time suggestions to edit as I wrote out an explanation of our plan.

Once we felt good about the wording and had read over the message approximately two hundred times, I hit send. I closed my laptop with a sigh.

"Okay, now tell me all about the scavenger hunt." Ripley bounced on the balls of her feet. "Who won?"

"The scavenger hunt?" I glanced over at Laurie. "Well, that's a longer story. Let's move to the couch."

THE NEXT AFTERNOON, those interested in participating in the one-clue-only, sudden-death, final, final, *final* round of the Morrisey Masterpiece Classic gathered in the building lobby. Zoe had to work again, but she saw us off before heading into the bar. Ripley was also sitting this one out, having made plans to hang out with Jade since she had to run off so quickly the other day.

Down in the lobby, Laurie eyed me, running his shoulder into me in a playful attempt to get my attention. "What do you say we team up for this one?"

Scoffing, I said, "Um... Didn't you hear? It's everyone for themselves. No holds barred. Cutthroat. All bets are off. Go for the throat. Full throttle." I stopped there, running out of competitive phrases.

He chuckled. "Sure. I heard. But I think I'd like to be on your team for once, for our last clue." The way his handsome face softened as he ran his fingers down the back of my arm made me melt. "And, for the first time ever, their insistence on no rules means they can't tell us what to do."

"You're right. I can't believe I didn't think of it." I curled my fingers into fists. "Yes. Absolutely. They are so going down."

Laurie lifted my chin. "I love it when you get bloodthirsty like this." He kissed me before adding, "Team Maurie is going to beat everyone."

Despite the kiss, and his deliciously competitive words, I

pulled back, brows tugging toward one another. "Maurie? That's, like, mostly *your* name."

He tilted his head. "Yes, but it starts with the first letter from *your* name, which is arguably more important. Plus, Laureg and Megrie don't exactly roll off the tongue."

Laughing, I conceded. "Okay, but only because you're cute, and I literally have no willpower when it comes to you."

"Noted," he whispered as Penny walked up to the podium in front of the group. "I definitely won't ever use that knowledge against you." His lip twitched as he turned his concentration toward my aunt.

"Okay," she said, projecting her voice to cut through the chatter. Once the noise died down, she continued. "Is everyone ready?"

The residents called out to confirm they were.

"Listen up for the rules. There's only one envelope, so whoever gets it first is the winner. That person will keep the trophy forever." She tried to make it sound desirable, but her voice caught on the last word, reminding us that this would be our last scavenger hunt.

Well, everyone else thought it was. Laurie and I had hope. We knew there was an email sitting in Wyatt Vandermeer's inbox that could change everything. I wasn't sure if he was the kind of person who checked his work email during the weekend, but I hoped come Monday we would at least hear from him and know if there was any reason to hope.

"Buuut..." Penny dragged out the word, surprising us all with more. "If I send you all out there at once, after one location, we're going to have a small mob on our hands. That's why I met with everyone this morning to make sure you all have my phone number. Before I give you the clue, you have to send me a picture of yourself in front of two items that feel quintessentially Seattle to you. One that shares the same initial letter with your first name, and one that shares the same initial letter with your last name. Once I get both texts from you, I'll send you the final clue."

Laurie's hand settled on my knee. This sounded fun.

Penny clapped her hands together. "Let the scavenger hunt begin."

We all stood at once, filing out the door and into the city. But Penny's plan worked. Everyone split up after that, searching for what they might use to represent their initials.

"I can use Merchant's Cafe for my M," I whispered as we walked. "And you can use the Tlingit totem pole for your Turner T."

Laurie snapped his fingers. "What about the bubble lights for my L?"

My eyes brightened at the idea. "And I could use the ferry dock for my Dawson D."

We split up while I took a selfie in front of Merchant's Cafe, one of the oldest bars in the city. And, yards away, Laurie took a photo of himself in front of the totem pole. After we had those, we walked toward the waterfront where I'd be able to take a picture of the ferry docks in the background. On the way, Laurie stopped next to an iconic downtown bubble light.

"I won't send mine yet," he said, catching up to me as the ferries came into view.

Once I had a picture of me with the docks behind me, we sent off our pictures with the text explanation under each one.

A moment later, and just a few seconds apart, we received a text with one sentence.

Where the piggy bank sits.

Laurie and I locked eyes as we read it aloud together.

"The market," I said.

"That's what I'm thinking too." Laurie grabbed my hand and started toward the Pike Place Market.

Next to the famous flying fish stand at the entrance on Pike Street, there was a big brass pig tourists loved taking their picture next to. But it wasn't just for looks. The pig was a functioning piggy bank. Any money donated via the piggy bank went to a foundation that helped the market community.

Laurie and I picked up the pace as we passed by the ferries and then the Ferris wheel on the waterfront. Though it gave me an uncomfortable flashback, we took the Harbor Steps up to First Avenue. But the knowledge that Art was still with us and might be on his way to the market ahead of us, had me breezing past the spot where he'd collapsed.

The slight incline to the road burned in my quads, especially after all those stairs. But we finally reached the entrance to the market. The pig stood there, like always.

Laurie pulled me back, hiding behind a magazine rack on the street corner. I was right to suspect someone might beat us, but I didn't think it would be Opal Halifax. She stood next to the pig.

"She got here before us," I whispered, unsure how that had happened. "Probably used a scooter again." I snapped my fingers in defeat.

"Look," Laurie said. "She's not holding an envelope, and no one's coming to give her anything."

He was right. She stood there, scratching her head and glancing around at the busy Sunday crowds as if she thought someone might jump out at any moment to give her the winning envelope.

I choked on my own spit as I sucked in a breath. Coughing for a moment while I cleared the obstruction, I said, "Aren't there *two* pigs?"

Laurie's eyes went wide. "You're right. There's another one at the other end of the market." He checked on Opal before pulling me across the street. "Come on. We can get to it this way."

Following Laurie up First Avenue, we broke into a jog as we closed in on Pine Street. Taking a left, we slowed our pace down the steep hill and then jogged across the cobblestones into a middle entrance into the market. This led to the extra pavilions, where artists and other crafters sold their wares. Brass pig tracks inlaid in the bricks of the market floor led us out to another covered section of the market.

There sat another piggy bank. But, while the first one stood on all four legs, the pig out here sat on its haunches.

"Where the piggy bank *sits*," I repeated the clue, understanding how literal my aunt had been with this one.

A line of tourists stood in front of this pig, too, waiting to take their pictures with it. Laurie and I queued up, bouncing on our toes in anticipation. Next to the pig, there was a booth filled with ceramic piggy banks. It was called Pike Place Pigs, and it sold colorful pigs of various sizes. The woman behind the booth watched me, bowing her head in greeting as I smiled at her creations.

Finally, it was our turn. Instead of posing like everyone else had, Laurie and I searched around the pig, hoping to glimpse one of the telltale golden envelopes.

"Looking for this?"

Our gazes snapped up to find the woman from the piggy bank booth smiling at us as she held on to a golden envelope. We surged toward her, making her take a step back in her surprise.

"Yes, we're from the scavenger hunt," I blurted, so excited we weren't too late.

She was about to hand it over, but she stopped. "I was told I was only supposed to give it to one winner. Which one of you is that?"

"We're sharing the victory," Laurie said, glancing down at me.

"But you can give it to him, because I'm going to need my hands free to hold the piggy bank I have to buy," I told her, pointing to a cute green one that had caught my eye.

The woman beamed, letting me know her name was Steph as she wrapped up my piggy.

"We originally went to the other pig," I explained to her.

"Ah, Rachel," Steph said.

"The pig has a name?" Laurie exhaled a puff of laughter through his nose.

Steph nodded. "Rachel was the first, and this here is Billie." She gestured to the seated pig before handing over my bag in exchange for my money. "Thanks so much."

"Thank *you*." I lifted the bag, and Laurie waved the golden envelope.

Just as we said our goodbyes, Opal, Darius, and Art came skidding to a stop in front of Billie.

"Aw, darn." Art snapped his fingers, moving his arm in a disappointed arc.

Opal shook her fist in the air. "I should've known it would be the two of you."

"What'd you get, Nutmeg?" Darius peered inside my bag.

"A piggy bank." I gestured toward the booth.

"Well, if we can't win the trophy, we might as well shop." Opal wiggled her fingers as she moved toward the booth. "I see one that matches the color of my glasses."

We left them to their shopping, passing by Bailey and Alyssa as they wandered through the vendors, having obviously gotten side tracked. The Rosenblooms were in the primary thorough-fare too. Their faces were red with frustration as they tried to move through the crowd.

Laurie and I headed for home. As we walked, Laurie opened the envelope, confirming the **Congratulations! You're the winner!** text on the card inside.

"We didn't quite think this plan through," I said with a sigh as I eyed the envelope Laurie tucked into his back pocket.

"How so?" His tone was teasing.

"Well, there's only one trophy. Whose apartment is it going to sit in?"

Laurie took a moment to consider this. He ran his tongue over his teeth as he smiled. "You're right. I think there's only one solution."

"What's that?" I readied myself for him to make up some reason why it would have to stay in his apartment.

"You'll have to move in with me," he said instead.

I stopped, then quickly apologized to the poor woman behind me, whom I'd caught by surprise, causing her to nearly run into me.

"What?" I finally asked as I stepped out of the way of foot traffic.

Laurie's mouth tipped up into a handsome smile. "Move in with me, Meg. I don't want to live in two different apartments in two different buildings."

My mouth opened in protest.

"I *know*," he said before I could respond. "You've sent the email to the Wyatt guy. But what if he says no, or it's not enough? It's too much uncertainty. If I have to get a new apartment, I want it to be with you."

I couldn't do anything but stand there, at first. My eyes locked with Laurie's just before I stepped toward him, leaning up to kiss him.

"Yes," I said into his lips. "Of course I'll move in with you."

TWENTY

There was more than one thing to celebrate as we returned to the Morrisey a short while later. Everyone groaned a little when they saw it was us.

"See? This is why they can't be partners," Ronnie whispered as we wandered by on our way to where Penny stood with our trophy.

But any animosity, faked or not, went out the front door when Penny asked which of us wanted the trophy and Laurie told everyone about our plans to move in together.

Nancy, always the planner, had purchased some sparkling wine and sparkling apple cider to commemorate the end of the scavenger hunt, and we "clinked" paper cups as our neighbors toasted our success. As we celebrated, more of the scavenger hunters wandered inside, back from their attempt to win the big prize.

There were two people who entered the building a short while later, however, who had not been part of the scavenger hunt. Edna Feldner's great-granddaughter, Taylor, stood just inside the lobby with her boyfriend. They observed the crowd of residents with confusion written across their faces.

"Taylor's back," Nancy announced, bringing everyone's attention to the new arrivals, much to the teenager's dismay.

A group of residents surged forward, surrounding Taylor and her boyfriend. They walked her over to the circle of chairs we'd set up in the lobby.

"What are you all doing?" Taylor rolled her eyes at us, but I caught a glimmer of a smile twitch over her lips.

"We just finished a scavenger hunt. Meg and Laurie won," Ronnie explained with only a small amount of bitterness in his tone.

"And they're getting married!" Edna said, clapping her hands together.

Taylor lifted an eyebrow at me, but I shook my head.

"Moving in together," I corrected.

But Taylor's interest only increased. "Really? What are you going to do with your place?" I could tell right away that she wanted it for herself.

She was right to assume we'd move into Laurie's apartment instead of mine. He had an actual bedroom with walls instead of my lofted sleeping area. But that wasn't the problem with Taylor's question, and we all studied our hands or the ground, not wanting to be the one to tell her the bad news.

"Oh, geez." Winnie huffed. "If none of you will get up the courage, I'll tell her." She stood, but once she was on her feet, the dramatic woman teetered as if she regretted her decision. "Well, the thing is"—she swallowed—"the man who owned our building died."

Taylor's eyes closed halfway. "Yeah, I know. Nana told my parents when they talked on the phone last week."

"What you might not have heard is that his children are going to sell the building. We have clauses in our contracts that say as long as they offer us fair market value, we have to sell. They're going to sell to a company that wants to gut the place and turn it into fancy condos," Wendell said, taking over the explanation.

Taylor, for once, was speechless. She didn't even have a rude face to fall back on, nor did she employ one of her usual dismissive throat-clearing noises. "Oh. Wow. Okay." Her eyes flashed to her great-grandmother. "That *is* a problem."

Edna teetered over to her, taking her hand and patting it gently. "Don't worry, dear. We'll find another place to live. I know you've been enjoying the city."

The way Taylor's gaze traveled over the group of us, I could tell that—however reluctantly—the people in this building had become part of why she liked it here so much.

"Oh, good." She feigned a dismissive wave. "Because after a couple of weeks back home, I realized I couldn't go back to living in Iowa."

From a few seats to my right, Alyssa tilted her head as she studied Taylor. "Is that my jacket?"

Glancing down at the rose-colored cropped corduroy jacket she wore, Taylor's cheeks turned a similar shade of pink. "Yeah. Sorry."

Alyssa held out her hands, obviously about to tell Taylor it was fine for her to borrow clothes like the rest of us did. But she didn't need to. Taylor wasn't apologizing for that.

She pulled a key out of one of the pockets. "I forgot to put your key back after I was done."

"You had it this whole time?" I blurted out, meeting Alyssa's eyes.

Taylor's attitude returned. She curled her lip and said, "Uh, yeah. You told me I could borrow stuff." Her tone was incredulous, like I'd set her up.

Alyssa jumped in to help. "No, we're not mad about that. We've just been—" She stopped herself as if realizing it would be too much to explain. "Is that the only thing you borrowed?"

Taylor ran her fingers over the corduroy material. "This and a dress. That's all. I promise."

A spark lit behind Alyssa's eyes.

Taylor misread her interest as anger yet again. "I-I don't have the dress right now. But I can get it back. I wore it out on Thursday night, and then my friend liked it so much she switched with me so she could wear it to a show she was going to on Friday night. She'd just broken up with her boyfriend and wanted to make him jealous. I told her she could only borrow it if she came and returned it to you on Saturday. She tried but texted me that there wasn't a key where I'd said there would be. That's when I realized I'd accidentally kept the key from the light fixture, so even though I gave her my spare key to the building, she couldn't get into your apartment. I told her she could just leave the dress outside your door ... but she actually wore it here because she thought she might borrow something else in exchange, so she couldn't even do that." Taylor cringed after admitting that her friend had been ready to borrow even more from Alyssa. "I'm so sorry. I'll text her now so I can return it to you."

The rest of the residents had been quiet as they listened, but as Taylor pulled out her phone, Ronnie Arbury let out a strangled groan, and a small squeak spilled out of Winnie.

Taylor stopped, glancing around the group. "What? Why are you all looking at me like that?"

"Your friend didn't happen to be named Quinn Garret?" Alyssa asked gently.

When Taylor nodded, reluctance written in the hard set of her mouth, Winnie, Ronnie, and a few other residents lost their cool.

"She's dead," Winnie wailed.

Taylor's features went pale, and her boyfriend swore under his breath, sitting back.

In a rare display of self-awareness, Ronnie scowled at Winnie and said, "You were supposed to ease her into that news, Winnifred."

Nancy saw her chance to step in and took command of the situation by giving Taylor the facts in a warm but firm tone. "On Saturday afternoon a few weeks ago, we found a young woman on the fifth floor, sitting in the hallway." Nancy softened her voice as she said, "She'd been strangled. And she was wearing the dress missing from Alyssa's apartment. We didn't know you had given her a key to the building, so we were confused as to who she was, how she'd gotten Alyssa's dress, and why she'd ended up here. I'm so sorry, dear."

Shock froze Taylor where she sat. Her face remained blank.

"That's messed up." Taylor's boyfriend shuddered.

As much as we were finally getting answers about Quinn's reason for being in our building, something still didn't make sense. "Taylor, you said you wore the dress Thursday night, but

Edna told us you were already in Iowa on Thursday, that you'd left shortly after you and I talked that morning."

Sniffling back the tears that were finally falling down her cheeks at the news, Taylor said, "Oh, well, I told Nana my flight was on Thursday, but I actually didn't leave until Friday morning." She gestured to her boyfriend. "Jay-J had a show, and I wanted to go, but didn't want her to worry about me." Her nose twitched. "Sorry, Nana."

Edna clicked her tongue at her great-granddaughter's lie but seemed to think she'd already gotten enough bad news for the day, so she merely patted her hand in sympathy.

"Show?" Laurie whispered next to me. "This guy's a musician too?"

"Jay-J?" I countered, interested to finally learn Taylor's boyfriend's name after all these months. Raising my voice, I asked, "I'm so sorry, Taylor, but your friend's ex-boyfriend... Do you think he might've followed her here? Was he ever violent?"

"Dark question," Jay-J whispered.

Taylor's expression showed her dismay as she considered my question. "I mean, maybe. She said he was cheating on her, and then acted surprised when she broke things off, like that wasn't a good enough reason for her to be upset." She scoffed.

Understanding flashed through me like a jolt of electricity. Maybe this had nothing to do with Alyssa's dress, designers, or contracts, after all. This could've been a relationship that turned violent and ended in tragedy. Alyssa must've come to the same conclusion, based on the awed look she adopted.

Taylor stood, wobbling slightly, and walked Alyssa's key over to her. She move to peel off the jacket, but Alyssa placed a hand on her arm to stop her.

"Keep it," she said with a warm smile. "It fits you better, anyway."

More tears filled Taylor's eyes. Jay-J swooped in and held her up as he directed her toward the elevator. Once she was standing on her own, he went back for her suitcase.

"I'm going to take her upstairs so she can sit down," Jay-J said, surprising me with the amount of care in his voice.

Edna tottered after him.

We all called various encouraging phrases after her until the elevator doors dinged closed behind the three of them.

I leaned forward, resting my head in my hands.

"Well, that was intense," Winnie murmured.

"No thanks to you," Bethy Rosenbloom said. "You really shouldn't blurt things out like that," she added.

I couldn't tell if it was ironic that Bethy was giving advice in this area or if she really had learned her lesson with Art. Despite all the questions running through my mind, there was one certainty.

"We need to call Detective Anthony," I told Laurie, hoping we'd finally found the break in this case we'd needed all along.

TWENTY-ONE

The next day, I was pacing around the apartment, not getting any painting done because I kept checking my email to see if Wyatt had messaged me back.

"Okay, tell me again how he said it," Ripley said.

Another reason I wasn't getting any work done was because I kept having to repeat everything that had happened yesterday for Ripley. The part she had me retell the most was when Laurie had asked me to move in with him.

I'd just opened my mouth to start—it was a short story, so why not indulge her—when the buzzer on my door stopped me. Peeking through the peephole, I found Taylor and her boyfriend standing there.

"What are they doing here?" Ripley asked after sticking her head through the door.

I shrugged toward Ripley and opened the door. "Taylor, hey."

"Hi, Meg." She shifted on her feet.

Jay-J leaned his forearm on my doorframe.

Taylor swallowed. "So, uh, I was wondering … if you weren't busy … if you wouldn't mind coming with me to the police station. That detective called. She wants to talk to me about Quinn."

It wasn't like I was getting any work done, and the overconfident nineteen-year-old looked worried for the first time in a while.

"Sure." I turned to grab my purse, eyeing Jay-J in the process. "Is Jay-J coming?"

He said, "Dope," which was not really an answer.

"I'm guessing that's a yes?" Ripley eyed him as he followed us to the elevator.

As much as I despised the elevator, Taylor didn't have a problem with it. I decided to cater to her needs today. The whole thing dipped as we stepped inside, making me clamp my eyes shut for a moment. Jay-J must've pressed the button because, instead of taking forever to start moving, the whole thing lurched downward surprisingly quickly. I swallowed, peeling open my eyes. My companions didn't seem concerned that we were diving through the floors of the building in a terrifying death trap. Ripley, however, wore a discomfited expression that matched my own, and she was already dead. If even *she* didn't feel comfortable in here, I knew I was in the right.

The lobby was empty this early in the day. The Conversationalists were late sleepers, and the other residents were doing a little hibernating after the drama of the weekend. I kept the silence going as we walked, not really sure what to talk about with the two of them. Taylor and Jay-J didn't seem to mind, likely feeling the same about me.

When we arrived at the station, the officer behind the reception desk asked to see Taylor's identification.

"Oh, happy belated birthday," he said, handing her license back to her.

I coughed. "Yesterday was your birthday?"

We'd told this poor girl that her friend had died on her birthday? And now she was spending the next day talking to the police about it?

"Last week," Taylor told me, so I wouldn't worry. "It's why I went back to see my parents. Twenty." She pulled a face as if it was a silly thing to be excited about, but there was a spark of light in her eyes that betrayed how much she cared.

"Same as me, now." Jay-J stepped up behind her and wrapped her in a hug, kissing her neck.

Taylor pushed him off her with a smirk that told me she loved it.

"Taylor Feldner?" Detective Anthony's stern voice cut through their public display of affection.

Jumping, Taylor whirled toward the detective. "That's me. Is it okay I brought some people with me?" She gestured behind her to the two of us.

Detective Anthony's eyes softened as she noticed me. "Uh, yes. Sure. Hey, Meg." That same gaze hardened as she took in Jay-J's swoopy, blond-tipped hair, ripped jeans, and bright orange sneakers. But she waved us back all the same.

Honestly, I was still reeling from the realization that Detective Anthony appeared happy to see me. I know she'd asked for my help with this case, which I should've seen as a sure sign that she no longer saw me as the problematic resident who always stuck her nose into local cases, but this was yet another instance I could tuck away in the box of evidence proving that there might be a friendship forming between the detective and myself.

I let Taylor and Jay-J take the two seats closest to Detective Anthony's desk as we arrived. There was a third chair at a desk nearby that I pulled over. Ripley stood next to me. By the time I sat down, the detective looked more than ready to begin.

"Thank you for coming." Detective Anthony folded her hands in front of her as she appraised the three of us. "Taylor, I got a call from Meg yesterday letting me know you were able to clear up a few things about our Quinn Garret case."

Taylor gave a quick, concise nod. "I was in Iowa visiting my parents. I'm so sorr—"

Detective Anthony held her hand up to stop Taylor from apologizing. "It's not a problem. We understand you weren't aware of what happened, nor would you have known to tell anyone about the dress." Tapping her pen on the paper in front of her, she added, "I'm just interested to hear your side of the story, starting with Thursday morning."

Glancing at me before she started speaking, Taylor told the detective about our conversation about clothes and how Alyssa let the girls on the fifth floor come over any time to borrow anything they wanted.

"I didn't know there was stuff that was off-limits," Taylor pleaded. "I just saw the dress and thought it would be perfect for Jay-J's show."

The man in question rubbed a hand over his girlfriend's back. Whatever criticisms I might have about Jay-J—his personality, the things he said, his general decision-making skills—the guy really was supportive of Taylor. He didn't have to come here today, but he was supporting her in the best way he knew how.

As if to add more proof to my opinion that he cared for Taylor, he said, "The dress *was* perfect. I didn't tell you this, but some guy came up to me the next night saying he'd seen a picture of us on socials. He was asking who you were and where you'd gotten the dress. He was so impressed with it and how beautiful you looked in it."

Detective Anthony and I both sat bolt upright at Jay-J's anecdote.

"Wait. A man approached you about the dress the next night?" Detective Anthony's brows furrowed, creating a shadow over her already dark eyes.

Ripley swore quietly, even though I was the only one who could hear her.

"Uh, yeah," Jay-J confirmed. "He said he wanted to know the designer and who the girl was wearing it. He said Taylor could totally be a model."

She placed a hand on her heart. "Really?"

"Of course, babe. You're a knockout."

Ripley and I swooned for a moment, watching the couple, but someone else wasn't as easily won over by romance.

Detective Anthony snapped her fingers. "Focus," she scolded the two of them. "Jay-J, what did you say to the man in response?" She poised over her notepad, ready to take it down in her notes.

Jay-J sniffed. "Well, I, uh, told him Taylor was my girlfriend, which he already knew from the caption of the picture, and that she lived at the Morrisey in apartment 5D if he wanted to get ahold of her. I also told him her Insta handle. As for the dress, I wasn't sure who'd made it, but her friend Quinn was wearing it to a show tonight, and she'd be returning it to the Morrisey by tomorrow." His shoulders jerked like he wasn't sure why any of that was a big deal.

Amaya's eyes flashed over to me, confirming that this was big. "Did you get a name from the man?"

Jay-J shook his head, flattening the hope I'd felt at the detective's question. "Nah. He just said he'd seen the picture of DJ Jay-J and his girlfriend online, and he knew he had to come talk to me."

He *was* actually a DJ? I'd been right about one of his jobs, after all. I clamped my lips together so my mouth wouldn't hang open in my shock. If the mood hadn't been so somber, I might have giggled. Also, DJ *Jay-J*? Really? The temptation to text Laurie was strong, but I settled for merely trading a brief, amused look with Ripley.

"Okay," Detective Anthony said, undeterred. "If you didn't get his name, can you describe what he looked like?"

Jay-J stroked his stubbly chin for a moment before saying, "He had a lot of facial piercings. That's what I remember." He pointed to his eyebrow, his nose, and his lip. "Other than that? He was kinda just a regular white guy. Older."

Eyes narrowing, Detective Anthony asked, "How old?"

Gesturing first to the detective and then to me, Jay-J made a noncommittal sound in his throat.

Excuse me? *We* were older? I was in my mid-twenties, and Amaya couldn't be much more than thirty.

"Late twenties?" Amaya asked, displaying none of the

resentment I felt. The consummate professional, she was focusing on the facts.

Jay-J pressed his lips forward. "Yeah, I think so."

"About how tall?" Amaya asked.

At that, Jay-J puffed out his cheeks. He held his hand until it was level with his stomach. I was about to wonder how such a short person could've strangled Quinn, when Jay-J said, "But that's while I was in my DJ booth. I'd bet he'd be around my same height if we stood next to one another."

"Six foot?" Detective Anthony guessed.

"Six two," he said defensively.

There was a flash of humor that crossed over Amaya's features in a way that made me sure she'd guessed low on purpose, knowing it would bug the guy. Maybe the age comment *had* annoyed her, after all, and she'd just gotten back at him for it.

As much as I was enjoying seeing the straitlaced detective mess with a witness, I turned my focus toward picturing every suspect we had at the moment, trying to remember if I'd noticed that number of facial piercings on anyone I'd talked to in connection with the case.

"Have we talked to anyone with piercings?" Ripley asked.

I jerked my head in the negative before I could stop myself. I hadn't noticed a single one.

My despair must've been written plainly on my face. Either that or Amaya caught my head shake, because the detective grimaced and turned to Taylor. "Quinn's ex-boyfriend. Did you ever meet him? Did he have any facial piercings?"

"Never met the guy," Taylor admitted. "I don't know if he had any."

"Do you have his name?" Amaya clicked her pen open.

"Sean?" Taylor asked. *Asked.*

Detective Anthony arched an eyebrow. "Are-are you asking me?"

Taylor winced. "She talked about him a lot, and I tuned her out. She mostly complained about him. It was a good thing she broke up with the guy."

A deep breath settled the detective's frustration. "I have a call in to Quinn's family. Maybe they'll know his name." Glancing over her notes, she said, "Okay, is there anything else you think I should know about the night or in connection with the dress?" Her concentration bounced between Taylor and Jay-J, then finally settled on me.

But I didn't know anything new, and the other two shook their heads.

"Okay, well, thank you for coming in." The detective stood, leading us out to the waiting room. "Meg, I'll be in touch."

I nodded, like I had any idea what that meant. Regardless of whether I understood it, it was *so* cool. My fantasy of us being a crime-fighting duo—well, trio with Ripley—replayed in my mind. The guitar solo from our awesome theme song I'd once imagined for us played in the background, making everything even more dramatic.

"Meg," Taylor said, obviously not for the first time. Once she could see I'd snapped out of whatever trance I'd been in, she added, "We're going to get lunch. Are you okay getting back to the Morrisey on your own?"

Was I okay? I'd lived in this city my whole life—well, most of it. I was apparently *super old*, according to her boyfriend. I'd faced down murderers and spoke to dead people daily. Was *I* going to be okay?

Ripley barked out a laugh.

"I think I'll be fine," I said, sounding way less sure of myself than I had in my head.

We split up, and I immediately texted Laurie.

> I was right! Jay-J is a DJ!

Laurie was working, but that also meant he was on his computer. His texts would pop up in the corner of his screen, and I was positive that message would be too much to ignore.

I was right. Two seconds later, I received an answer.

> So he's DJ Jay-J?

A guffaw exploded from me as I started walking toward home.

> He is. And he also had some interesting insights into the case. He was approached by an OLD man (*cough* our age) on Friday night who was looking for the dress and Taylor. He had facial piercings. Sorry, I know you're working. I have so much to tell you when you're done for the day.

Laurie answered immediately.

> Dinner? I'll cook so you can tell me all about it.

"The two of you are disgusting," Ripley deadpanned as she

rolled her eyes at my phone. But she couldn't keep the smile from her face.

Neither could I as I gave his invitation a thumbs-up. I started to see what living together might be like. In no way was I happy that the Morrisey was being sold, but if I got to live with Laurie, the whole ordeal might not be so terrible.

Twenty-Two

It was a good thing I'd found a way to look on the bright side of losing the Morrisey, because as the week progressed without word from the Pacific Investment guy, that eventuality became more and more likely.

By the time Thursday rolled around, the reality had begun to sink in.

"Yikes," Ripley whispered as she took in the painting I was working on. "This is depressing."

I leaned back, taking in the scene of Elliott Bay I'd been working on. "Too dark of a color scheme?" I gestured to the grays, dark blues, and purples I'd been using to create a stormy sky.

Ripley tilted her head in concern. "I think maybe it has more to do with the ferry." She pointed to the ferryboat I'd painted in the middle ground of the canvas. "It's sinking."

"I mean, sure, but there aren't any cars or people on it."

"Right. Well, I still think you should get some fresh air.

Take a walk or something," she said, shooting one more look of concern at the sinking boat in my painting.

"Fine," I said, standing up. I stretched out my back and grabbed my phone, making sure I hadn't missed any messages while I was working. "Ripley," I said, her name trembling as much as my fingers were, clutched around my phone.

"What?" She raced over, squinting at the screen.

I held her gaze with mine. "It's an email from Wyatt Vandermeer."

Her features cycled through half a dozen emotions in the following moments. "Oh, wow. Well, you've gotta open it. Just take a deep breath."

I followed her instructions before clicking open the email. Once I did, my eyes pored over the text, rereading everything to make sure I was understanding correctly. Ripley's gasp of surprise from over my shoulder confirmed that I was.

"He wants to meet," she said, her voice breathy with disbelief.

"He wants to meet," I repeated, needing to hear myself say the words. Then I jumped, eyes wide with excitement. "He wants to meet!"

Ripley bounced around with me before halting. "When?"

Reading more of the email, I finally found it. "This evening. Oh, wow. That's fast." Glancing at the clock, I added, "That only gives me, like, six hours to prepare."

"Okay," Ripley said, obviously not understanding. "What do you need to prepare?"

"I've got to tell the building, and close to half of them are at work right now." Grimacing, I began to pace. "I really should've told them what I'd done earlier. This was stupid. Now I'm not sure if the rest of them are even okay with the plan."

Ripley moved toward the door. "Well, the only thing you can do is tell them and see."

I chewed on the inside of my cheek.

"I think you should at least start by telling Nancy," Ripley advised.

An hour later, I stood behind Nancy's podium in the lobby. Only the retired residents and the ones who worked from home sat in front of me, but Nancy was ready to send messages to the others to give them a heads-up about our plan, as long as everyone agreed.

Heat flooded my cheeks. "Yikes, standing up here is a lot more nerve-racking than Nancy makes it look," I told my neighbors, fingers gripping the podium for strength.

Laurie's eyes met mine from the small group in front of me, and he grinned, trying to encourage me.

"It's okay, Nutmeg. You've got this," Darius called out from his seat next to Art in the front row.

"Thank you for coming on such short notice," I started. "I didn't share any of this with you before because I wasn't sure if it would work, and frankly, it still could fall apart spectacularly," I mumbled to myself.

A gentle hand landed on my arm. I glanced over to see Nancy's kind eyes peering at me through her thin glasses.

"Right. Stick to the facts. Sorry, Nance." I shook my head as a physical reset.

She took a step back.

"I think there's a way we might be able to save the Morrisey," I said, restarting, focusing on the heart of the matter. "I can't tell you how I know, but I found out that the bidder coming in second for this building has some sort of personal connection to it. I emailed their CEO and asked to meet with him. I explained that we might make up the difference between the highest bidder and what they can allocate for the project, as long as it's understood that we would get to keep our apartments and continue living here. We'd also collectively own a small part of the building."

Stopping, I coughed, realizing I'd barely taken a breath.

"How much are we talking?" Art raised his hand.

I had anticipated that question. "The current highest bid is about fifty thousand more than what Pacific Investment can pay. With twenty-five of us, it would only take roughly two thousand each to put them above the highest bidder."

Murmuring moved through the group, but from the higher pitch of the whispers, it sounded like that number was lower than they were expecting.

"If you're not sure if you can swing that much, you can come speak to me," Nancy said, stepping next to me again. "We have a few residents who are able to give a little more and are happy to cover for others. Penny has also graciously offered to help where she can."

That made me smile. Having just purchased her dream house on a large parcel of land in Scotland, she wasn't as flush as she normally was, but a few thousand would definitely be doable for her.

"Okay, what do we do next? Write out checks?" Opal asked,

fidgeting as if she might run to get her checkbook at that moment.

"Not yet." I put up a hand. "The CEO has asked to meet with us. Today, actually. That's why I needed to talk to you all now."

"We have to convince him we can come up with the funds," Nancy added. "That we're serious about this."

"Maybe Laurence can put together a nifty-looking spreadsheet for us to show the breakdown of how we'll pay." Art found Laurie in the crowd.

Hiding a smirk at the fact that the other residents never knew what exactly he did at Microsoft, only that he worked with computers, Laurie said, "I can definitely do that."

"And we should all dress up," Zoe said from her spot next to Laurie. "It'll help us look like we're serious."

I smiled gratefully at her support, and I was happy to hear she had the night off so she'd be able to join us. Agreement swept through the small group.

"Uh, Nutmeg?" Darius ran a hand over his chin. "You know we love you, but maybe you should take time to go shopping."

Scoffing, I said, "What? My clothes are..." My protest died on my lips as I glanced down at my paint-spattered clothes.

Alyssa's generosity had made me lazy about getting anything nice of my own. And I would've simply borrowed something from her, but I knew she hadn't put the key back in the light fixture. In fact, she'd mentioned putting a temporary hold on the fashion philanthropy program, in light of the current events.

"Okay, I'll ask Alyssa when she gets home," I said, giving in.

Surely Alyssa would make a fashion exception for me in this situation.

"What if she can't make it to the meeting?" Shirley Rosenbloom asked.

Her sister backed her up by adding, "Yeah, that girl works late all the time. What will you wear if she's not here in time?"

Checking my watch, I inhaled. "Fine. I'll go out and grab something. Are you happy?"

My neighbors pushed back their shoulders and sat up straighter. "Yes," Bethy Rosenbloom spoke for them.

Laurie hid a laugh behind his hand.

Nancy stepped up again. "Penny and I will contact those in the building who are at work right now, but if anyone wants to help, come see me so we can coordinate."

"Not you, Meg." Art pointed in my direction. "You'll be shopping."

I ignored his comment and pulled out my phone. "I'll email him now to confirm, letting him know that the time he gave works for us. Then we should all meet back here at four thirty since he's supposed to be here at five," I reminded them, stepping out from behind the podium and moving straight toward Laurie.

"This is all your fault, you know." My eyelids slitted.

"Me?" He placed a hand on his chest, but it shook with a suppressed chuckle.

"Yes, you. You've turned me into a comfortable, happy slob, apparently." I stuck out my bottom lip.

Laurie planted a kiss on my cheek and then my lips. "I can't help it if a paint-spattered Meg is my favorite kind." He pulled me close, hugging me to him. "It's too bad your Jerome outfit won't be ready in time. I'd bet they'd think that was professional."

My smile dissolved. "I know, but I still haven't heard back about my fitting, so I'm sure one day wouldn't be enough notice. Which means, I'm going shopping," I said, lobbing the sentence over my shoulder toward my neighbors.

"I would join you, but I've got to get back to work. And then I've got to cook up a spiffy spreadsheet." Laurie wet his lips to hide his grin.

"That's fine. I'll go find something on my own," I said. "At least one person won't abandon me."

Ripley cocked an eyebrow. "Literally can't." She cackled with delight.

"Keep her company, Rip," Laurie whispered before returning to the stairwell as I made my way out into the city.

It was a beautiful day. I pulled in a lungful of fresh air as I glanced around at my different directional options.

"Pioneer Square is going to have boutiques, more like Dirk's place," I said. "Which might be preferable to the department stores." I shuddered.

"Because of the mannequins." Ripley understood my reasoning immediately.

"Dirk didn't have any, and neither did Jerome. Maybe it's a boutique thing," I said, hopefully.

"But we saw Dirk's prices," Ripley reminded me. "If you're already paying for an outfit from Jerome, and chipping in to help save the building, that doesn't leave much for something like this."

"True." I pursed my lips as I turned north. "The Rack?"

"I think that's your best bet." Ripley started in that direction. "Plus, if you strike out, you'll be near Westlake, and you can find a different place to shop."

It turned out that Laurie's mention of my Jerome outfit set me up for failure. Nothing I tried on made me feel even remotely as good as my consultation with Jerome had, and I found myself wondering if I should just call and ask *him* what I should wear.

But it wasn't only the thought of Jerome's outfit that had me stalled. Ripley agreed that everything I tried on was either trying too hard, or not good enough.

I was on my third hour of unsuccessfully trying to find a professional-looking outfit for the meeting today, felt clammy from all the mannequins I'd seen, and was about to enter my fifth store, when my phone began ringing. Thinking it might be something to do with our meeting today, I plastered myself against the side of the nearest building, so I'd be out of the way of the other pedestrians and grabbed my phone out of my bag. It was an unknown number.

"Hello?" I answered.

"Meg?"

"Yep. That's me." I tried to place the male voice.

"This is Atlas, from Jerome Arundel Designs."

"Oh! Hi, Atlas."

Ripley cocked her head to one side with interest as she recognized the name.

"I wanted to call to let you know Jerome has your order ready for you. You can come in any time to do your fitting."

Hope sprang inside my chest. This was the good omen I needed for today. Maybe I'd be able to wear my new outfit for the meeting this evening, after all.

"Any time?" I asked. "Like, would right now work?" I only had two more hours until the meeting at the Morrisey, and I was losing hope that I'd find anything in a regular store.

I'd also seen more than my fair share of mannequins and was feeling a little tense about going into another store where I knew I'd find even more.

Atlas flipped through some papers in the background. "Uh, sure." There was a scuffling sound as Atlas held his hand over the speaker. "Jerome, can we do that fitting with Meg today?"

In the background, I heard a faint, "Absolutely," in a deep baritone voice.

Atlas was back. "Yes, he can see you today."

"Omigosh, that's amazing, Atlas. I'm actually in Westlake, so I could be there in twenty minutes?" I tried to remember how long it had taken me and Laurie to walk that distance the other day.

"Perfect. See you soon, Meg."

I hung up the call, jumped in a happy circle, and then started walking again. Ripley beamed next to me.

"Looks like things are finally going your way today," she said, obviously tired of following me around and hearing me complain.

I nodded. "Let's hope this is just the first of many pieces of good news that the day holds."

TWENTY-THREE

"Okay, this time the walk feels much more inconvenient," I whispered as Ripley and I approached Jerome's studio in the shadow of the Space Needle.

"Because you actually have to put the clothes on, and he's going to see how sweaty you are?" Ripley chuckled.

"Yes," I scoffed, fanning myself to cool down. "I'd never be silly enough to curse a sunny day in the Pacific Northwest, but I almost wish it had been overcast today."

Ripley shot me a sidelong glance before saying, "If you want, I'll pass through you a few times to cool you off." The offer was flat, showing how much she wasn't looking forward to it. Her hatred for walking through a living person was only slightly outweighed by her love for me.

I placed a hand over my heart. "You'd do that for me?" Now my hand was fanning the tears gathering in my eyes. "You're the best friend."

Closing her eyes tight, she rushed through me once, twice,

three times. A whole-body shiver moved from the back of my neck, down my spine. I danced around to get through the worst of the chill, then I exhaled.

"Thank you. That feels so much better." I patted my face with the backs of my hands, dabbing away the sweat, knowing that it would be less likely to return now that my body temperature had lowered considerably.

Despite her faux annoyance, Ripley smiled at me. "You're welcome. Now go get that cute outfit."

"Here's hoping it's ready today, so I don't have to do any more shopping." I crossed my fingers and walked inside.

Neither Jerome nor Atlas was there to greet me. I stepped forward into the studio space, threading my way through the shelves to the consultation area. Also empty.

"Hello?" I called. "Jerome? Atlas?" The hairs on my arms raised as a chill washed over me. Was I scared? Was something wrong here?

"Sorry," Ripley said, so close to me that she must've passed through me again. "Didn't see you stop."

Relief filled me. I wasn't scared. It had been Ripley accidentally walking through me. This was fine.

"Ah, Meg." Jerome's voice called out from the back of the studio. "There you are."

I turned in a circle. "Where are *you*, though?"

Jerome expelled an echoing laugh. "In the back. I'll be just a moment. Have a seat."

Settling on the green sofa, I closed my eyes and let the worry abandon me as quickly as my overheated state had left me outside. A minute later, Jerome came bustling over. He beamed when he saw me.

"Okay, are you ready?" When I said I was, he fixed me with a devious grin as he took my hands. "Follow me."

Excitement bubbled in my chest as he led me over to a group of dress forms. I sucked in a breath as I realized the outfit represented on the forms was mine.

"Oh, Meg. It's perfect." Ripley moved closer to get a better look at the outfit.

It was three pieces, not two or one, as I'd expected. The first piece I noticed were the pants. They were ... beautiful. I don't think I'd ever said that about pants before, but these were. Made of a cotton material that had structure but still looked buttery soft, they were high-waisted, wide-legged, slightly cropped, and a slate-gray color that called to mind the Seattle sky on a foggy fall day.

Then there was the sweater. Yes, a sweater. But it was better than any sweater I'd ever seen. It looked like it was hand-painted with large splotches of black, white, slate gray, and a shimmery gold. The tip of the right sleeve was the same color as the pants, tying the two items together in the most elegant way. The painted sections weren't splattered like the paint littering my overalls, though. They were large, sophisticated swaths, with just enough random roughness around the edges to look artsy.

"I started with the sweater, but then I got to thinking it might be too hot in the summer, so I made this as well," Jerome motioned to a blouse on the second form.

It was black, with a deep V-neck leading into delicate buttons. But the truly eye-catching part was the sleeves. They were large, but not in a balloony way. They were structured in their volume, sticking out behind and giving such interesting dimension to the piece.

"Jerome," I whispered his name. "I don't know how you did it, but these are better than anything I could've hoped for." When his gaze met mine, we were both tearing up.

"I'm so glad." He beamed, then clapped his hands to get us both refocused. "Okay, let's get them on you so we can see how they fit."

He didn't have to tell me twice. I followed instructions, careful around the pins present in the few areas he hadn't finished yet in case the pieces needed alterations. I tried the pants with the black blouse first.

"Jerome, I think I'm going to cry again," I called as I stepped out from behind the divider he had up as a makeshift changing room.

Stepping out, I let him take in the outfit. "Just like I pictured it." His hands splayed out in front of him, and he beckoned me forward to a small stand in the middle of the space, like I was a bride trying on a dress. Fussing with a few things here and there, he muttered to himself about measurements.

"I think this could be taken in here. Oh, and an inch shorter on the pants." He moved around me in a whirlwind, pinning and repinning.

The sweater, stretchy as it was, didn't have any pins in it, and it fit perfectly. No alterations needed. I took off the items, changing back into my original clothes.

"Okay, just a few changes. That's not too bad at all," he said, when I emerged from the dressing room. He made a final note on a pad on the worktable next to him. "This shouldn't take me too long to finish."

Eyeing him warily, I chewed on my lip as I got up the

courage to ask him what I really wanted. "*How* long? Could I pay extra to have it done today?" My teeth raked over my lip again as I waited for his answer.

I had just over an hour until the meeting. If I went back to shopping now, I might find something and get it back to the Morrisey in time, but this would be so much easier.

Jerome's eyes traveled over the garments. "Hmmm... Maybe? If Atlas were here, he could have these alterations done in ten minutes, but it'll probably take me thirty."

"That's great," I blurted in my excitement. "I have a really important meeting in an hour, but I can take a cab back home, so it'll be fine. How much can I pay for the rush?"

"My fee for the rush is that I need to hear all about this important meeting." Jerome gathered up the pants and blouse. "Come with me." After I paid the remaining balance on my account, he led me to a station where there were three different sewing machines, each looking more complicated than the last.

When he pointed to a stool, I perched on it as he took a seat in front of one of the machines. Ripley hovered nearby.

"Where *is* Atlas?" I asked, looking around. "I talked to him on the phone earlier. Did he leave?"

Jerome clicked his tongue. "Just after the call with you, actually. I sent him on an in-home client consultation." Arching an eyebrow, he added, "Well, to be honest, I was going to go but Atlas insisted." Lining up the fabric, Jerome began sewing. "It's one of our ... more difficult clients."

"Oh?" I tucked my feet onto the footrail of the stool as I listened. "Why would Atlas choose to go?"

"I think he still feels bad. A few weeks ago, a dress was stolen on his watch." Jerome flinched. "I told him it wasn't a big deal, but I can tell the guilt is eating him alive."

"That's awful." The words *dress* and *stolen* caught my attention. "Someone broke in?"

Jerome shook his head, a pin sticking out from between his teeth. "That would've been preferable, actually. We might've caught them on our security cameras if that had been the case. No. This was right in the middle of the day. Someone came in and grabbed it right off the rack where I had it waiting for a client to pick up." He grabbed the pin and weaved it into the garment to hold two pieces together, then used the machine to secure them. "It was such a pretty piece too. Glittery. Gold. Gorgeous. The police found the dress, but it was destroyed. The girl who'd been wearing it had been killed, and they were running a whole investigation into what happened." He winced.

My mouth fell open. What if Dirk hadn't merely stolen Jerome's design, but the entire dress?

"Atlas was in the back when the dress was taken?" I guessed.

Focusing on the sewing, Jerome said, "He was. Didn't even hear them enter."

Another designer might know that they often spend time in the back of the shop. Dirk was the same in that respect, after all. I'd had to make quite a bit of noise to get his attention.

Glancing up from his work for the first time in minutes, Jerome checked all around to make sure we were alone. Once he was sure, he tapped the garment in front of him proudly. "Look at that. Atlas might be faster than me, but I'm more precise. Take these darts, for instance." He motioned to a seam running down the front of the blouse.

"I can't even see them." I snorted.

Jerome pointed at me as if I'd just won a game show. "Exactly. Atlas can't make darts like this. So, even though I know he thinks he's ready for his own studio he's still got a lot left to learn." The machine whirred in the background, each stitch precise. "Now, tell me about this meeting."

"Oh. Well, it's actually to save my building."

The story took the rest of the blouse alterations and the hemming of the pants. I tried everything on once more, coming out to show Jerome.

"So, that's why I have to get back to the Morrisey." I finished the story as Jerome circled me, fussing here and there with the pieces.

"You live at the Morrisey?"

I jolted at the unexpected voice. Turning, I found Atlas had returned. He stood near the far wall, staring at us, wide-eyed.

"I do. I have most of my life." I smiled at him.

"We're getting her ready for an important meeting," Jerome explained. "Real life-or-death stuff." He smiled at me, checking his watch. "I know you have to go, but let me run a lint roller over you so you don't look like you rolled around in loose threads."

Jerome left to find the roller, and Atlas stepped forward. Once he moved closer, I realized he looked different than he had the first time I'd seen him. The light glinted off a silver hoop in his lip, a septum piercing in his nose, and a few studs in his left eyebrow.

Next to me, Ripley let out a nervous hum. "Piercings, Meg?" Her question was ominous. "Like the guy who approached Jay-J during his set the day before Quinn died?"

But she didn't need to remind me. It was the first thing I'd thought of when I'd seen him. Despite my racing heart, I needed to stay calm.

"Oh, I didn't realize you had so many piercings," I said conversationally as he inspected Jerome's work. "You didn't have them in the last time I was here."

Atlas cleared his throat. "Yeah, they were irritated. I used a different face wash, and it made them all inflamed for a while."

"Or they got irritated after someone shot him in the face with pepper spray," Ripley countered.

With as many grunge friends as Ripley had, I didn't doubt her knowledge of piercings. Swallowing thickly, I willed Jerome to come back.

But everything took a turn for the worse as Atlas grabbed my wrist. His genial smile was gone, his eyes dark with a threat. "What are you *really* doing here? Tell me the truth." His voice was low but menacing in a way that couldn't be called a whisper. It was ragged. Dangerous.

I tried to shake him off, but he only gripped tighter. Fear flashed in Ripley's eyes, and I tried to free my wrist again. This time, Ripley positioned herself between us and shoved him back with all her ghostly might.

The energy knocked Atlas back, and he finally released my hand. "I don't know what you're talking about." I played dumb.

Confusion flashed across his features as he glanced from me to his hand, likely wondering how I was so strong. But his anger won out, and he craned his neck, looking too much like an apex predator sizing up its prey. "Oh, really? Then what's this important meeting you're going to? Let me guess. It's with the police?" He came at me again.

I held my hands up in front of me, and Ripley, still standing in between me and Atlas, sent a pulse of energy toward him the moment he ran into my palms. I pushed him at the same time, the combination of me and Ripley together, sending him staggering back again.

But that only infuriated him more.

Growling in frustration, he came at me again. And again. Ripley pushed him back, but her spirit was weakening fast. She rarely used her energy, and this kind of thing drained her. Terror pulsed behind her transparent eyes as she turned toward me, saying a ghostly, "Run" before she vanished.

Before I could, Atlas lunged forward, succeeding in grabbing me now that Ripley was gone. He yanked my arm, causing me to cry out in pain. "Come on," he growled. "There's no way this is a coincidence. You know something, and I'm going to make sure you don't make it to that meeting."

"Atlas!" Jerome came rushing into the room, moving himself in between us.

In his surprise, Atlas let go of my arm, and I rubbed at it.

"What's gotten into you?" Jerome might wear soft sweaters and talk about color theory, but he was kind of intimidating when he was upset.

Atlas moved in a manic pattern in front of us and raked his hands over his face, coming dangerously close to snagging a few of his piercings in the process.

"I can't let her go to that meeting, Jerome. She knows. I can't." There was agony in his tone and the shiftiness of a cornered animal in his eyes.

Jerome lifted a hand to calm him. "Knows what?"

Tensing in a way that made him seem like he might explode, Atlas let out a frustrated scream. "It wasn't supposed to happen like this."

Jerome's arm came up to shield me in case Atlas came at me again. He pushed me back until I was stepping off the pedestal.

Atlas noticed the action and lurched forward. "No, you can't let her go. She's going to tell them."

"Tell who? I don't know what's gotten you so upset." Jerome kept his voice even, a feat in the presence of such an angry, spiraling man. "Of course we're going to let her go. It's a very important meeting, and she's going to be late if—"

"I'll pay you ... both." Atlas stepped forward. "What do you want?" The question was frantic. "I could threaten you, but we could do this the easier way if you just agree not to say anything."

I was frozen. I couldn't speak. Jerome kept looking at me, confusion creasing his forehead.

"Say anything about what?" Jerome bellowed, tired of being out of the loop.

"The dress!" Atlas broke, the guilt he'd been feeling over the past few weeks finally becoming too much. "It was me. I stole it. Dirk Evans and I had the chance to get a contract with Nordstroms, and I took the dress. But then it went missing, and I freaked out. I was just trying to get it back, but the girl with pink hair wouldn't give it to me." Tears rolled down his red cheeks. "She wouldn't give it to me, and then she sprayed me with pepper spray, and it hurt so bad, and I just ... I just wanted her to stop." He crouched nearby.

Jerome swallowed. "Son, I'm not following. You took the

sequin dress? What did you want to stop?" He glanced at me. "Stop Meg from going to her meeting with a buyer for her building?"

Atlas blinked red eyes at me. "Your meeting isn't with the police?"

I shook my head slowly, feeling every centimeter of the movement.

Atlas broke down, but as Jerome comforted his apprentice, I crept over to my phone and texted Detective Anthony.

> I'm at Arundel Designs. Jerome's assistant Atlas is the killer. I'm safe, I think, but I could really use some backup.

She texted right back.

> Stay put. I'll be there as soon as I can.

Glancing at the clock, I released a defeated breath. The Morrisey meeting was set to start in fifteen minutes. There was no way I was going to make it now.

Twenty-Four

I texted Laurie to let him know what was happening, and that I wouldn't be able to make it.

My eyes stayed glued to the screen for a few moments, waiting to see if Laurie was writing back, but what was happening in front of me soon stole away my focus. Atlas must have been carrying *a lot* of guilt around because he spilled everything to Jerome.

"Dirk and I know each other from school. I was the one who convinced him to move up here." Atlas's voice was raw. "Dirk got frustrated when his styles didn't take off, and I guess I felt a little responsible since I'd told him how great the fashion scene was up here. Anyway, I mentioned that he might try something a little more formfitting, to show off his sewing skills. He thought it would dilute his brand to change styles, but I told him how you believe in constantly adding to your design aesthetic. Like, even though you've gone back to the formfitting dress quite a few times, you find a way to make it unique each time."

"Dirk doesn't do darts, though," I said from where I stood off to the side.

"Right," Atlas agreed. "But I suggested that he might go to Jerome for lessons. I mentioned how much I've learned from you already."

Jerome's posture softened even more at that comment.

"But Dirk became furious with me. He said he didn't need lessons, that he could make a dart dress better than you. So, I found him the same gold sequin material you'd been using for the one you were working on, and he started his own. He quickly grew frustrated and left it on his dress form, and a Nordstrom buyer came by and said she wanted to take it to her bosses for a potential deal." Atlas unleashed a laugh. "It was the first hint of interest he'd had, and it wasn't even his style."

"He couldn't make it work, though, could he?" I guessed. "That's why you stole Jerome's version of it."

"Yeah," Atlas admitted. "I'm still not great at darts, especially not compared to you," he told Jerome, "and if we wanted to impress Nordstroms, it had to be perfect. But then Dirk called to tell me the Nordstrom buyer had lost the dress." Atlas raked his fingers through his hair. "I got so paranoid, thinking that you'd find out and fire me, and then I'd be out my job as well as the contract. But then, on my social media feed, I recognized the dress. It was on some young woman next to a local DJ, and I tracked him down. I waited at your building that day until I saw that girl with the pink hair approach in the dress. She used the back entrance, and I slipped in behind her."

My fingers gripped my phone as we reached the part of the story I was most dreading.

"I tried to reason with her, to ask for the dress, but she

freaked out on me, moved to run away. When I reached out, I caught the fabric, and it ripped right along the dart." He exhaled. "I got so mad at that moment, I lost it. Everything felt like it was going wrong. And then she sprayed me with pepper spray." His throat bobbed with a hard swallow. "I was so mad. Between finding the dress, then having her refuse to give it to me, and it ripping, I snapped. I reached forward and ... squeezed so hard." Tears leaked from his eyes.

I found myself crying too. To distract myself, I checked my messages and found that Laurie had texted back.

> Okay. You're safe?

> I am. Tell everyone I'm sorry. I'll get there as soon as I can, but the police haven't even arrived yet.

> It's okay. I think we've got it covered. Gotta go. He just arrived.

Jerome patted Atlas on the back, but he didn't berate the man or even show any anger that his apprentice had gone behind his back to try to sell his design and take credit for it. His sad eyes merely met mine.

We all jumped as the front door opened.

"Meg?" Detective Anthony called into the space.

"Over here," I said, not knowing how to describe where we were, and realizing she'd just have to follow the sound of my voice.

"Take a right at the brocades and slip in between the opening between the silks," Jerome called out.

I figured that the detective would be just as confused by

those directions as I was, but she emerged into the space a few seconds later, followed by a few officers. Detective Anthony glanced over at the scene in front of her, scrunching her eyes shut for a moment in her confusion.

Jerome stood. "Atlas has some things to tell you, Detective. And while he does, I need to take Megan back to her building so she can help save it." He checked his watch. "That is, if we're not too late, Meg?"

The combination of his soft tone, the kindness he was showing in such a difficult situation, my frustration that Atlas had done any of this, and the way I'd resigned myself to not being able to get back home in time made a few more tears slide down my cheeks. "Um, I'm not sure."

"But I am. It's worth a try." He grinned.

"Save the building?" Amaya asked.

Turning to her, I said, "It's a long story, one I'll tell you later. I promise I'll answer any questions you have about this." I gestured toward Atlas. "But right now I really do have to go."

Jerome drove a zippy little vintage car that was in perfect condition, which felt all too fitting for the man. But even though he drove as quickly as he could through the crowded streets, it was rush hour, and it took us close to half an hour to get through downtown.

Pulling up next to the Morrisey, Jerome said, "Good luck. Come back when you can for the sweater." Both of us had forgotten it back at the studio.

I glanced down at my perfect outfit, the one I'd forgotten I still wore. Swiping a finger under each eye, I hoped I didn't look like too much of a mess from my crying. "Thank you. For everything." And with that, I bolted from the car, toward my home, hoping I wasn't too late to help save it.

But as I reached the front doors of the Morrisey, and let myself inside, I found I didn't need to unlock the door. A man was walking out, and he held the door open, his gaze lingering on me for more than a second.

"Thanks," I whispered, watching him too.

Was he the Pacific Investment guy? He was leaving already? Was I too late?

Rushing inside, I found the residents seated in the normal spot in the lobby where we held meetings. Nancy stood at the front of the group, behind the podium, saying something that didn't register because I immediately zeroed in on Aunt Penny.

My aunt's entire body was rigid, her face red. I don't think I'd ever seen her so angry.

My stomach plummeted, and I almost sank into a crouch right there from the weight of disappointment.

He'd said no.

We'd failed.

And now I'd never know if it was because I hadn't been there.

But just as soon as my hope left me, someone caught sight of me and yelled out, "Meg's here, everyone."

A cheer went up from the gathered group.

I slammed my eyes shut, hoping everything would make more sense once I opened them again.

"Meg!" they called, getting to their feet. "We did it! Your plan worked!"

The mental and emotional overwhelmingness I was experiencing became physical as well when the residents raced over to me, led by Laurie.

He beamed, his phone in his hand. "Sorry, I was just about to text you. I didn't want to say anything until we were sure." A quick widening of his eyes as he scanned the lobby told me he for sure thought Ripley was here and had kept me informed.

"We... we did it?"

Everyone cheered again.

Looking to Laurie, I asked, "And that was him? Leaving as I got here?"

"Yep," Laurie confirmed. "He wanted to leave as quickly as possible, so he can contact the Kincaids and let them know of his revised offer."

Relief pushed through the worries, and I breathed easily for a moment. That was until I remembered Penny.

"Why does Penny look so upset, then?" I asked, as the residents filed back to their seats to stack them.

Laurie frowned. "I'm not sure, but I think she knows the guy. They exchanged some heated words before the meeting began and glared at one another the whole time. Other than that, she hasn't told us why she's upset."

We were about to find out. Penny stormed over with so much fury emanating off her that Laurie placed himself between me and my aunt.

"How'd you find him?" Penny's tone wobbled like a hot corn kernel about to pop.

"Find who, Pen?" I stepped out from behind Laurie.

But she was spiraling into her anger. A laugh careened out of her. "I should've known better than to tell Iris. You got his name out of her, didn't you?" Penny scowled at Iris, who hung back with the other residents.

"Penny—"

"No, it's not okay, Meg. This is literally the one thing your mom asked of me, and I've failed at it." Despite her tight posture, her shoulders sagged forward at the admission.

Everything felt overwhelming, but those words clicked in my brain. We'd saved the building. I didn't have to move out. The only other thing Penny had promised my mom had been... "That man was my father?"

Penny scoffed. "Like you didn't know. This was your idea. You found him and convinced him to help us. He even told me he agreed to come because he recognized your last name."

"I swear, I didn't know, Penny," I pleaded. "He was just the second-highest bidder, and I reached out to him."

It was hard to watch the devastation cross my aunt's features. She squeezed her eyes shut for a moment, shaking her head, like she wished she could have a do-over. "You didn't know?"

"No. Like I told you all, I heard the company who was bidding second for the building had a personal connection..." My sentence petered out as I realized exactly what that personal connection had been. "Mom." The word was a whisper. "He wanted to buy this building because of Mom," I repeated.

Penny realized her mistake in stages. First, there was denial. She tried to convince herself that I was lying about not knowing he was my father. Then the anger came. This time, it wasn't directed at me, but at herself. She paced, grumbling her frustration.

At that point, the other residents had crept closer. From the tight set to most of their expressions, they'd heard the part about Wyatt being my father.

"Penny, is everything okay?" Opal was the bravest of the lot, stepping forward first.

Whirling on the older woman, Penny huffed out a breath. "Oh, everything's *great*," she said in the least great tone ever. "I'm going to pack now that everything's *great*."

"Pack?" I stood there, stunned.

Aunt Penny didn't stop, though. She stomped off toward the elevator, disappearing behind its doors with an ironically chipper *ding*. The residents must've understood that I didn't have the capacity to answer their questions, either, because they wandered away, whispering among themselves.

Laurie's arm was around me in an instant. "Hey, that was... What *was* that?"

I slumped against him. "That man was my *dad*. That man was *my* dad." Repeating it, emphasizing different words, none of it helped the truth sink in.

"And Penny just accidentally spilled the secret," Laurie summarized.

Running my hand over my forehead, I pressed my fingers into my temple to relieve some of the pressure. "I have to go talk to her."

Laurie nodded. "Want me to come with?"

"No." I squeezed his hand. "I've got this."

He held on to me for a moment, not letting go just yet. A grin took over his expression. "I'm glad you're okay, and I like your new outfit. It's perfect."

"Thanks," I said with a small smile.

His fingers opened, and I rushed off to follow my aunt,

passing by the huddle of our concerned neighbors. I couldn't stop to talk to them, as much as I wanted to ease their worries. I had to fix this first.

Iris's door was open a few inches when I reached the fifth floor. The sounds coming from inside the apartment were frantic.

"Pen?" I knocked on the door, causing it to swing open even wider. "Pen, can we talk?" I took a tentative step inside.

My aunt was folding clothes, setting them in her suitcase, and sniffling back tears. She cringed as I came closer. "I'm fine, Meg. I'm sorry for causing a scene."

"No, it's... I'm sorry for my part in it all. I didn't realize."

Penny's chest moved up and down with an inhale. She tossed the shirt she'd been folding into the suitcase and closed the distance between us, setting her hand on my cheek. "Kiddo, you did nothing wrong down there. I'm sorry I jumped to that conclusion. To be frank with you, I mostly feel stupid about blurting that out." She glanced over at her suitcase. "And I've already stayed longer than I expected. As fun as it's been being back at the Morrisey, I need to get back to my life."

Gulping, I held back tears. It was an emotional day. "Okay, I understand. Do you need help?" I motioned to her pile of clothes.

Penny snorted out something that was half laugh, half sob. "I'd love it. You're way better at folding than I am."

We folded in silence for a minute before I said, "So that was the guy who walked out on Mom when she told him she was pregnant?"

Setting her mouth in a grim line, Penny said, "Yep, and based on what I saw today, he hasn't gotten any nicer as he's gotten older. When he first arrived, he came right up to me and asked if this was my idea of a joke. Apparently, your last name caught his attention in your email, especially in conjunction with the Morrisey, and he thought maybe *my daughter* and I were trying to use him for his money, to guilt him into buying the place."

My mind returned to the way the man had stared at me when we'd passed one another. It was almost like he'd seen a ghost. But I remembered Penny saying how they'd kept all mention of me out of the obituary and the news stories surrounding my mother's accident. Of course, my father would have believed I'd died with her in that accident, and if I was a Dawson, I must be Penny's daughter.

She continued. "He admitted that he mostly responded out of curiosity. I told him you had no idea who he was—something I thought was a lie, at the time—but at that point, the rest of the residents took over and really seemed to wow him with their presentation."

"They did?" I asked.

"I think he was on the fence. It's why he didn't up his bid right away to beat out the other company. When he asked the residents why this building meant so much to them, I used my turn to speak to make sure he knew that I no longer lived here. Once he knew that, he gave this whole speech about loving the community here, and that someone he loved used to feel the same way." Penny rolled her eyes. "Yeah, right. More like he feels guilty, and he's finally trying to atone for leaving Charlotte. Just like always, throw some money at the problem and it'll go away. That's the kind of man your father is. The fact that he took our money when he could easily pay for it himself proves that."

"It is kind of nice that we'll be part owners," I admitted, folding another shirt and handing it over. "Also, in your defense, I probably would've found out eventually."

She looked up from the suitcase.

"If everything goes well, he'll own the building. He's going to be around. And I'd bet he would've said something to me about being your daughter. I would've slipped and said something about my mom having died, since I wouldn't have known who he was." I shrugged. "It's better this way. Now I know to be careful around him, to keep him at arm's length. The guy's just here because he felt guilty for what he did to Mom, but if he can save our building? I'll take it. And that's all I'll take from him." I held her gaze to show I was serious.

Reaching over, Penny pulled me into a tight hug. "I love you, kid. I know your mom would be so proud of you."

I set my head on her shoulder and closed my eyes. "All that matters to me is that you are."

TWENTY-FIVE

I wrinkled my nose at my savings account. "This number has me feeling depressed."

"Not as depressed as you'd be if you had to move apartments," Ripley countered.

Laurie chuckled from across the room. "I'm guessing from the sour face you just made that Ripley told you to stop complaining."

Ripley cackled.

I tossed her a side-eyed glance before turning it on Laurie. "Possibly."

He walked over to where I sat on a stool, looking at my computer at the breakfast bar next to my kitchen. Wrapping his arms around me, he whispered in my ear. "You know, we never revisited the conversation about moving in together."

Ripley, who'd been about to leave so we could have privacy, stopped in her retreat. Interest tilted her head.

Craning my neck so I could see him better, I said, "What do you mean?"

"We decided to get a place together before you came up with your brilliant plan," he said, like I could've forgotten. "But we haven't talked about it since."

"Yeah, because we're not moving. Everything went through with the Kincaids and *dear old Dad* owns ninety-nine percent of our building now."

Our Morrisey contribution of fifty thousand wasn't anything to scoff at—especially when you asked my bank account—but in the grand scheme of the cost of a historic building in downtown Seattle, it wasn't much.

Laurie swiveled me around so I faced him. "Yeah, sure. But that doesn't mean we can't still take that step."

"Laurie, I can't sell this place. It's—"

But he cut me off. "I'm not saying you should. But you could keep this as your art studio. I work from home most of the time, so us both being in the apartment all day probably wouldn't work very well."

Ripley grunted. "If that's not the understatement of the century."

I ignored her as my mind built upon the image Laurie had started. My place was a studio, so it made sense that we would use Laurie's one bedroom as our primary residence. But the thought of keeping this place, designating it solely for my art, sounded amazing.

"Are you sure?" I asked, unable to keep the smile from my lips.

He nodded, his own grin spreading. Then he pulled me into a kiss.

"Okay, now I'm out." Ripley disappeared through the door.

I laughed into the kiss, and Laurie pulled back for a moment. "Ripley gone?" When I nodded, he went back to kissing me.

But it was my turn to pull back. "Are you sure about this?"

"One hundred percent. Plus, living together means we could cut down on some costs, and you could help your savings account get back up to where it used to be." Laurie waggled his eyebrows at me.

I gave him a light smack on the arm. "Laurence Aaron Turner, you don't have to convince me to move in with you. I already said yes."

"Did you?" he asked with a teasing smirk. "I feel like you got distracted in the middle, and sort of forgot the yes part."

I leaned back toward him. "Hmmm. I wonder whose fault that was?"

He hugged me closer. "Definitely not mine. Let's blame Ripley."

There was a knock on the door, and we both groaned.

"Okay, we're on our way," I called, knowing it was Zoe.

I could practically hear the attitude in her stance as she waited at the door. "I'm *not* going to this thing alone, so you'd better hurry."

I slipped off the barstool. "You don't think my dad will come to this, do you?" I asked Laurie as I moved toward the door.

He shook his head. "From what I saw at the meeting, he didn't seem like a party person. Plus, he hasn't been back once since we signed the sale paperwork and transferred the money."

"Who?" Zoe asked when I opened the door.

"Meg's dad," Laurie told her as we stepped out into the hallway. "She's worried he'll be at the celebration party."

Zoe scoffed. "No way. I think you're safe."

That settled my gut, at least for the moment. I knew I'd have to see him again someday, but at least I wouldn't have to worry about it today. The other nice thing about the entire building being present for my fight with Penny was that I didn't have to break the news about Wyatt to anyone. They'd all heard.

Inwardly smiling affectionately as I thought about the other Morrisey residents, I couldn't help but feel immense love for them as I recalled how they'd, each and every one of them, come to see me at one moment or another over the past week to ask me how I felt about learning the identity of my father after all these years.

My conversation with Zoe had been the hardest, knowing her own search for her birth father had ended much differently than mine. But she assured me that she didn't begrudge me for having a father who was alive when hers wasn't. I'd pointed out that it wasn't like mine was likely to become my best friend anytime soon, and that seemed to have softened the blow as well.

Alyssa and Brad came out of apartment 5C as Laurie pulled my apartment door closed behind him.

"Hey," Alyssa said with a smile. "We're not supposed to bring anything, are we?"

Zoe shook her head. "Nancy said all refreshments are covered. Apparently, Mr. Moneybags gave her a small allowance for the celebration."

That was what we'd taken to calling him, since *Dad* felt too weird.

"I also heard he's promised to fix the elevator," Alyssa whispered, as if it were a secret.

Zoe, Laurie, and I blinked in surprise.

"That would be amazing. I'd love to not feel like I'm going to be part of some horror film where the elevator plummets to the basement each time I have to take it," Zoe said.

It wasn't lost on me that we all headed for the stairwell, not even considering the elevator an option.

"Maybe he will be more hands on than I thought," Laurie said, bringing back our earlier conversation.

My gut twisted with an odd sense of anticipation that wasn't entirely dread as I thought of my promise to Penny to stay away from him as much as possible. Knowing what he did to my mom was awful, but people changed, and maybe this was all to make amends. Who knew?

Speaking of amends, Alyssa caught my arm as we descended the stairs. I moved behind Laurie to walk next to her.

"I got a call from that detective yesterday," she said as we walked. "She said Atlas pled guilty and they're working on charges."

I'd gotten a similar call from Amaya, but didn't want to take away from Alyssa sharing the information with me, so I said, "Oh? How are you feeling about everything?"

Alyssa looked down. "I mean, I feel bad that I had any part in it. If I hadn't convinced myself it was okay to buy that design, even though I knew it was so close to Jerome's—well, now I know it *was* Jerome's—then Atlas wouldn't have been so motivated to get the thing back and hurt Quinn."

"Lyss, you can't blame yourself for what someone else did.

You would've never guessed that the situation would end in murder."

She nodded. "I guess. It's definitely taught me a lesson, though."

"Me too," I said, smiling at my people, my Morrisey family.

The reality was, I didn't need things to end in any sort of happily ever after with my father. No matter what happened with him, I had the people I loved most around me. They were my true family.

MORRISEY MASTERPIECE CLASSIC MAP

Dear readers,

If you'd like to see a map of the places Meg, Laurie, and the rest of the Morrisey residents visited during their scavenger hunt, I've created a Google map of the sites for you to view!

(Below is just a screenshot, but you'll find a link to view the map on my website. Visit erynscott.com and hover over the Extras tab at the top menu. Click on Bonus Scenes, and that's where you'll find a link to the map.)

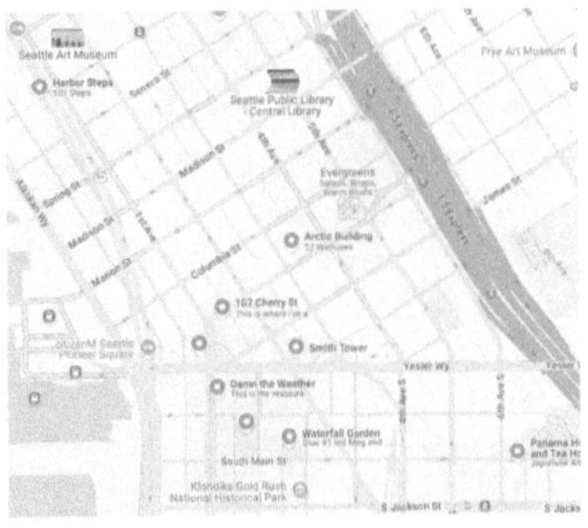

Take me to the map!

Special thanks to Ericka, Melena, and Carol for sharing some of your favorite local spots with me!

THE MORRISEY WILL RETURN ...

Book five, A BULLET IN THE BASEMENT, will be coming this winter.

The worst ice storm in recent history is about to hit Seattle.

When the city suggests that residents ride out the storm inside, Meg Dawson and the Morrisey residents stock up on essentials. They embrace the forced lock down with fun, games, and apartment-hopping festivities. It all comes to a stop when a trail of blood is discovered in the lobby, leading to a used bullet in the basement.

Where did the bullet come from? Where's the victim of the shooting? And who pulled the trigger?

The residents of the Morrisey are about to find out that the storm inside might be more treacherous than the one raging outside.

Get your copy today!

Join Eryn's mailing list to be notified about updates.

Whiskers and Words Mysteries

Ongoing series * Best friends *
Bookshop full of cats

PEPPER BROOKS
COZY MYSTERY SERIES

Completed series * Literary mysteries * Sweet romance * Cute dog

About the Author

Eryn Scott lives in the Pacific Northwest with her husband and their quirky animals. She loves classic literature, musicals, knitting, and hiking. She writes cozy mysteries and women's fiction. Join her mailing list to learn about new releases and sales!

www.erynscott.com